Who is Elizabeth Bennet's Soulmate?

A Pride and Prejudice Variation

Laura Moretti

ISBN-13: 9781234567890
ISBN-10: 1477123456

Library of Congress Control Number: 2018675309
Printed in the United States of America

Prologue

It started with a whisper.

A few notes. A short musical phrase.

Darcy's soulmate music swelled when he entered the assembly rooms in Meryton.

His arrival in Hertfordshire was very recent. Darcy was staying with his friend Bingley, who had just rented an estate—an elegant, respectable place called Netherfield. And now... this. This dark series of rooms, reeking of sweat and dirt. A public ball, to mingle with their new neighbours.

When their party was announced, the dance had already started. Darcy felt his entire being vibrate with the strength of his soulmate melody and knew *she* must be present.

She. Darcy had always supposed his unknown soulmate was a 'she'. He could almost see her, sometimes. She had kind eyes.

Then he looked around.

No. No, *she* would not be here, in this vulgar place. *She* would not be dancing here, in questionable company, among the scents of old varnish, cheap wax, and stale wine. *She* would not be one of those... 'Ladies' was too amiable a term.

A Mrs Bennet was talking to them, introducing a gaggle of daughters. Darcy's inner music was screaming.

No. No. Please no.

Darcy retreated as soon as he could, keeping to the corners, to the dark. The sudden strength of the soulmate song must mean something else. Maybe *she* was not present today, but merely living in the area. Darcy imagined her, a proper, well-behaved young lady, an excellent horse woman, riding home, right at this moment. Outside, the sun was setting. *She* would be in a dark green velvet riding dress—practical, elegant attire. Soon *she* would arrive at the main house, on her parents' estate. Old money, not necessarily a lot of it. Darcy did not require a good dowry; what he demanded was impeccable parentage, impeccable lineage, and yes, elegance, in character and in attitude.

His soulmate's thoughts—the young lady's—were certainly wandering. *She* must have heard Darcy's melody also, heard his harmonies, sensed that her soulmate was getting nearer. Yes, this must be the explanation. Maybe her parents' estate was close by, only a few miles away. *She* must be feeling Darcy's presence, and this was why his music—

Bingley interrupted his thoughts.

"Come, Darcy, I must have you dance. I hate to see you standing about by yourself in this stupid manner. You had much better dance."

Darcy glanced at one of the Bennet girls, Jane, whose company Bingley had kept all evening.

"You are dancing with the only handsome girl in the room."

"But there is one of her sisters sitting down just behind you. She is very pretty, and I dare say very agreeable."

A look. "She is tolerable, but not handsome enough to tempt me; I am in no humour at present to give consequence to young ladies who are slighted by other men."

She had heard. The young lady Darcy had just thoughtlessly insulted had heard him; she had reacted, Darcy *knew*.

Except how exactly had he known? How had he been aware of her reaction? He had not given her a second glance. He *knew* though that the young woman was amused. He could pinpoint, without looking, the moment she rose from her chair...

She crossed the room, a secret, light smile on her lips, and Darcy's music—

Oh no. Please no.

Part One

Two years before.

Elizabeth heard her soulmate's melody for the first time when she was nineteen. The notes sounded faraway; *he* was faraway, or *she*. Faraway in spirit, or maybe literally far—oceans, continents separating them.

"*He* will be a romantic," Jane decided, when Elizabeth told her. The two young women were ensconced in the safety of their bedroom; candlelight flickered in Jane's hair, her grey eyes tender with a wistful light. If Jane Bennet was a reputed beauty, Elizabeth thought, it was not because of her handsome, classical features. It was because her spirit shined through.

"Do you think we ever hear each other's soul music?" Elizabeth asked her sister. "You and me, Jane. Can you hear my melodies sometimes? A note, a phrase?"

"Lizzy, do you mean… Are you asking whether sisters can be soulmates?"

"No, not in the habitual way, obviously," Elizabeth answered with amusement. "But we are so close, Jane. You are as dear to me as a husband or a wife could be. Shouldn't we hear each other's harmonies?"

"I…" Jane hesitated. "Maybe. When you were in London last year, Lizzy, and I missed you so much, I believed I could hear an echo. But it might have been only fancy." She briefly blushed. "Though, these thoughts…you know the church see them as anathema."

'Anathema' was maybe too strong a word, but the Church of England frowned on the mere idea of perceiving—in your heart, in your mind—any music that was not your soulmate's. There had been countless treatises written about the subject, and some debate two hundred years ago when a courtier stated he heard the soul music of his king—as his faithful vassal, not as someone he was destined to love. But the church ruled this as impossible and blasphemous, and the poor man had been sent into an unpleasant exile.

Ah well. Elizabeth sighed and lay down on the linen covers. Hearing music was so abstract. Her soulmate, whoever they were, was more a concept than a human being. Someone, faraway, was hearing Elizabeth's music in their soul, as she was hearing theirs. She could not picture them; she could hardly believe them to be real.

While Jane, their special bond, their sisterly affection—this was true. This was now.

"Why did you say 'he' must be a romantic, Jane? My soulmate? Why a 'he'?"

"Oh, forgive me, Lizzy, of course, they can be anyone. I suppose I have been applying my dreams to yours. I have been hearing *him*—my soulmate... I have been hearing his music for so long, Lizzy, I feel like I know *him*. Lately, it is like I see *him*, even."

Elizabeth raised herself up onto her elbows with a smile. "So? Pray tell! What does the mystery gentleman look like?"

Jane paused. "The vision is blurry. I think I see his bright eyes, a bright smile...a kind voice, and, er, soft hands..." Jane turned crimson. "But those are just silly imaginings. Enough about me. Your soulmate, Lizzy. See, you just heard *him* for the first time on your nineteenth birthday. Nineteen is rather late…"

"It is. But through which peculiar Jane logic do you deduce 'he' must be a romantic?"

"Because *he* is thinking of love late in his life. So…maybe *he* has never fallen in love before. Maybe *he* was waiting for you."

Elizabeth blushed, and laughed, and shook her head again.

∞ ∞ ∞

When, two years later, a gentleman named Charles Bingley let Netherfield Park at last, the melody swelled in Jane's soul. "His soul music is full of emotion," Jane described, tears in her eyes. "Full of hope, of repressed melancholy, of decided joy. Oh Lizzy, his song is ever so gorgeous."

"Dear Jane, I hate to be the ugly, cold voice of doubt, but…are you sure? How can you be certain you are hearing Mr Bingley, of all men?"

"I *know*, Lizzy. When I saw him the first time, when Charles Bingley entered the assembly rooms, during the ball, while we were dancing, I just knew. See, the melody in my heart…it is so much clearer, stronger now. It goes like this…" Jane tried to hum. Her fingers searched for the rhythm playing in her mind, tapping on the old, beaten oak table till, frustrated, she walked to the pianoforte.

"No—there are several voices..." Jane began to play. "Lizzy, will you transcribe? If I dictate?"

"Of course," her sister said, grabbing some manuscript paper. With the importance of solfège in mating and marrying customs, there was not a woman in the kingdom—and hardly a man—who did not know how to compose, read, or write music. Educated gentlemen and ladies all played; even the merest peasant, the poorest shepherdess, knew their notes.

"Here I am, ready to serve Cupid's will," Elizabeth stated, sitting at the writing desk, pen in hand.

"If he—if Mr Bingley ever died, or left," Jane whispered, "I would want to keep his music. To preserve a part of him."

It was a dark and illogical idea, but when you are in love, you are allowed some unreasonableness, Elizabeth decided. Not that it would ever happen to her. She was not like Jane; she was too headstrong, too logical. No, that was untrue, Elizabeth mused, while Jane sung to herself, searching for the right notes. Elizabeth knew how to love; her heart was capable of stout, loyal affection, but she had never been *in love.* She hoped she would be one day; she could not imagine herself so lost that she would lose reason though, or her sense of humour. She would never be lost in romantic fancies, like Jane was.

Her sister had begun to play and sing. Not words, just humming a part of the melody. Elizabeth frantically scribbled.

The exercise was complex. Soulmates' harmonies were always sophisticated and difficult to put down on paper. "Soul music shows that us humans are intricate beings," Mr Bennet, Jane and Elizabeth's father, had commented one day. "Although, in some cases, it seems difficult to believe."

The two sisters worked for hours and covered five sheets of paper with Jane's soulmate notes before they stopped, exhausted. "I've lost him," Jane explained smilingly. "The music has stopped."

Elizabeth smiled. "Mr Bingley must be talking to his sisters—or to Mr Darcy. That would be enough to chase thoughts of romance out of anyone's head."

"Come on, Lizzy. You are being unfair. Mr Darcy has always been civil," Jane protested.

"If you say so."

Jane shook her head with amusement— Elizabeth had met Bingley's friend Mr Darcy only twice, but she already heartily disliked him. "What about yours, Lizzy? Have you heard… *their* music recently?"

"Indeed, I have." Elizabeth paused for a while. Her soulmate's music had recently grown stronger. Its appearance was still infrequent, but when the melody was present, it was strong, resonating in her mind, sharp enough that Elizabeth could not help but wonder.

Was *he*—or *she*—getting close? Recently, so much had changed in their neighbourhood. There were the new residents of Netherfield Park, of course: Mr Bingley and his sisters, his brother-in-law Mr Hurst, and Mr Darcy. But they were not the only recent arrivals. The regiment —hundreds of soldiers—had recently settled in the nearby town… Hordes of red-clad men now walking and laughing in the streets. There was also a new reverend in a town ten miles from their home, and some comings and goings in the prevalent families of the area.

In truth, the increased power of her soulmate music seemed connected to the arrival of the regiment in their home town. Elizabeth remembered it well; her mother had just told them the juicy piece of gossip at luncheon. Officers! Dozens of them! Quartered for half a year in Meryton! And Lizzy's soul had sung—yes, when did it happen exactly? Just a few days before Bingley and his group of unpleasant companions had set foot at Netherfield.

Elizabeth's soulmate music. Was it connected…to the regiment? To one of the officers, maybe?

∞ ∞ ∞

"A stronger soulmate melody does not necessarily mean a closer connection, not closer geographically at least," Mr Darcy stated, at Netherfield's dinner table. "Have you heard about the Oxford Soulmates' Experiments, Miss Elizabeth?"

"Indeed, I have, sir."

Elizabeth was always a little surprised when Mr Darcy addressed her directly—it was so rare. Their mutual dislike did not promote easy conversation. When Elizabeth and Mr Darcy had debated, the topic had generally been initiated by someone else, and Elizabeth had let herself be swept into the discussion.

Like this evening. Jane had fallen ill at Netherfield during a visit and was now secluded in a bedchamber upstairs. Elizabeth had been invited to stay for a few days to care for her sister. Fortunately, Jane was doing better, so tonight, Elizabeth had gone down to eat dinner with Mr Bingley, his sister Caroline, Mr and Mrs Hurst, and of course, Mr Darcy.

Who was now staring at her across the elegant table, waiting for a more elaborate answer.

Elizabeth slowly put her glass down. "My father subscribes to the Oxford Soulmates' reports, Mr Darcy. We read them together each month. The information is fascinating, I must own. The analysis of the experts I love the most —it is amusing seeing how learned men disagree so often."

Mr Darcy frowned. "May I ask which experience you are referring to?"

Elizabeth smiled with the utmost politeness. Of course, Mr Darcy would test her, to see if she had really read the reports. To try catching her in a lie, or to see whether she overestimated her knowledge.

"Oh, several, sir. But I was thinking about, specifically...the research about silences."

Everyone around the table was listening intently. Discussions of soulmates' music, of soulmates' bonds usually drew a lot of interest, even if, or maybe because, so little was known about the process.

Even Mr Bingley's eldest sister, Louisa Hurst, seemed drawn to the conversation, and Mr Hurst momentarily lifted his eyes from his plate of roasted duck. Elizabeth briefly wondered about them—not every marriage was a soulmates' union, of course.

"Most do not hear their soulmate's music continuously," Elizabeth continued. "Generally, it comes and goes. But why? Of course, those silences often correspond to sleep, unconsciousness, intoxication...or a different focus, or even, alas, inconstancy of feeling. But these reasons, as compelling as they are, do not account for all pauses."

Elizabeth was conscious of Mr Darcy's attention. His serious gaze was not leaving her face—she coloured a little.

"Mr Blackmore believes that those silences are an involuntary process that we humans cannot control," she continued. "But Mr Blackmore's colleague Mr Thrupp thinks some humans are able to control their inner melody. It would need a strong energy though, a strong character, to willingly block the...the emission of the music."

A pause ensued, that Elizabeth broke with a smile. "You can now despise me, Mr Darcy, for my lack of scientific accuracy, and my use of profane, simplistic words to describe such an intricate subject."

"Quite the opposite. That was very well said, madam, and exposed the issue quite clearly."

Elizabeth was so surprised by the compliment she did not even think of thanking him.

Caroline Bingley seemed vaguely exasperated, maybe with the fact that another young lady had been the focus of attention.

"What a strange area of study for a woman, Miss Elizabeth," she began with a sweet voice, and the smile of a shark. "Do you not fear it will pollute your innocence, stain your purity of thought, to get so interested in...the human bonding process?"

"I hope not, Miss Bingley."

Caroline was taken aback—Elizabeth's answer left no possibility to argue.

"Well, I disapprove of all this research!" Bingley protested with his usual cheer. "Not of young ladies being interested in the studies," he added with a smile in Elizabeth's direction. "Curiosity is natural. But to be honest—I do not want to know! The soulmate attraction is mystic, magical. I do not want some dusty old Oxford professor dissecting the process and spoiling all the fun!"

A lively discussion ensued, in which Elizabeth happily took part. Mr Darcy said not a word. She met his eyes once; he was observing her. Elizabeth just averted her gaze and smiled. Let him disapprove all he wished; he had broached the subject, after all.

But maybe she had misjudged. Mr Darcy turned his attention to the table centrepiece; there was no censure on his expression, he seemed solemn, sombre even.

Elizabeth's thoughts wandered. The music in her heart had been particularly intense lately, even piercing in some moments. Her soulmate was having difficulties, she supposed.

She should have been worried, for their sake. But call her cold, she could not muster ready empathy for someone she had not even met. *They* were still so abstract, a mental construction more than a reality. Maybe her soulmate did not even exist, she mused. Maybe melodies were random, and the whole marriage system of society was built on a lie… Elizabeth did not really believe it, but it was an interesting thought experiment.

She shared it with the table and was amused to hear the vehement protests of all, except Hurst and Darcy. The former poured himself another large glass of wine; the latter gave a wry smile.

"A lie? If only it were so."

"Oh Mr Darcy," Caroline readily intervened, her hand on her heart, "you do not hope for a soulmate? How awful!"

"We would be free, Miss Bingley," Darcy argued. "Would you not wish to wed whom you liked—and not whom the music chose for you? Would you not want to be liberated from irrationality and the random cruelties of fate?"

"Do not reduce music to obligation, Darcy!" Bingley protested. "You forget the beauty of falling in love, whether or not it's connected to melodies, or soulmates, or whatnot. Yes, love— it makes it all worth it. And when you feel it, when you feel your heart is being conquered, it is the most wonderful sensation in the world, is it not?"

Elizabeth was sure Darcy was going to scoff at such romantic notions, but strangely enough, he did not. A shadow passed across his face. Mr Bingley, without much subtlety, turned to Elizabeth and asked, "What does your sister Jane think of the soulmate bond?"

Caroline's face darkened. Mr Darcy raised his eyes—he did not seem happy either. The truth was, the Bingley family had money, and the Bennets did not. A marriage between Jane Bennet and Charles Bingley would not be considered joyful news by Caroline, or by Mr Darcy, who must wish for a higher connection for his friend. *But still*, Elizabeth wondered, with a pinch of fear, *they would not oppose a soulmates' union, would they?*

"Jane is an obedient daughter, so she dutifully listens when our father reads the Oxford reports," Elizabeth answered with prudence. "But I do not believe she has much interest in the scientific aspect. Jane is more captivated by what the poets have to say. And we both read novels —not for pleasure, only to be instructed further about soulmates' bonds, of course."

"Oh, of course." Mr Bingley laughed, and cheese was passed around.

"It is difficult to know for sure…when you… when you *hear* the music. Interpretations are… easy, but drawing conclusions too fast could be dangerous," Mr Darcy said hesitantly to Elizabeth, later, when they had all retired to the blue saloon for the evening. "Even when you hear…" he paused. "You cannot blame…anyone for a restrained attitude, when prudence is necessary."

Darcy's voice was low. He was standing near

the fireplace, close to Elizabeth. Miss Bingley was at the pianoforte, showing off her talent in a difficult concerto. The others were conversing, or, in the case of Mr Hurst, sleeping.

Elizabeth frowned. Mr Darcy's meaning was unclear. He wanted to continue the conversation started at dinner about soulmates, that much was clear, but to what aim? Was Mr Darcy saying —was he suggesting—that Jane was getting her hopes up for nothing, imagining her soulmate bond with Mr Bingley while there was none?

Elizabeth's heart swelled with indignation. If Mr Darcy was asking her to warn her sister off, she would have none of it.

"Wise advice, sir," she answered with a cold smile. She dropped a curtsey, then walked away from the gentleman, before wishing good night to the company and gratefully joining Jane upstairs.

∞∞∞

"Do you *hear*...anything, Miss Bennet, when you think of me?" Charles Bingley asked Jane Bennet a month later, during the Netherfield ball.

Jane turned crimson. It was late, Charles

Bingley was holding her hand. Their dance had just ended, the orchestra were preparing for the next. She averted her gaze; Charles Bingley's expression was too full of love—of hope. If she looked at him, she believed she would faint.

Though, she must answer. It was time. It was right.

"Mr Bingley, if you visited me tomorrow at home, I believe I could... I would have something to share with you, sir. A—a melody." Jane's voice was barely a whisper now. "I could play for you, if you would—if you would do me the honour of hearing it."

"I shall be there. I shall be there." Bingley held Jane's hand tighter. "Miss Bennet, nothing on earth could prevent me from coming."

"Charles, you cannot seriously think... You cannot mean to propose *marriage* to Jane Bennet!" Caroline protested the next morning during breakfast and after a lot of coffee. "I know she lets you believe that she is your soulmate—that you *believe* you hear her music..."

"That I *believe*? Caroline, you are not in my

head! How can you doubt..."

"Miss Bingley is right, Charles," Darcy said, pacing the room. He seemed tense, unhappy. "Emotion is not proof. Jane Bennet is beautiful of course..."

"But Charles, you could do so much better!"

"Jane Bennet is indeed a beauty," Darcy repeated, ignoring Caroline's interruption, "but her family is extremely objectionable, as was amply proved yesterday by their behaviour at your ball. Not... Not Miss Elizabeth's conduct, but—the younger sisters. Also, please keep in mind, Charles, that Jane Bennet's dowry is non-existent, while you are wealthy. Imagine the pressure her mother certainly exerts on her— rich husbands are hard to find..." Darcy sighed. "In short, I do not believe you could trust the sincerity of Jane Bennet's feelings towards you."

"Darcy, you are an ass."

"Charles!" Caroline squealed, but Darcy ignored her again.

"Bingley," he continued, "did Jane Bennet tell you... Did she irrevocably swear that she—that your melody resonated in her soul?"

"She will tell me this morning, I hope, when I go and visit her," Bingley said, standing up. He coldly bowed in the direction of his sister and his guest. "Now, if you will excuse me, I have a rendezvous I cannot miss."

∞∞∞

When Mr Bingley threw thirty pages of music paper on the Netherfield dinner table, black with the tight and well written notes of *his* soul music, dictated by Jane Bennet to her sister weeks ago, Mr Darcy had nothing further to object to.

Caroline Bingley was not to be so easily deterred. "This is a lie!" she protested, gesturing at the sheets with anger and disdain. "That is not your music, Charles!"

"It is."

"Well, Jane manufactured this somehow…"

Bingley crossed his arms. "How?"

"I do not know! Did you…tell her beforehand… about your melody? Did you sing it to her?"

"No!"

"Did you hum your harmonies to someone? Someday, mayhap last year, amongst the ton? Perhaps a transcript was made—and stolen, or maybe Jane's mother bribed some other woman to obtain—"

"Caroline, do you think your brother a complete simpleton? No, I did not reveal my music to anyone. And even if I did whisper a musical phrase, here or there, to another lady, or two—or three—in London, when I wanted to, er, test the waters, so to speak..." Bingley shook his head, grabbed the papers, and raised them before his sister's eyes. "These are not a dozen notes. This is the entire symphony. This is...this is *me*, Caroline, the entirety of who I am. Nobody has ever...known me like this, understood me like Jane did, when she dictated this."

"Mr Darcy! Say something!"

Darcy shook his head. "They are soulmates, Miss Bingley, this is proof. Your brother is a gentleman, he loves the lady, they share their music. There is no force on earth that can prevent this marriage now—and none that should. Bingley, let me give you my heartiest congratulations. Finding your soulmate, being blessed with mutual affection—it is a rare feat."

"It is! And thank you, Darcy. Will you extend your stay with us—here at Netherfield? Now that Jane and I are engaged, I want to give another ball in her honour, as my *betrothed*, officially this time. And I shall need your advice for the estate! I want to take this landowner business seriously if I am to be married—come on, man, will you stay?"

A hundred emotions played on Darcy's face.

"Maybe. Maybe for a few more days."

∞ ∞ ∞

Three weeks later, Darcy was still at Netherfield, but Caroline Bingley was gone.

Gossip reached the Bennet family. Caroline had tried to force the issue, it was said. Caroline Bingley had told Mr Darcy she was his soulmate and had tried to prove it somehow—at night, in his *bedchamber*, the servants whispered.

The attempt had not gone well.

As his betrothed, Jane was now in Bingley's confidence, but what she learned, she only told Elizabeth. "Caroline seemed desperate, Lizzy, and I do not fathom why. It was after we all dined together at Netherfield on Friday— remember how pleasant a party it was?"

Elizabeth smiled but did not answer. She had not appreciated the evening as much as her sister. Charles Bingley had invited a few friends to his beautiful home for a meal and an impromptu dance; as a resident guest, Mr Darcy was present, of course. He was in one of his disagreeable moods, but for some perverse reason, he still tried to dance with Elizabeth twice. She had to pretend fatigue to refuse him, and then could not accept another partner all night.

Jane shook her head and sighed. "After that evening, it was as if time and hope were slipping through Caroline's fingers. I understand though. I understand her. I know all too well the power that draws you to a man you believe you *hear*. And Caroline…if she thought she *heard* Mr Darcy, I suppose she wanted to…to act. And that night…" Jane shook her head. "As much as I love Caroline, now that she is to be my sister— she did not act as prudently as she should have. Afterwards, Mr Darcy was pale with rage."

Elizabeth imagined it all quite well. The arrogant Mr Darcy, being wooed by a woman with connections *in trade*. His paleness, she decided, must be due to contempt.

Caroline was sent to London, to the house of an aunt.

∞∞∞

Another month passed. Christmas came and went.

∞∞∞

The day was grey.

In Netherfield's blue drawing room, a feeble sun barely crept its way in. Darcy read in an armchair, Elizabeth on the sofa. An hour drifted away, Elizabeth engrossed in her book, the gentleman and the lady not uttering a word to each other.

Somewhere, church bells rang, their sound muffled by wind and distance. Then the world was silent again.

Darcy stood up.

He walked to the window—then walked back.

"Miss Elizabeth…"

Elizabeth lowered her book. Darcy's voice was strangely rough. A peculiar tension floated in the room; it was so dark, you could almost imagine night was falling. She felt pressure— waves crashing on a shore somewhere. What a strange, senseless thought.

"I suppose I should accustom myself to calling you by another name, Miss Elizabeth," Mr Darcy finally said, with a slight bow. Elizabeth had the irrational impression that he had switched topics at the last possible moment. "As soon as your sister takes the name of Bingley, you will become Miss Bennet."

"Indeed, I shall." Elizabeth smiled, trying to shake the eerie sensation. "Can you imagine the greatness of my new position—my elevated consequence in the world? I am not sure I shall be able to bear the change."

Amusement flickered in Darcy's eyes. "I am certain you will."

Silence, again. Yes, a storm was building somewhere.

The gentleman hesitated. He walked to the table, before turning back to her with a dry, odd smile.

"Miss Elizabeth, I—I find myself with a sort of headache—a family affliction, I fear. My sister's music generally works wonders. Would you... We have such a fine instrument here, could I prevail on you to play a piece?"

"Of course, sir," said Elizabeth, surprised, although not unwilling. It was an unexpected request, but she loved playing, and as unpleasant as Mr Darcy could be, she did not want him to needlessly suffer. She walked to the instrument, feeling his eyes on her all the while. When she looked through the music sheets, he seemed strangely expectant, strained even. Waiting for *something*—or maybe it was Elizabeth's fancy at work.

"Do you wish for something in particular, sir?"

"I wish for you...to choose," he said, his voice even lower than usual. "A...personal piece, maybe?"

Elizabeth nodded, but she did not want too difficult a song, so after some thought, she decided on a sweet Scottish composition. "Shall I sing?"

"Please."

Elizabeth acquitted herself as best she could and was satisfied with her performance. Despite the gentleman's clear unease, there was an unexpected peace in the secluded room, with the curtains half drawn and the dark slivers of sky. The moment felt suspended; in the confines of her mind, Elizabeth's soulmate music rose, as if *they* were close, as if *they* were thinking of her. Elizabeth had to check the impression; she had to quell the harmonies of her soul, to prevent the notes of her soulmate's melody seeping into her music. She had to stay focused on her light, hopeful song.

Once she had finished playing, she turned to her companion.

Darcy observed her in silence. He was

serious, then an expression crossed his face that Elizabeth could not interpret. Relief, she thought, soon followed by its exact opposite, some unexpected, but bitter disappointment. *I do not know this man at all*, Elizabeth decided.

Some people were so open, she could interpret any of their expressions. Fitzwilliam Darcy was a cypher.

"Do you feel better, sir? Was it in any way helpful?"

Darcy did not answer—instead he began to pace the room again. Elizabeth was rather offended. She had played as best she could. Surely her talent was not great, but she deserved at least a courteous thanks.

Still, Darcy kept silent. Elizabeth fiddled with the keys, wondering whether she should leave, or maybe begin to play another song, when the gentleman turned to her at last.

"With my friend and your sister in such an interesting situation, we have often discussed the intricacies of soulmates' bonds... But we have never discussed the opposite situation, Miss Elizabeth."

"The opposite, sir?"

"There are people who— What do you think of—the morality, the risks... The likely consequences of marrying someone who…may *not* be your soulmate?"

Darcy's colour was high. Elizabeth did not react at first, her hands were still distractedly playing on the pianoforte keys. *What on earth was Mr Darcy's purpose? Was he still opposed to Mr Bingley's betrothal? Did he still believe Jane had lied? No, it could not be.*

Was Darcy asking for advice for himself, maybe? Rumour had it that Darcy's family was trying to promote a marriage between him and his rich cousin Anne de Bourgh. But… The powerful Mr Darcy, taking Elizabeth Bennet as a confidante? She could not fathom such a turn of events. No, it had to be some sort of test again, but why? Elizabeth played a slow musical phrase, to give herself time to think.

"What was that?" Darcy asked, rather brusquely.

"I am sorry?"

"That—the notes you just played."

It was fortunate Elizabeth had her back to him and Darcy could not witness her horrified reaction. She had been so distracted her hands had erred and played a phrase of her soul music—her soulmate's melody. Panic rose. Elizabeth quickly played again, her cheeks burning, adding notes, transforming the phrase into something else—into a completely different song.

Oh, her shame was intense. She would not open herself up before this man. She would not bare her soul to him.

Worse, Darcy would interpret it as an attempt to entrap him. Young ladies everywhere must be attempting to seduce the rich and eligible Fitzwilliam Darcy. Of course, the Caroline Bingleys of the world would have taken advantage of such a moment to try their notes —to try their luck—to play their soulmate's melody before Darcy and hope for the best. And now, she... Now Darcy would believe the worst of her. Elizabeth was humiliated, she was mortified; her fingers unsteady, she played the musical phrase for a third time, transforming it even further, till it became quite unrecognisable.

"This is the introduction of Mozart's Seventh Concerto, sir," she said, trying for a light tone and failing, hating her weakness and the sound of her voice. "A lesser known variation. Maybe you remember, Mrs Hurst spoke of it yesterday?"

The silence was deafening.

Elizabeth thought she could hear the storm, but outside, the skies were calm.

(The sea was deep and wild.)

"Indeed."

A pause. Then Mr Darcy bowed; he turned on his heels and left the room.

The next day, he was gone.

The soulmate music was savage after Darcy's departure from Netherfield. Not that Elizabeth connected the two events. For her, the melody haunting her days and nights had possibly found its explanation in the return to Meryton of an old favourite—a handsome gentleman named George Wickham.

Mr George Wickham was a poor but dashing lieutenant. He disliked Mr Darcy very much, which only elevated him in Elizabeth's mind. It seemed Mr Wickham and Mr Darcy had an history; the story was unclear, but Mr Darcy had played a villainous role in Wickham's tale, so Elizabeth was happy to accept it as truth.

Elizabeth and Wickham had flirted a few months ago, before Jane's betrothal. Then Wickham had had to leave, but now he was back, now he danced with Elizabeth again.

Wickham was so very charming, and so

clearly attracted to Elizabeth, and so very gallant with all of Elizabeth's sisters. It was whispered that he had suffered a recent romantic disappointment with a Miss King, but oddly, the rumour only increased the suave officer's popularity. In Meryton, every young lady sighed when Wickham smiled, but the officer only had eyes for Elizabeth, or so it seemed.

Elizabeth played with the idea for a while. That Wickham was the one, that her music would match his. She imagined it all. The handsome lieutenant would present himself at her father's door one day; he would declare, in the most passionate tones, that he was the soulmate of Mr Bennet's beautiful, clever, second daughter. "Dear sir," Wickham would say to Elizabeth's father, "it is true, I do not yet have the financial means to offer Elizabeth a respectable establishment, but…"

But…what? There Elizabeth's romantic fancy ended. Would they marry? Would Elizabeth marry Wickham without a penny to live on? Or would she accept a long engagement, hoping for the hazards and vagaries of fortune? For such a step, Elizabeth would have to be very, very much in love, and she suspected she was not. Dancing, flirting, conversing, it was all very agreeable, but if Wickham left the neighbourhood again, she would miss the distraction he brought more than the man himself.

If Wickham was indeed her soulmate though? He could be. The timing fitted; Elizabeth's soul music had grown stronger around his arrival. Yes, what if? What if Elizabeth was driving her soulmate away because the man had not completely won her affections yet? Perhaps she was being too cold, too guarded. Mayhap she should give it time, try to know him better. They were already good friends—real love, mayhap, could come.

Except Elizabeth's father did not like Wickham.

"My dear Lizzy," Mr Bennet said, one afternoon, after drawing his daughter into his study for a serious conversation, "I shall play the role of the stern father for once and tell you that I do not approve of this growing intimacy with your simpering lieutenant. If he was a poor, but admirable young man...clever, brave, and worthy of you, then, if he was your soulmate, and only in that case, we could consider the possibility of a union. It is very disagreeable to be without money, but something could be contrived, I am sure. I could borrow a sum, we could enlist your uncle's help—you know I would not like to break your heart, my dear."

"You have always been very kind, Father."

"But admirable George Wickham is not. Maybe

I am wrong, but...I know you well, Lizzy. I cannot perceive that you hold a strong affection for such a man."

Elizabeth should have protested, she should have taken the side of her favourite with passion. What did it say about the state of her affections, she wondered, that she felt no such desire?

"May I ask, Father, why you hold such an opinion?"

"Your young man talks a great deal, but he does nothing much. He plays cards, he complains that the cruel Mr Darcy stole his inheritance, and that is all. Oh, he enthusiastically partakes of our mutton cutlets, our lemon pies, and our Madeira wine. He likes your spirited conversation, and Lydia's too, have you noticed? I understand—our living room is more pleasant a prospect than his lodgings or the habitual regime of the military mess. But I am not sure he has marriage in mind. Has he ever uttered a word on the subject?"

Elizabeth paced the room. Her father gave her time to gather her thoughts. Finally, she sat down.

"He has not. And indeed, sir, I am not seriously attached. But still, would you give me a few weeks—no more than three, to... I hardly know how to define it. To think about what you just told me. And to test him, I suppose. To test Mr Wickham's character, to test his affections—to test mine, possibly. I promise I shall do nothing, say nothing to entangle myself. I just need…" Elizabeth sighed, "I need to know more. I would ask for your trust, sir."

"Very well, Lizzy…I can give you three weeks."

Elizabeth remembered her father's wise advice in the weeks that followed. She watched Mr Wickham with a scrutinising eye. The officer enjoyed the comforts of the Bennets' home maybe more than was entirely proper; he flirted with Lydia more than he ought. Although it could be said that Lydia flirted with him, and Wickham did not dislike it.

All forgivable behaviours perhaps, in a happy, energetic young man who enjoyed laughter and the comforts of life. After all, Charles Bingley, who came every day to visit Jane, his beautiful betrothed, certainly also sang the praises of Mrs Bennet's table, and ate the lemon cakes, and drank the Madeira wine, and he was also very kind to the younger girls.

But somehow, it did not feel the same.

∞ ∞ ∞

One afternoon, Wickham and Elizabeth found themselves alone. Kitty and Lydia had walked to Meryton. Mrs Bennet was busy upstairs with Mrs Hill, the housekeeper. Jane had been whisked away by Bingley for a carriage ride, Mary serving as a reluctant chaperone.

After tea and some entertaining conversation, Elizabeth led Lieutenant Wickham to the Bennets' cramped music room. The curtains were half drawn. It was dark in the house, although outside the sun was shining... And suddenly Elizabeth was seized by the memory of Netherfield, of that grey day, the half-lit blue drawing room, Mr Darcy watching her while she played.

The sensation was so strong, it was as if Elizabeth had been transported there again. She felt the power of Mr Darcy's gaze on her, the peculiar, charged atmosphere of the moment— then she was back in reality, in her home's familiar surroundings.

Wickham was close, watching her with an unusual, hungry smile.

"Am I to hope, Miss Elizabeth, that we are finding ourselves isolated in this room on purpose, and that you were dying for a moment with me?"

Elizabeth laughed but took a prudent step back. "No, Mr Wickham. I sincerely wish to talk about music."

Wickham closed the door behind them. Elizabeth remembered her father's admonitions. "Do you mind opening the door again, sir? This room is not often aired."

Wickham obeyed without a word.

"I have been practising a new musical creation of mine," Elizabeth explained, sitting at the pianoforte. "I was hoping you could give me your opinion—and maybe play yourself if you wish to. I do not believe I have ever heard you at the instrument?"

She was having fun with the keys; Wickham drew over a chair. "Oh, I am far from gifted," he answered amiably, "but I would love to try and entertain you, Miss Elizabeth, if only to hear that delicious laugh of yours." He gestured in direction of the instrument, "But, as always, ladies first."

Elizabeth started to play.

Personal musical creations were very popular; any accomplished young lady must invent a few of her own to shew her imagination and her sensitivity. But there were more to those artistic inventions than just posture. Music was a language, a secret way of conveying feelings and information. If a dear friend—or a lover— shared a phrase of their soul music with you, you could incorporate it into your compositions, as a secret, as an intimate and clandestine gift. And none would know when you played, except the one it was intended for. In novels, captive heroines—or adulteresses—performed complicated sonatas, intertwining them with secret musical phrases stolen from their loved one's soul melody, to send a message... Stories varied and could be quite wicked.

Elizabeth knew of those methods; Lieutenant Wickham certainly did too. Thus, Elizabeth was aware of the likely consequences when she incorporated a particular phrase into the music, and let it appear again and again.

As if it were important. As if she were giving Wickham a clue, a key.

(The sea, faraway. Her melody—her soulmate's music—roaring on the shore.)

(Silver skies in the Netherfield music room. Heaviness in the air.)

The music came to an end; Elizabeth did not move, waiting for Wickham's reaction.

He rose. "I am stunned," he whispered,

"stunned and bewildered. I had hoped...but hoped only. I could not be certain... Oh, beautiful Elizabeth," said he, taking her hand and trying to draw her to him.

Elizabeth gave him a smile but refused to stand. "Dear Elizabeth," George Wickham began again, "at last I have found you. All these years, I was desperately searching for—"

The lady interrupted him politely. "Must I deduce from your reaction, Lieutenant Wickham, that you...recognise these harmonies? This music?"

"Recognise it? This particular phrase... This phrase you have chosen has been resonating in my soul since I was fifteen."

"This is useful information to have," Elizabeth commented, drawing her hand back. Her smile did not waver. "But this is not my soulmate melody, Lieutenant Wickham, just a new musical harmony I invented. I was, as I told you, only practising." She stood. "I am sorry I led you astray, I believe you will soon find the lady of your notes, sir," she added, walking towards the door.

There was silence.

"You little—" The man growled a terrifying slur; Elizabeth stilled and turned to him, aghast. Wickham pushed her violently against the wall.

"A fake soulmate melody, oh, that was a clever trap," he hissed. "Very clever, testing me, yes, you got me, but after all this work, I believe I am owed…" He tried to kiss her, his hands roaming over her body. Elizabeth cried out, she bit him, pushed him away. Wickham's hand grabbed her throat (somewhere, the sea was roaring, her soulmate music swelling in her brain, like a friend, an ally, carrying her, giving her strength.)

"Mrs Hill!" Elizabeth screamed, hearing familiar footsteps. The housekeeper hastened into the room—Elizabeth's aggressor had already drawn back.

He looked at the two women, and after a despicable curse, he made for the door.

∞∞∞

Lieutenant Wickham never set foot at Longbourn again.

∞∞∞

What Wickham had really wanted from her Elizabeth would never know. He was clearly not in love, and Elizabeth had no fortune, so he had no reason to force a marriage. Maybe Wickham was ready to lie about the existence of a soulmate's bond just in the hope of obtaining a few kisses...or more substantial favours. Or perhaps Elizabeth's father had been right, and the impoverished officer had no particular plan; he mainly wished to enjoy good food and amiable conversation, but was open to other, more...carnal possibilities, if the opportunity arose.

Elizabeth shivered sometimes, thinking of what could have happened if she had believed Wickham was her soulmate. If she had trusted him. If the man had led her into some secluded place... Of course, Elizabeth never would have willingly submitted to—

But Wickham was strong, and if, later, she had found herself with child...

One mistake, and her whole life could have ended in shame and despair.

Mr Bennet hesitated, but after some discussion, he and Elizabeth finally decided to keep the incident secret. They did not warn the army authorities of the lieutenant's disgraceful conduct. Colonel Forster, Wickham's superior officer, was a jolly man. He liked to drink, and neither he nor his pretty young bride were the soul of discretion. If Mr Bennet told them what had happened, someone would talk, and

Elizabeth's reputation would be greatly harmed.

But Wickham's conduct had one important repercussion. Weeks later, Elizabeth's younger sister Lydia was invited to stay in Brighton by Colonel Forster's young wife. The regiment would be quartered there for a while, and the two young ladies could have a merry time under Colonel Forster's protection.

Mr Bennet sternly refused to let his younger daughter go. To let Lydia live in the Forster's home as a guest, while Wickham was a close friend of theirs, while he would be an intimate of the family, in and out of their house at all hours...

Never.

Lydia cried, protested and wept, but she never left home.

∞∞∞

Then came blissful months.

Strange, to talk about happiness after such a harrowing incident. But paradoxically enough, with Lieutenant Wickham's elimination as a soulmate possibility, Elizabeth was now free to hope and imagine.

There was someone else out there, waiting for her.

Her soul music was intense and clear. Elizabeth's soulmate was somewhere, thinking about her. And *they* could be anyone. Everything was possible, every future was hers; life was open, exhilarating.

Elizabeth could meet her soulmate any day; maybe she already had.

There was a joy in not knowing, in waiting for the Fates to show their hand. And Elizabeth had decided, at last, to study her soulmate's music.

Elizabeth's soulmate's chords were deep and powerful, dark even, at times. Profound and moving like the sea, like the images of the ocean that had lately invaded Elizabeth's psyche. To make sense of those visions, she read the Oxford Soulmates' reports again. She understood then the waves to be a metaphor—*phantasmagorias*— the visual that her brain created to illustrate the notes she heard.

Translating *audire* to *videre*, Mr Blackmore, one of the Oxford experts, had written. Elizabeth studied everything on the subject.

It was now Jane's turn to write Elizabeth's soulmate music under dictation. Elizabeth should have felt embarrassed, opening the recesses of her heart to another human being. But with Jane it did not feel like trespassing; with Jane it felt like she should know.

Once the dictation was over, Jane played Elizabeth's soul music at her sister's request.

"Should I be worried that *they* are so sad?" Elizabeth asked, listening to a particularly nostalgic passage.

Jane shook her head, smiling, and finished playing the part before turning to her sister.

"There is melancholy in the music indeed, but—listen, Lizzy... Here." Jane played a few more notes. "This is joy, or at least the hope, the possibility of joy. And there is so much"— Jane hesitated—"strength, but also generosity. Your soulmate is someone...good," she finally concluded. "I am sorry, I wish I could I express myself better."

Elizabeth smiled. "I am perfectly satisfied with your analysis."

"Let us not forget," Jane added with a smile, "that it could be *your* sadness that we are hearing. These are not only your soulmate's harmonies. The soul music is a combination of both your inner themes."

Indeed, Jane was right. Humans hearing their soulmates simplified the matter by talking of "his" or "her" music, and this was how the concept was referred to in casual conversation. But a soulmate's melody was a blend of both spirits, both souls. Soulmates heard the same music, it was *their* melody, a song that they both shared.

"Then, I challenge the muses," Elizabeth protested laughingly. "You are perfectly right, Jane, this is my music also. But then these chords are much too solemn! Where is the happiness? I have never been sad a day in my life."

Jane looked at her sister with surprise. "Do you really believe so, Lizzy? I believe you are very often sad—often disillusioned by people. That is why you hide behind jokes and witticisms."

Elizabeth seemed stricken. Her sister continued, "Do you not say that you are disappointed with the world?"

"Yes," her sister protested. "But I hope for a better one."

Jane smiled and looked at the music sheets. "*They* do too."

∞∞∞

Mr Darcy staggered when Elizabeth walked out of Meryton Church.

∞∞∞

Mr Darcy had come back to Netherfield to stand up with Mr Bingley at his wedding. It was a cold morning; Jane was still at Longbourn, busy with the final arrangements of her bridal attire. Elizabeth had walked early to church, wishing to talk to the reverend before the marriage ceremony about a few adjustments her mother desired.

The sun was feeble, but once the discussion was over, Elizabeth stepped outside the ancient building to enjoy the light.

Maybe 'staggered' had been too strong a word. When Mr Darcy saw Elizabeth appear on the church steps, he stilled, and turned pale for the merest moment. Elizabeth could not make sense of it.

Darcy finally averted his gaze and resumed his discussion with Bingley, while Elizabeth conversed with the reverend's wife. A few minutes passed before Darcy at last came to coldly salute Elizabeth. The delay bordered on rudeness, considering their level of acquaintance. But hearing Darcy's strained voice, Elizabeth's thoughts flew again, with a combination of unease and fascination, to their bizarre moment in the Netherfield music room.

(A storm was building.)

During Jane and Bingley's wedding ceremony, Darcy's gaze hardly left Elizabeth. It could be attributed to distraction of mind, or to disapproval. Elizabeth decided it was the latter; she was very ready to dislike him again. Alas, she was prevented from a complete return to her old prejudices by the gentleman's polite approach during the wedding breakfast.

"I can call you Miss Bennet now, as foreseen," Mr Darcy began with a smile.

Elizabeth gave a smile back. "And as foreseen, sir, I shall bear the title with fortitude."

"Were the days uneventful at Longbourn after I left?"

Elizabeth answered merrily, talking about the suffering of young ladies in the country due to the lack of distractions. But Mr Darcy, she felt, had a precise intention in mind. He was very diplomatic and never pushed too far, but it seemed he wanted the confirmation, or the contradiction, that *something*—an unpleasant event—had happened to Elizabeth during his absence.

Elizabeth thought briefly of the Wickham incident, but—it could not be. How would Mr Darcy know?

It was certainly not in her interest to confide in him though, so she stayed perfectly smiling while assuring the gentleman that nothing could be safer or more boring than life in Meryton.

Darcy nodded once, his expression unreadable, and dropped the subject.

But he would not let Elizabeth leave. To her surprise, he tried one topic, then another. Elizabeth was too polite not to help him in his endeavours; the discussion which followed was uneasy at first, but after some exertion from the gentleman, and some goodwill from the lady, they had an earnest discussion about books, a conversation Elizabeth enjoyed more than she thought she would. Mr Darcy had a very informed mind and read a lot. What a pity he was so disagreeable! When he was silent again, it was with that thought in mind, and the memory of their old dislike, that she added laughingly, "You cannot have missed the pleasures of my conversation, sir."

He was silent for a moment and seemed very surprised. "On the contrary, Miss Bennet," was all he said.

She laughed it off like the gallant lie it was, and after a curtsey, she left him. She wanted to talk to Henry Tilney, the new reverend of a prosperous village ten miles from Meryton. Mr Tilney was clever, funny, and handsome enough; soon he had Elizabeth laughing, and they were swept into a fiery debate. To Elizabeth's surprise, Mr Darcy joined them. Maybe the topic was of interest to him, though he did not participate much. His presence at Elizabeth's side was unsettling, though—she wondered what he was thinking, if he was judging her still, if he found her manners and her family wanting. It was an unpleasant sensation; she soon left the two gentlemen to themselves under the pretext of helping her mother.

Half an hour passed. Elizabeth was still surrounded by guests when she realised her soulmate music's sudden strength.

The harmonies. Vibrating, almost screaming in her soul.

Why? How? She had long stopped trying to make sense of the bizarre timings and irregularities in her soulmate music's surges of power; nothing seemed logical, nothing made sense. She walked into the garden, to catch her breath, to *listen*.

There she stayed alone for a while. The music was poignant. She did not move, just let the harmonies take hold of her, wash over her, waves on a distant shore.

When she came back into the parlour, Mr Darcy had already left.

∞∞∞

He did not stay at Netherfield as he was invited to, but departed for Pemberley, his home, the very same day.

Elizabeth did not give it much thought.

∞∞∞

She had other matters on her mind. Her confrontation with Lieutenant Wickham had at least one advantage: to Elizabeth, her soulmate had ceased to be abstract. Yes, now they were not a concept anymore, they were...someone. Alive, palpable.

Flesh.

At night, Elizabeth's imagination wandered. Her soulmate was a living person, made for her, moulded for her by destiny. Waiting for her as she was waiting for them. Someone with a smile and tender eyes and a ready joke; someone who would kiss her—touch her—in ways she could not imagine yet.

After some languorous, languid dreams, Elizabeth's cheeks were rather red in the morning.

Elizabeth made a list. Of soulmate possibilities in her area. She did not write the list down, but she talked about it at length with the new Mrs Jane Bingley, whom Elizabeth visited almost every day at Netherfield, her sister's new and beautiful home.

The two young women drew great enjoyment from considering all the attractive gentlemen and ladies in the vicinity of Meryton and deciding if they were, yes or no, worthy of being Elizabeth's potential soulmate. The task was amusing, but at the end, only three individuals made the cut.

The first soulmate possibility was a young lady named Elinor Dashwood. The Dashwood sisters were not from the area; they had recently been visiting a friend in Meryton. Elinor and Marianne were their names; two single young women of excellent birth, sadly now in reduced financial circumstances.

Elinor Dashwood, the eldest sister, was twenty-three, discreet, and serious. She was also very clever and not an easy creature to befriend. Elizabeth never knew, really, whether Elinor liked her or not, but *she* liked Elinor, and the young woman's character and recent arrival fit with the new vigour of Elizabeth's soul music.

"I believe it fits," Elizabeth commented with amusement to Jane. "Elinor Dashwood is certainly as stern and grave as the harmonies I hear. But I have succeeded in making her laugh! I did, at least twice. You must believe me when I say it was quite the feat."

This discussion of the utmost importance was happening at Netherfield, where Elizabeth and Jane were having tea in the library. The room had been sadly empty for years but was not anymore. Indeed, every month, thanks to Mr Darcy's suggestions, new books arrived to ornament the elegant shelves. Bingley was in regular correspondence with his friend; he was following his advice and duly ordering new tomes.

Jane and Elizabeth always read them, if

Bingley did not. Thus, Mr Darcy's literary taste and choices were often a subject at dinner. Jane, being a married lady, could write back to Mr Darcy, thanking him for his counsel, and explaining how much she and Elizabeth had appreciated his recommendations, and why.

This sometimes led to scholarly debate by proxy. If Elizabeth disliked an author, Jane told Mr Darcy in written form, and the gentleman answered with some compelling arguments. Elizabeth thought, amused, that she could not help disagreeing with Mr Darcy, even when he was distant and all communication went through letters written by another.

But enough of Mr Darcy—back to Elizabeth's possible soulmates, and Elinor Dashwood.

Elizabeth could see it. Elizabeth Bennet and Elinor Dashwood—soulmates. A calm little life, a cottage near the sea. They would read, they would talk, they would play on an old, beaten pianoforte. Two women could not have children, but they could take care of their nephews and nieces, adopt a child from an impoverished family—or stay childless, just the two of them. There would not be a lot of money —very limited means, even. Books would be rare, but certainly Longbourn and Netherfield's libraries would stay open to them.

"But would such a quiet and retiring life

suit you, Lizzy?" Jane worried. "You are not materialistic, I know, but you and I were raised in comfort."

Elizabeth drank more tea and gave it real thought, and decided that yes, such an existence would suit her. "I would visit you at Netherfield when I was in need of luxury, but really, Jane... what I fear in life is intellectual solitude, not lack of financial means. I need...a spirit ready to understand and challenge mine. I have to get to know Elinor better, but I believe she has just the mind and character to suit me."

This was all well and good, and fed Elizabeth's fancy for a few weeks, but nothing in Elinor Dashwood's conduct seemed to lead towards a soulmates' union. Elinor remained perfectly polite, and perfectly indifferent. There was a sheet of glass between Elinor Dashwood and the world, Elizabeth decided, and whether fire or ice lurked behind, she did not know, and after a while did not much want to know.

Yet Elizabeth's soul music sang, as strong as ever. But it did not sing any more—or less —in Elinor's presence. Elizabeth did not yearn for her. When the Dashwood sisters were gone again, it was, after all, as if they had never been there.

∞∞∞

Very different, and fiery, if short, were Elizabeth's interests in Reverend Henry Tilney and the beautiful Claire de Verneuil.

Claire de Verneuil was the impoverished daughter of some French noble who had fled the revolution. She was also a friend of Bingley's eldest sister, Louisa Hurst, and on Bingley's invitation, the charming Claire came to reside at Netherfield for three months, in the company of Mr and Mrs Hurst. Despite her impressive name, Mademoiselle Claire de Verneuil had not much money, but what she lacked in fortune she made up for in brilliance.

Claire loved dinners and parties, and the generous Charles Bingley was only too happy to have an excuse to show off his hospitality. Never had Meryton known such a flurry of balls and receptions than during the stay of the beautiful Parisian *demoiselle*. This state of affairs was an unexpected and rather consuming task for the new Jane Bingley; after all, each time her husband so liberally bestowed a new invitation, Jane was the one who had to organise the practical matters.

But, to her own surprise maybe, Jane was a

born hostess, and despite her quiet manners, enjoyed seeing her friends and her husband happy. Once reassured that her sister was not unduly suffering, Elizabeth was taken in by the whirlwind of celebrations, and very pleased with them. Claire de Verneuil longed for sparkling conversation, intelligence, and humour, and found them all in Elizabeth.

Soon the two women were inseparable. Was it flirtation, or was it rational affinity? Sometimes it is difficult to know, sometimes you may not want to. Claire even invited Elizabeth to dance with her during the balls, quite scandalising the neighbourhood.

If same sex marriages had been made legal in England almost three centuries ago, after Henry VIII had fought with the Pope for the right to gleefully behead his husbands as well as his wives, there was still reluctance in the more old-fashioned English families, especially in isolated neighbourhoods. Couples of the same sex may dance together in some circles, in a few fashionable ballrooms, in London or in Paris—but in Meryton, such conduct was quite unheard of.

Despite it all, Elizabeth accepted Claire's invitations to stand up with her during the Netherfield balls. Her cheeks were burning, and she felt very modern.

Elizabeth's father drew great amusement from the shocked glances. Elizabeth's mother did not know quite what to feel. It was certainly irregular, and Mrs Bennet was old fashioned. She would have preferred a man for her daughter, and Mademoiselle de Verneuil was not rich enough to be forgiven for being female.

But…if it really must be so—well, a marriage to a member of French nobility, you know—so very elegant… Elizabeth Bennet de Verneuil—how well that sounded!

Elizabeth reflected about it all when she was alone, one rainy afternoon, at Netherfield.

The library there had soon become her favourite room to think. For some mysterious reason, her soul music was stronger there. Sometimes the calm and the semi darkness strangely seemed to invoke Mr Darcy's image. Elizabeth imagined him, walking along the shelves, looking at a book, putting it back in its place.

It was a pleasant enough idea—she did not feel any dislike towards the illusion of the man. Why would her fancy fly to Mr Darcy though? *Phantasmagoria*… Elizabeth decided that her mind must invoke the serious gentleman's presence as a metaphor for study or reflection.

Sometimes, the sensation was so strong, she felt as if he was really present.

One day, curled up on the sofa, Elizabeth closed her eyes, and the library morphed around her, becoming a different one. Vaster, more luminous. Pemberley's library, she *knew*.

Darcy was looking at the tomes. He felt her presence. He turned to her…

Elizabeth woke up.

A future with Mademoiselle de Verneuil. A small, elegant apartment in London, maybe even in Paris one day, when the war was over. Not much money, but many friends. Noble connections. Clever, shocking, modern theories. Dinners, balls, routs, laughs.

Why not?

But—there was another soulmate possibility, in the presence of Reverend Henry Tilney. The man was funny, he was kind, he liked Elizabeth. Mr Tilney and Elizabeth even spent an entire day together, walking in the gardens, then conversing in Longbourn's drawing room all evening, and that night, after the gentleman left, Elizabeth really wondered if...

A reverend's wife. A nice house. Mr Tilney was wealthy—there would be money enough to not worry about life's inconstancies and perils. Enough money to help people, as Elizabeth ought in her role, if such a union came to be. Comfort, duty, community. Elizabeth would be useful and merry, settled close to her family. She would be happy.

Three different soulmates, three different futures.

But Elinor Dashwood was already gone. Claire de Verneuil left for London without Elizabeth feeling a strong enough impulse to share her melody with her. Reverend Henry Tilney met his soulmate, a sweet, younger girl named Catherine who revealed her music to him as soon as they met and gazed at him with adoration in her eyes.

None of this broke Elizabeth's heart. On the contrary, she was free again. Her destiny was still not settled. Life was long, and again full of possibilities.

Someone, somewhere, was waiting for her.

Charlotte Lucas, Elizabeth's closest friend in Meryton, had felt somewhat neglected as Elizabeth began spending much of her time at Netherfield, in Jane's company. Charlotte was not the type to be offended easily though, and just joked about it...and then, all of a sudden it felt like, she was engaged. To a Mr Collins, a cousin of the Bennets. A week after Charlotte was married, the next day she was gone with her husband, or at least it felt that way to Elizabeth, taken aback by the rapidity of the events.

Charlotte had invited Elizabeth to visit her in her new home for a few weeks though, and Elizabeth prepared for her trip to Kent with only joy and hope in her soul.

∞∞∞

Charlotte and her new husband lived in the parsonage in the village of Hunsford, under the patronage of Lady Catherine de Bourgh of Rosings Park. As fate would have it, Lady Catherine was Mr Darcy's aunt, and Mr Darcy and his cousin Colonel Fitzwilliam came for their annual stay with the exalted lady a few days after Elizabeth's more discreet arrival.

Then, Elizabeth's soulmate music brutally stopped.

It happened at Hunsford Parsonage, Charlotte's home. Mr Darcy and the colonel had come to pay a visit. They all crammed themselves into the minuscule sitting room. Elizabeth, Charlotte, and her husband, Mr Collins, and their guests—Darcy and his cousin Colonel Fitzwilliam.

Tea was served; Mr Darcy was pretending to listen to Mr Collins's eulogies. At a nearby table, Elizabeth was talking to the colonel when her soulmate melody went suddenly silent.

Elizabeth blinked, stilled, and stopped talking right in the middle of a sentence. The music, the harmonies that had accompanied her for so long had just…vanished.

Silence. Absolute silence in her soul.

Mr Darcy was watching her.

"Miss Bennet?" the colonel asked with the utmost politeness.

"I—I apologise, Colonel. I believe I had a

moment of distraction," Elizabeth said, forcing a smile.

The colonel gave a cheerful answer; Elizabeth did not really listen. She sipped her tea, fighting dread. Why had the music stopped? What had happened? Was her soulmate in danger? Hurt? Or…dead? Behind her, Charlotte was offering Mr Darcy more refreshments.

The music started again, weakly, to evaporate again a few moments after. Elizabeth hid her relief. Whatever happened, *they* were not completely gone, but she was glad when the visitors went away, and she could hide in her room to think.

Elizabeth listened. After an hour, the music was back. Thank the Lord, thank heavens, the music was back.

Hushed, in low tones. Sometimes it went completely silent.

Charlotte's soulmate was dead.

Charlotte Collins, née Lucas, had begun to hear her soulmate's music at the tender age of nine. She had grown up with the melody; the notes had moulded her. "I was carrying my best friend with me, at all times," Charlotte had explained to Elizabeth, years later. "I had never met her—or him—but *they* were always with me."

Then, when she was twenty, Charlotte's music stopped, and never started again.

Charlotte said the worst thing was not knowing. A young man, lost at sea, or on the battlefield? A young woman, consumed by an early illness, or forced into a marriage she did not desire—then dying in childbirth after an interminable agony? Charlotte would never know.

What Charlotte had now was a broken heart, no soulmate, no dowry, and no prospects.

Mr Collins had a sizable income; he was also not the cleverest of men. When he first came to visit Longbourn, it was with the intention of marrying one of his pretty Bennet cousins. At first, he had persuaded himself he could hear Jane's soul music, but the lady was revealed to be betrothed to Mr Bingley. Mr Collins almost never saw Elizabeth, who was, at the time, always in Claire de Verneuil's company, so he proposed to Mary Bennet, the middle sister. But Mary, who considered herself very virtuous, was waiting for her soulmate, and would not fathom any other option. She refused Mr Collins on the spot.

Thus, the gentleman, offended by all these disagreeable contretemps, left the Bennets' home in a huff and took advantage of Charlotte Lucas's parents' hospitality to go and sulk in their house. What Charlotte said during Mr Collins's visit to make him believe *they* were soulmates must ever remain a mystery. But the blatant lie earned Charlotte a husband, a nice house, and a comfortable income.

Elizabeth had never quite known how she ought to react to her friend's marriage. Pretending to be someone's soulmate was a major moral violation—but Charlotte was almost an old maid. If she had not acted, she was destined for solitude and poverty. The untruths Elizabeth could not forgive in George Wickham, or in Caroline Bingley, she excused in her friend —humans are irrational beings.

However, Elizabeth could not open her heart to Charlotte. Between the two of them, soulmates were too tender and too dangerous a topic. The sudden anomalies, the sudden silences of her melody, Elizabeth had to keep to herself.

She was alone with her fears.

Days passed in the Collinses' parsonage. Elizabeth's soulmate music was still irregular.

Solitary walks in the beautiful grounds of Rosings Park. Charlotte's clever conversation. Visiting their condescending neighbour, Lady Catherine, a pompous and uninteresting woman.

Being witty in Colonel Fitzwilliam's company, polite in Mr Darcy's.

Elizabeth's heart was sick. Was her music going to simply disappear?

Mr Darcy was as quiet and as disagreeable in his aunt's grandiose house as he was everywhere else.

The Collinses and Elizabeth had been invited to Rosings Park for dinner. The meal had been a boring affair. Now, in the large and formal drawing room, Mr Collins conversed with her ladyship, Darcy was haughtily silent, Lady Catherine's daughter Anne de Bourgh and her companion Mrs Jenkinson were too proud or too shy to try for conversation. And in the presence of Lady Catherine, Charlotte was as always politely silent, and silently amused.

Thankfully, Darcy's cousin Colonel Richard Fitzwilliam was funny and gallant. In his company Elizabeth was well entertained and could almost forget her soul music had stopped again, the very moment of their arrival in the house.

"Darcy," Lady Catherine de Bourgh asked in her usual brusque manner, "are you still studying the concerto Georgiana was speaking about in her letter this spring? Go to the pianoforte—show us your progress, will you? It has been a while since we had good music in this house. Only Mrs Jenkinson plays, you know."

"No," was Mr Darcy's abrupt answer.

The room stilled. Darcy must have realised his rudeness because he hastily added, "Forgive me, your ladyship. I cannot play. I have the most serious headache."

"True, you do not look well at all," was Lady Catherine's pondering statement, and Elizabeth had to agree. Fitzwilliam Darcy was indeed quite pale, his eyes red, like he had not slept much. Ill, possibly, or in the throes of some deep, inner conflict.

Strangely enough, Elizabeth had seen Darcy often during these last few days. Quite frequently, in truth. More even, than when the gentleman resided at Netherfield. Elizabeth kept meeting him in the woods when she went for her early promenade. Those were not pleasant encounters; Mr Darcy had never been a great conversationalist, and those walks were no exception. Sometimes, he scarcely even spoke, and Elizabeth had to hide her silent exasperation.

But she quite pitied him now—migraines, poor man. They could be awful things. So, when Lady Catherine called her to the pianoforte in Darcy's stead, she did not protest.

Elizabeth played. Colonel Fitzwilliam and Darcy both approached the instrument to better listen. After Elizabeth finished her piece, the three of them had a slow, pleasant conversation around the instrument. When Colonel Fitzwilliam stepped away, summoned by his aunt, Darcy and Elizabeth continued to converse.

Elizabeth teased him, but her voice was gentle, her smile kind; she knew he was unwell and did not wish to add to his discomfort.

"Did it help?" she asked, after a few sentences. Darcy looked at her uncomprehendingly and

Elizabeth explained, "The music? I was hoping to soothe your headache."

A strange expression flitted in his eyes. "Yes," he said, his voice soft. "It did. Thank you, Miss Bennet."

Her soul melody had reappeared, Elizabeth realised, a few moments later. And somewhere that night, before she drifted off to sleep, the music was back to its normal strength.

It never faltered again.

Except during those horrid nights in London. But those events were still months away.

"In vain I have struggled. My feelings will not be repressed. You must allow me to tell you how passionately I admire and love you."

Darcy and Elizabeth were alone in the sitting

room of the Hunsford parsonage. Mr Darcy was pacing the parlour, offering her marriage. In the moments it took Elizabeth to overcome her surprise, the gentleman had already explained, in no uncertain terms, how difficult the decision to propose to her had been—how degrading was an alliance with Elizabeth, how great her inferiority in the eyes of society. He then proceeded to insult Elizabeth's family, her upbringing, and her connections.

When Elizabeth was free to utter a word, she declined Darcy's offer as politely as she was able to.

Mr Darcy paused and raised his eyes to her.

"You cannot refuse, Miss Bennet. We are soulmates."

A laugh. Dry. Incredulous. "No, sir. Of course we're not."

"Yes, we are, Miss Bennet. How…how on earth can you deny the truth?"

Elizabeth did not believe him—not yet—but unpleasant sensations began shifting in her soul. Was it cold in the room? It felt cold.

"Mr Darcy, indeed, you are mistaken. I—"

Saying that the gentleman interrupted her would not be fair; truth was, he had not even heard her objection.

"I had—it was very difficult for me to admit the truth at first," he said grimly. "It seemed so preposterous, ridiculous, even." Elizabeth was getting even colder. "I thought there must be some other young lady in the area who I had not yet met, and that would explain the strength of the melody. And you, Miss Elizabeth, you would dance around the matter, you would refuse to give proof. When I left Hertfordshire, I was certain I had been mistaken, that it could not be you. I was—glad of it… Rather, I thought, at first, I was glad of it, but then…"

His voice faltered, but the sinking horror in Elizabeth's heart prevented her from noticing the gentleman's emotion. *No. It could not be. Of course, he was mistaken. Soulmates? It was preposterous*—she shivered.

"I do not know, Miss Bennet, if your reserved attitude was an attempt to increase my desire, or if you were, on the contrary, thinking the difference of rank and position prevented us from forming a respectable alliance…"

Anger replaced horror. "Mr Darcy, let me put an end to these insulting suppositions. We are not soulmates, sir, and even if we were, I would not dream, in any circumstances, of linking my destiny to yours. I do not admire you, sir. Your arrogance, your conceit… Your attitude towards my family, towards my sister—your constant rudeness, even to me—"

"This is absurd," Darcy interrupted. "I was not... I always behaved in a perfectly—" He paused, pale with anger, then, after a short silence, he waved her objections away. "We have no choice anyway, Miss Bennet. The music..."

"No—*no!*" Elizabeth repeated.

She stood up, her heart beating wildly, feeling almost faint. If it were true, if Darcy was her soulmate, then all her hopes were dashed, reduced to ashes. All her possible futures— dreams, phantasms, would be crushed by dire reality. She would not, could not marry Mr Darcy, and then? There would be no one else; the Fates just offered you one soulmate.

It would all have been the cruellest joke.

"You are wildly mistaken, Mr Darcy. I do not know what strange fancy has risen in your mind, but—I do not hear your music. I hear someone...someone close, mayhap, but—"

"You are my soulmate, Miss Bennet. I *know*. When I saw you at the assembly I just—"

"No."

"I tried to deny it. All those weeks at Netherfield, I tried to fight it. Then, when you came out of the church on the day of your sister's wedding, I— The music swelled, and... Still—still I foolishly hoped it could be a mistake. Then you came here, to Rosings Park, two weeks ago. When I saw you again, after months of separation, in this very parlour..."

"No."

"The music goes like this." Darcy tried to hum, but at first he could not find the right key, so he played with his fingers on the table, searching for the tempo. This was all very similar to Jane's actions, during these happy days at Longbourn, when Elizabeth's sister wanted to share her soul music, except—except this was not a happy moment, this was—Elizabeth's world was crumbling.

Darcy found what he was looking for, he hummed again, his fingers playing on an imaginary pianoforte.

"Can you take dictation?" he asked in a harsh tone.

Elizabeth had the strength to be appalled still. "No, sir, I was raised by wolves." The gentleman watched her without understanding. "That was sarcasm, Mr Darcy, I believe you are acquainted with the concept."

He did not answer; Elizabeth took possession of whatever paper was on Charlotte's writing desk and drew hasty staves. She wrote under Darcy's impatient dictation, and thank God, it did not sound like…

Of course. Of course, he was mistaken. "Mr Darcy, this is a very different music— This is not what I hear at all…"

"Will you let me finish? I do not… I have not yet found the exact…" He hummed again, before correcting his interpretation. Then he dictated a new series of measures. "This is just the first voice, the second goes like this…"

Elizabeth jotted down the notes. And…

She… He…

The music…

"This is the third voice," Darcy said, starting anew, his voice still simmering with rage, and—

Elizabeth had stopped writing.

Oh God. Oh no.

Darcy paused and looked at her. She was livid. So still.

It was like he saw her, really saw her, for the first time.

"No," Elizabeth whispered. "Please, no."

Darcy tried to speak. He could not.

"Please, no."

Now Elizabeth was crying. A few tears, she wiped them off as soon as she could.

"No. No, please no. Please, please no. Please."

Silence.

"Please," she repeated.

Darcy watched her for a few moments—his face ashen. Then he turned away and left.

∞∞∞

The night was long. The soulmate music was strong, desperate, swelling, disappearing before rising again, stronger still. Elizabeth's head was hurting, she could not sleep because of the abhorrent melody; she stayed in bed, eyes open, tears slowly falling. In novels, the young lady fleeing from the love of her life would hear the notes shrieking, pounding in her brain, till she fell on her knees on the floor and cried, "Stop it! Please stop it! For the love of Heavens, make it stop!"

Theatrics, Elizabeth had always thought; real human beings did not behave in this dramatic way. But now, she could understand. She did not, of course, throw herself on her knees and curse the skies, but her mind was exploding.

The deep, solemn notes. *Please no. No, please no.*

The expression on Darcy's face when he left. His insults.

"We are soulmates, Miss Bennet."

No. Please, no.

Morning came as a deliverance. Elizabeth left her room as soon as was respectable. She had not slept at all, but there was a relief in the habitual, trivial activities—washing her face, getting dressed. There was no way she could face Mr Collins for breakfast today, or even Charlotte. She went down to the kitchen to beg for coffee and bread; she and the cook had a quick chat about headaches.

"Yes, miss, see, coffee will do you good—with a lot of sugar—but butter your bread, or you'll feel it in your stomach."

Elizabeth did as the kind woman ordered; a quick word to Charlotte and her husband, and at last she was out.

Coffee, fresh air, and activity work wonders

against most ailments, at least ailments of the soul. It also brought some clarity. Elizabeth knew, of course, that the omnipresence of the melody—this sensation that the music was devouring her—was only partly true. The phenomenon was fed by her own obsession and dismay; indeed, she was feeling so much better now. The music had receded to a distance, like a line of fog faraway on the sea while you are walking on a cliff and pausing to look towards the horizon. She was glad of it—would she miss the melody if the circumstances were different? If she had loved Darcy, would she wish for the music to be constant? Would she miss it if it was go—

"Miss Bennet." Darcy's voice.

Elizabeth stopped. Two venerable oaks, on the top of a hill. A path, the trees. She almost fled, then thought the better of it.

Darcy stepped closer. "Miss Bennet, would you do me the honour of reading this letter?"

In a moment, the missive was in her hand; Darcy had turned away to leave. "Sir, wait," she cried.

Darcy stopped. "Wait, please," Elizabeth whispered. His eyes, when he turned to her— then he stepped forward and bowed in silence, to show he was at her disposal.

She could not hold his gaze for long.

"We…" Elizabeth sighed. Her head was hurting again. "I believe we must talk."

She sat on a log, under the branches of the tallest oak, then gestured for him to join her.

"If it is true that we are soulmates…" Elizabeth voice failed. "I mean, it is true. I apologise for doubting it earlier."

"You did not know." Darcy's voice was hoarse. "I was convinced you did."

Silence. He was so pale. Black circles under his eyes. Clearly, he had been up all night, too. Did he hear *her* music? Of course, he did.

Did it scream?

"Would you read my letter?" he asked, glancing briefly at her.

"Here? Now?"

"Why not?"

Elizabeth nodded, then turned her attention to the epistle. It had been written in haste, and in the throes of anger. Inside, Darcy had tried to answer Elizabeth's accusations of arrogance and discourtesy. If Darcy had been cold, he wrote, it was in reaction to the general vulgarity of the neighbourhood and the distasteful conduct of the Bennet family. He exempted Elizabeth and Jane of any reproach but did not help his case by explaining that his distant attitude was also due to his early discomfort in seeing Charles Bingley court Jane.

At first, Darcy had written, he was convinced the attraction between his friend and Elizabeth's sister was a trick, an attempt at seduction on Jane's part, and Elizabeth's blood boiled. On this point, time had proved Darcy wrong, he wrote, and he wholeheartedly approved of his friend's happiness, but in his case—in Darcy's case—the situation was quite different, he wrote, and all his misgivings were perfectly natural.

The letter was over. There was hardly an apology. Elizabeth lowered the sheets of paper; she was so weary.

So disappointed.

All her dreams, and nothing.

"Why is your melody so sad, Mr Darcy?" she asked, after a while.

"Maybe the melancholy is yours," the gentleman answered slowly, still looking far away, in the direction of the main house. "Maybe it is your soul the harmonies illustrate."

He sounded like Jane. Elizabeth gave a dry, tense laugh. "Sadness is not in my character."

"Says the lady who was inconsolable last night, and who is almost crying now."

"These are peculiar circumstances, sir."

"Indeed."

"Are you going to sue? Prove I am your soulmate in front of a court, to force the union?" Elizabeth asked, turning to him.

Darcy swore, then he shook his head, still looking anywhere but at her. "Interesting opinion you have of me, Miss Bennet. No. I shall not sue."

Silence. He sighed. "I am sorry. I did not express myself well yesterday, and might have dwelt too long on my misgivings, and not enough on…"

A pause. The winds, playing with the leaves.

"I love you, Elizabeth. Of course, the fact that you are refusing your soulmate's offer, denying your music's call, denying our bond, is… thoroughly unpleasant…" Elizabeth could see Darcy struggling, choosing his words with care. "But it is not my main concern. My main concern is…" He shook his head. "Soulmate situation aside, the situation is as old as time, I suppose. I love you, and—you do not love me."

Elizabeth's eyes were long dry. "You do not love

me, sir."

"Really?"

"This is not love."

"Could have fooled me."

"This is not love when you insult the woman you admire and treat her like an inferior. This is not love when you wish the object of your affections were different, or not destined for you. This is not love when you think a woman unworthy of you, when you pray each day that the music will be revealed to belong to someone else. This is not love when—how did you say it? When you felt *glad* I was not your soulmate..."

Darcy rested the back of his head upon the oak tree behind him. "Mayhap I should have lied to spare your pride." He laughed dryly. "Miss Bennet, do not play the fool. You are a clever woman. Do not pretend you do not know of contradictory feelings—of humans' inner paradoxes. I could wish you on the other side of the earth and at the same time miss you bitterly in your absence. I could hope for someone else for my soulmate, and still be tremendously hurt when I convinced myself, wrongly, that you were not. I could feel cursed by the choices of the Fates—and wake up every morning at Pemberley wishing you were by my side..."

Again, silence.

"But no, I shall not sue. I do not want you trapped in a marriage with a man you despise. I want…to laugh with you, to debate with you, to share my life with you," Darcy explained, before adding, "That afternoon at Netherfield… I thought you were pursuing me. But you would not reveal yourself. The music you chose to play did not match mine. And despite it—despite the fact that I was convinced you were, in truth, *not* my soulmate—I even considered…I seriously considered asking, despite the circumstances…"

"Pursuing you?" Elizabeth interrupted, aghast. "How could you think… When did I ever…?" Another thought crossed Elizabeth's mind and her anger soared. "When we met again, two weeks ago, in Charlotte's sitting room, you—you stopped the music. Our soulmate music, you stifled it. Willingly."

Darcy rose from his seat on the log and took a few steps.

"I did."

"Why?"

"I wanted to—to test it. To test you. To be sure."

"Do you realise the fear you caused me—the anguish of the next few hours? I thought you were dead—I thought *he* was, *they* were dead—

and it was all a game? Do not say it was to verify the truth of our bond, sir. Not when you admitted your opinion was already formed. No, you wanted to try to get rid of the pressure of the music, you wanted to see if you could—ignore the pull, ignore our bond... Free yourself from me forever..."

"Maybe I did!" Darcy said, pacing the grass. "Maybe—maybe I wanted to assess my strength of will. Or maybe I wanted to get a reaction from you, any reaction. To get a show of emotion, of worry, of fragility...anything other than your usual perfect, icy composure..."

"Icy? I..."

"I was a fool. It is of no importance now."

The wind played in the leaves. Darcy took a step forward and bowed. "Goodbye, Miss Bennet. I wish you all possible happiness."

Part Two

Seven months earlier.

After the assembly ball, where he first met Elizabeth, Darcy's stay at Netherfield was a nightmare.

Was the music *hers*?

Was the music Elizabeth Bennet's?

His soul melody was screaming, driving him into madness. And now *she* was here—Elizabeth —at Netherfield, in Bingley's house. For a week. Jane Bennet had fallen suddenly ill and could not leave, so Elizabeth had been invited to stay to care for her sister.

It was as if the Fates were conspiring against Darcy. He was driving himself demented, listening every night in the solitude of his room, examining every note, every measure. Trying to name the sensations the music created to see whether it applied to her—to Elizabeth—to her character.

Trying to see if the music fit.

Maybe it did. Maybe Elizabeth Bennet was his soulmate. True, the harmonies were grave, and Miss Elizabeth was merry, but the melancholy could be Darcy's—his own darkness. Had he ever been happy, since his mother died, so young, so unexpectedly? Since he had seen his father wither away after the demise of his soulmate; his father, brutally deprived of his wife's music, a man weaned from his daily dose of opium, losing all will to live?

There had been no lightness, no joy in Darcy's life since he had inherited Pemberley and the guardianship of his lovely, fragile younger sister.

But the eternal good humour of Elizabeth Bennet did not fool Darcy either. He could see the deepness in her eyes. He recognised the seriousness, the cleverness hidden behind Elizabeth's polite restraint, he could guess the thousand opinions playing in her mind behind the barrier of her amiability.

Maybe his intuition was right. Maybe she...

No.

Enough nonsense. Enough sentimentality. Elizabeth could not be destined for him. Her family... The Bennet family, the mother, the mother's parentage, the vulgar, shrill younger sisters, the tastelessness of it all. Of all but her. At night, Darcy could hear Elizabeth's soft laugh. He invoked her voice. If they were married, she would bring him hope and joy—but—no. No. He was falling into a trap—not set by her, he could not believe it of her; indeed, if Elizabeth was aware of Darcy's attentions, she had not acted in an unseemly manner to try to retain them.

No, the trap was of Darcy's own making.

See, he was spying on all of Elizabeth's movements, to decide if she was his soulmate or not. He was dissecting each of her sentences, watching her expressions, divining her thoughts. And oh, such a dangerous game it was. Getting too close to a pretty girl with a generous heart, a quick mind, and a beautiful smile—of course Darcy would get attached.

Was it not an interesting irony? Getting closer to a lady to prove to himself she was unworthy and getting his heart stolen in the process?

Except Elizabeth was not unworthy— *unsuitable* certainly, but worthy. And...

No. Stop. The trap. Beware of the trap.

(The waves were crashing on the shore, and the tempest was raging.)

Darcy's soulmate—he wanted, he needed someone kind, someone bright. With grace of beauty and of mind.

"Miss Eliza Bennet," said Caroline Bingley, "despises cards. She is a great reader and has no pleasure in anything else."

"I deserve neither such praise nor such censure," Elizabeth answered. "I am *not* a great reader, and I have pleasure in many things."

"In nursing your sister I am sure you have pleasure," said Bingley, "and I hope it will be soon increased by seeing her quite well."

Lord. Her smile.

∞∞∞

Now.

After his conversation under the oak with Elizabeth, Mr Darcy left. He bid his adieux to Rosings Park and to his aunt Lady Catherine and was gone the next day.

Elizabeth's visit to Charlotte was also coming to an end. A week later, Elizabeth said her goodbyes, and after a long carriage ride to

Longbourn, she was back home at last.

Elizabeth burned her soulmate's music sheets as soon as she set foot in her room.

His sheets. *His* music. Elizabeth's soulmate melodies that Jane had so painstakingly recreated under Elizabeth's dictation. *Mr Darcy's music.* Every line, every note now contaminated, ugly. Poisoned.

Jane was not even there, in their bedroom, to soothe Elizabeth; Jane was Mrs Bingley after all, living in the company of *her* soulmate.

Elizabeth would have no soulmate. No hope, no future.

It was all gone.

Months passed.

Elizabeth stayed at Longbourn with her family and felt the hopelessness of each new day.

Jane and her new husband were so happy in their beautiful home. Bingley's joy was effusive, Jane's was quieter, but Elizabeth knew her sister; she saw deep affection in all Jane's looks, in all her actions. She saw wonder and pleasure in Jane's eyes at the sight of the man she loved;

she felt her sister's silent pride when Bingley's words or decisions daily proved his worth, his generosity, and his sense of justice.

"Mr and Mrs Bingley, the shining example of a magnificent soulmates' union," Sir William Lucas—Charlotte's father—commented one day with his usual goodhearted pomposity. "Just as it should be. Would give anyone a yearning for tying the knot, hey, Miss Elizabeth? Sorry, I mean, Miss Bennet?"

**

Elizabeth still heard the soul music faraway. Sometimes—when the melody was really low, almost undistinguishable—she thought she had dreamt it, she had dreamt it all.

Charles Bingley took his responsibilities towards the Netherfield estate seriously. Settling down and becoming a gentleman had been his long-held dream and the wish of his late parents. He applied himself with his wife's counsel. The wellbeing of his tenants, the interest of every soul on his land were frequent subjects of conversation over dinner at Netherfield, where Elizabeth was a regular guest.

Darcy's steady advice, given through his frequent letters to Bingley, was often discussed there.

The advice was wise, and kind.

Bingley regularly invited Darcy to Netherfield. Each time, his friend refused and sent his regrets.

Elizabeth wondered whether he also heard about her. Whether Bingley mentioned her in his letters sometimes.

∞ ∞ ∞

"Are you well, Lizzy?" Mr Bennet asked.

Elizabeth raised her eyes to her father and gave a strained smile.

"Of course, Papa." She tried to laugh. "I am always well."

"I fear that you are a little less sprightly, and more prone to missish melancholy, since you came back from Rosings Park, my dear. Did anything happen there that would require a father's intervention? I greatly hope you do not have any drama to relate which would force me into action. You know how little I like it."

Elizabeth shook her head, which seemed to satisfy Mr Bennet. "Father," she added after some reflection, "I have a question. It is rather unseemly for me to ask, so I shall... I shall phrase it as a statement instead..."

Mr Bennet waited. "You and Mother were soulmates, of course," Elizabeth stated.

It was indeed a disrespectful topic, but Mr Bennet just glanced towards the window and smiled.

"We thought we were. At the very least, *I* thought we were. Is this what it is all about, Lizzy? Did you suffer a romantic disappointment that I am unaware of? This is not still about Lieutenant Wickham, I dare say?"

Elizabeth laughed. "No, Papa."

They joked for a while, then Elizabeth retreated to the drawing room, the short conversation having the benefit of recalling her to her duties and shaking her out of her sombre, selfish mood. *Enough melancholy*, she told herself. Near the sofa, Kitty and Lydia were fighting over a ribbon. Mary was playing the pianoforte. Her mother was wailing about some neighbour's gossip. The sun was shining though; Elizabeth put on her bonnet and prepared for a walk in the golden light of midmorning.

Enough. Enough thoughts of woe, enough self-centred misery. Elizabeth was living in a comfortable house, with parents who both loved her—in their very different ways. She was living the easy, comfortable life of a gentleman's daughter, while half of the population was at war, starving, or sinking deeper into poverty. She had a good life, good food, good friends...and here she was, falling into melancholy, like those fictional heroines Elizabeth thoroughly despised. And all over a 'romantic disappointment' as her father called it.

No. Life was long, and happiness had many faces, Elizabeth decided, walking with energy along the familiar lanes, rejoicing in the shape of the patches of the sky between the leaves, in the dancing shadows created by the breeze. She could still marry, still find a man or a woman to cherish—and who would cherish her. It would not be her soulmate, but non-soulmate unions were possible, frequent even, if held in lower esteem.

Why should Elizabeth not find contentment—or even joy—in such an alliance? If she found someone—or if someone found her—and they decided to wed, it would be at least an informed choice. And not, as Darcy had said months ago at Netherfield, obeying 'the random cruelties of fate'.

And could not Elizabeth be happy alone? Reading, laughing, writing letters, providing help and support for people around her? Now that her sister had made a good alliance, Elizabeth could stay unmarried and not sink into poverty. As much as it pained Elizabeth to think, their mother had been right—Jane's marriage to Charles Bingley had changed all their futures for the better. If the Bennet ladies found themselves thrown out of their house at the death of her father, they would not need to sell their services as governesses or cram themselves into a tiny cottage with no way to survive in a respectable manner. Elizabeth would always be welcome at Netherfield, at Jane's side, or if she chose to be alone, Charles Bingley would make sure she did not starve.

Elizabeth could see herself living with a respectable companion in a tiny little house, close to her family. Soulmates were an important part of life, indeed, but so was love, free love, offered without obligation. And so were friends, and so were affectionate, tender sisters. And so was reading and playing music and being part of the community… And with those reflections, the clouds parted; the future that had closed before Elizabeth's eyes began to open again.

Life would go on. She would be well.

She would ignore *him* now, ignore the distant sound of his melodies. Certainly, Darcy must be doing the same.

Maybe the soulmate music, if starved of hope, would just fade away?

He would be well.

Life would go on.

Darcy would rally, he was sure of it. He would find a mistress or take a society wife. Being joined in holy matrimony to your soulmate was, of course, the desirable situation, but many members of the ton, many heirs of good families married for money, to make a brilliant alliance, or sometimes even just because their heart called them elsewhere.

It was well—it was all well. Elizabeth Bennet had refused him, but the world still turned. What had happened was no great drama after all. Darcy was a man of action, he would not fall into despondency. As soon as that horrid conversation with Elizabeth was over—at Rosings Park, when she read his letter, the tree shaking above them—Darcy had told Colonel Fitzwilliam they were leaving, and the next morning, he and his cousin were for London.

For the first time in his existence Darcy needed the exhausting whirlwind of the town, the useless chatter of balls, the relentless attacks of mothers throwing their panicked daughters at his feet. This was life, those were...possibilities.

This was his future.

Hundreds, maybe thousands of single, eligible young maids were tossed each year into the London marriage market. Because of the war, and of the steady emigration of men to the British Empire's colonies, husbands were scarce and females desperate.

Yes, it was time to get married. Darcy just had to pick and choose—and he would.

The first ball was all Darcy had hoped for. He had decided to go about this marriage business in a rational manner. He danced with every suitable young lady he knew or was introduced to by a trusted acquaintance. He chose a woman, led her to the set, drew her into conversation, then assessed her beauty, her education, and her level of fortune. Then he drank some water—one does not want to be inebriated while conducting such a sensible search—before asking another young lady to dance and starting the whole process again.

Not an unpleasant way to pass the evening after all. The orchestra was talented, the *décor* of impeccable taste, and it was not before Darcy was offering his arm to his sixth prospect of the evening that he was assailed by the bitter memory of how, months ago, Elizabeth had refused to dance with him.

She had refused to stand up with him twice. Once in the Lucases' home, one evening, and once at Netherfield, after Bingley and Jane were betrothed. At the time, Darcy had not attributed Elizabeth's reluctance to dance with him to dislike. He had just thought she… He had not thought at all really. He was too swept up in his own inner battle to even wonder about Elizabeth's opinion of him.

Of course, all she had said to him —Elizabeth's declared aversion of him—was ridiculous. Her repugnance was based on errors of interpretation, on over-romantic female standards. Not that Darcy cared. She had made her choice and pretended it was his fault. She pretended he had not treated her or her friends well. It was preposterous of course. Darcy thought Elizabeth was clever; clearly, he had been mistaken... A good thing he had discovered his error before standing with her at the altar—yes, an excellent outcome after all. Now he was free, free from her, free to make a magnificent union. Elizabeth Bennet would languish in the country alone—not that Darcy was angry or wished her ill. He was not angry. Not in the slightest.

Relieved, really.

The music of the dance was particularly wild; he accelerated the steps to follow the rhythm. Faster. And faster.

"Mr Darcy..." a soft voice protested. His dance partner. The young woman watched him with a bemused expression; Darcy realised it was not the orchestra his steps had been following, but his inner music.

His soulmate melody, going feral.

Did Elizabeth hear his music still?

Not that he cared.

Darcy apologised and began to converse with his pretty companion. Pretty she was, and charming, funny even. Her hair was such a golden nuance of blonde some might call it red, but Darcy did not mind, it suited the lady. In fact, after the dance and a few moments' conversation, he decided he quite liked Miss Diana Stiles—such was the lady's name. There was life and humour in those eyes; the young woman was also bringing to the table a thirty-five thousand pound dowry and some connection to a marchioness. Darcy led her back to her uncle, making a mental note to go and visit her the next day.

Then he started the process again, with another woman.

He made some preliminary choices, and the next day, went to visit all four.

An efficient evening indeed.

A second ball. More dances, more forced conversations. Darcy's dislike of the task grew stronger. Everything felt stale and forced, and he longed to be at Pemberley, to walk out of the house on a bright autumn day. To stride along the meandering lanes, under the venerable ash trees. To go round the lake through the path between the willows. Or just to ride, for pleasure, through the woods. He would go and visit the tenants—as was his duty—a duty Darcy did well. He cared for Pemberley well. Even *she* would not find anything to reproach him for there—he was not cold and uncaring there—*no* —*stop*—who cared about *her* opinion—this was a dangerous line of thought.

Back to the ball.

More young ladies. When the evening came to an end, only one of them had been deemed worthy of a second glance. Darcy was clever enough to know the quality of the women he met was not in question. It was his mood— or maybe a part of him was beginning to find the process of evaluating human beings like horses on market day morally distasteful. But it had to be done. The whole unpleasant affair would soon be over. He would choose a suitable woman, some business with the lawyers would ensue, and then he would have a wife at his side —with shining eyes, and a smile to light up the darkest room at Pemberley. He would treat her well—more than well. He would show Elizabeth what a happy union was—he would make her regret she ever doubted his—*no*—*stop.*

Dangerous thoughts.

**

"Why is there sand in the library?"

"This, Miss Bennet, is the beach. The sand is still wet. Listen… Don't you hear the waves?"

"This must be your dream then, Mr Darcy. I

have never been to the seaside."

"Never? This is quite scandalous, Miss Bennet, and I shall not let this situation stand. We shall rent a house with a view of the sea—June would be the best choice, I believe. But I protest—that we find ourselves walking on a beach does not infer that this is necessarily my dream. You have seen paintings of the sea, I suppose. Your imagination could easily recreate the scene."

"True, Mr Darcy. But I could not imagine this smell, nor the strange patterns of the seaweed on the sand. I could not make up the taste of salt on my lips. This is your dream."

Elizabeth woke up.

Darcy woke up.

Darcy paid another visit to the lady he had met at the first ball, Miss Diana Stiles, with the 'golden'...with the red hair. Then he met her again unexpectedly, at a private party, hardly a week later. Miss Stiles was indeed an agreeable conversationalist; Darcy spent a charming evening in her company.

"Darcy, this is not at all how you should go about finding the future mother of your children!" Lady Matlock protested at dinner the next day, when Darcy told her of his plan.

Lady Matlock was Darcy's aunt—his other aunt, the wife of Darcy's uncle, the earl. If Lady Catherine de Bourgh never moved from Rosings Park, to better be able to torture her tenants in all seasons, Lady Matlock was the opposite—a fashionable woman who very much enjoyed the gaieties of London. She would stay in the capital all year, if doing so was not considered bad taste.

Lady Matlock was also sincerely attached to Darcy, and she proved her affection by instantly listing all the things her nephew had done wrong in his search for a suitable wife.

"You will not meet your future bride at a ball! The best young ladies—the true gems—are snatched up well before they are out, Darcy. They would never show themselves in public before they are married. You hear about them through friends or family connections; that is how I met your uncle."

Lady Matlock proceeded to give her nephew a list of names and proposed to arrange meetings.

Darcy agreed to it all.

"Do not mind my mother. She can be overbearing sometimes, but she means well," Colonel Fitzwilliam said after the meal, when the two cousins were left alone with a decanter of brandy. "But I thought you were waiting to find your soulmate, Darcy."

"I found her. She refused me."

Richard's eyes widened. "What? Really? Who…when did that happen?"

Darcy did not provide an answer, so his cousin added, "Well, I may not know her name, but I can safely say she is an idiot."

"I agree."

Two months earlier, Rosings Park.

Before Darcy's proposal.

Another interminable evening in Lady Catherine's company. Charlotte and Mr Collins had been summoned for dinner, and to her dismay Elizabeth had been invited too. Her ladyship was insufferable but had to be suffered.

The meal was a subdued affair. Mr Darcy was quiet and solemn as usual, hardly speaking, even though he had, again, met Elizabeth that very morning for a walk in the woods. Colonel Fitzwilliam, who had just taken a hearty second serving of potatoes, was conversing with Charlotte.

"Oh no, Mrs Collins, the soulmate bond is so much more than just hearing music," Darcy's cousin explained. "Soulmates share dreams. And in certain circumstances, they can also see images of their soulmate's daily life—their location, mostly. Sometimes the visions are metaphoric, symbols constructed by the mind... dream places, in dreamland. Phantasmagoria indeed. But sometimes, the images are genuine visions of an actual locale."

"Really?" Elizabeth cried, with more eagerness than politeness. Those dinners had been such a dreadful bore, and she had been starved for an interesting topic. "I beg your pardon, Colonel," she added, feeling Darcy's eyes on her. "It is just...I thought those were old wives' tales— sharing dreams, I mean. The Oxford reports state those visions—showing the location of your soulmate—they believe those to be falsehoods, imagined by over-excitable female minds..."

"Oxford fellas!" Colonel Fitzwilliam sighed, with all the spite men in uniform could muster against lovers of science. "They have a preposterous idea coming in and will twist the facts to prove whatever they have already set their mind on. We in the army do not have preconceived opinions. Our experiments are unbiased. We just want to discover what's true, and furthermore, what's useful to us."

"You are unfairly harsh, Fitzwilliam," Darcy protested. "The Oxford researchers do have their blind spots, but their work is quite interesting. I would agree though, that they are sometimes blinded by misogyny—by their prejudice against the fairer sex, madam," Darcy added, turning to his aunt.

"I know what 'misogyny' means, Darcy," Lady Catherine protested with irritation. "Fitzwilliam is right, these men are idiots. What is the matter, Miss Elizabeth Bennet?" her ladyship added, her annoyance heightened by Elizabeth's discreet laugh. "What I say does not have the honour of agreeing with you?"

"Quite the opposite, your ladyship, I am wholeheartedly on your side."

Lady Catherine did not seem mollified—freely agreeing meant one could be freely dissenting, and she highly disliked even the possibility of such a liberty. Elizabeth turned to Darcy with a smile. "Sir, in explaining unnecessarily to a lady the word 'misogyny', you might have been guilty of the actual concept you were trying to define."

Darcy smiled. A real, sincere smile directed right at her. "Indeed, Miss Bennet. You are perfectly right."

Elizabeth never knew what to do when Darcy pretended to compliment her, so she just smiled again before turning to Colonel Fitzwilliam. "Colonel, do I understand correctly —do you mean to say that the King's army is experimenting on soulmates?"

"Of course, they are," Lady Catherine said with hauteur. "Every army in the world does. Why wouldn't we?"

Colonel Fitzwilliam raised an amused eyebrow. "My aunt is right, Miss Bennet. They all do it, why not us?"

"Using soulmates for...spying?" Elizabeth asked, fascinated.

"If by spying you mean rightly collecting military information in the name of king and country, yes, this is what we do. Imagine soulmates hundreds of miles apart, one of them far in enemy territory, and the other feeling— maybe seeing—their situation, their location... Consider how useful the information gathered could be to our military strategies."

"Can you code the soulmate music?" Charlotte asked. "To send information?"

The colonel did not answer straight away, but watched the lady with a cautious smile, as though he was assessing her. "You think like an officer, Mrs Collins. I feel sorry for your parishioners. We have tried it, of course," he added, "but the process seems out of our reach, at least for now."

Darcy did not seem surprised; certainly, he had discussed the subject with his cousin many times.

"Fitzwilliam," he began thoughtfully, "what about believing—having the illusion that you and your soulmate are both in the same place —together? Like a dream, but you may not necessarily be sleeping… It could happen during the day, when…" Darcy paused in the middle of a sentence, and if Elizabeth did not know him better, she could have sworn he was horribly embarrassed.

"Sadly, I must ignore your query, Darcy," Colonel Fitzwilliam replied in a light tone. "If I say any more, I shall be in danger of revealing state secrets. I shall be hanged, and you will all be sorry, I hope." The colonel raised his glass to the ladies. "So, the conversation will end there, and as a highly useless conclusion I shall only tell you my personal opinion—which is, there is much more to soulmate music that we humans know, and more than we probably will be able to ever discover."

Now.

Night.

In Pemberley library. But also on the beach.

Sand. Waves.

"This is a fantasy, Mr Darcy. In real life, you are not…so amiable, nor so kind. Not in truth."

"Yes, I am. I can be, Miss Bennet." Darcy's voice was soft. "This—this is what we could be."

They both woke up.

Darcy's realisation happened thanks to Miss Diana Stiles, or more precisely thanks to one of Miss Stiles's clever friends.

Miss Diana Stiles and her shiny red hair. The

more Darcy thought about it, the more he liked that the lady had a certain something that made her different. Miss Stiles remained Darcy's favourite, even after he had duly visited each and every one of the perfectly educated ladies Lady Matlock had laid out for him like jewels on a table. Young, aristocratic beauties, unsullied by the public eye, his aunt stated. But maybe they were too unsullied because Darcy found them quite boring. The ones he liked reminded him of his sister Georgiana. They were shy and sweet; they did not challenge him or add the spark which made existence quite bearable after all.

So, Darcy kept visiting Miss Stiles. Not too often—he did not want to reveal himself quite so early—but enough to learn to know her better. Diana Stiles also knew how to play the game; she was utterly charming, but not only to Darcy. She was pleasant and teasing, but she did not give him the whole of her attention, which suited Darcy perfectly.

One afternoon, while paying a visit, he found himself the only gentleman in a lively group of young ladies. Miss Stiles had invited five of her friends for luncheon before a promenade in Bond Street. The party was supposed to have broken up afterwards, but it was such a merry afternoon, the young women had come back to Miss Stiles's beautiful home for tea. This was when Darcy entered. He was ready to run away, but the ladies insisted so much on keeping him there that he could not disobey without being abominably rude.

Five young women! He feared the worst, but it was not so bad. Miss Stiles was always interesting—even more so among trusted friends. Darcy did not speak much, and soon the young ladies forgot all about his presence.

It was sunny outside. The drawing room had grown quite warm. Darcy was comfortably settled in an armchair, a little apart from the group, while rays of light played on the carpet. The conversation turned to many subjects, till it landed on one which got the gentleman's full attention—soulmates, of course.

A young woman, recently betrothed, was in the middle of her tale.

"...I did not play any games with him— I forsook feminine delicacy, modesty, and even restraint," she explained, finishing her story. "When I realised he was my soulmate, I threw myself at his feet. Not literally, of course, but in all the ways that mattered."

The other ladies asked many questions. They were well educated, and their opinions— whether in favour of or against their friend's artless behaviour—were given with sense and diplomacy. Darcy listened eagerly while the young woman answered every objection.

"No, I understand, Elena, my sincerity was not fashionable, or even modest... This is not the conduct that society would wish us females to follow. But—do you fathom how low the chances of meeting your soulmate actually are? With the war, and the likelihood of dying young, for men and women alike? As for those of us who survive, how do you even find your soulmate, considering the size of the British Empire—of the world? Then...imagine you are one of the lucky ones. You meet your soulmate, against all the odds, and they are...awful. Selfish, stupid, vain, or vicious and violent. We have all seen these, in our families, those terrible soulmate unions, and we all thought— why didn't she run? Instead of meeting him on the church steps? Why didn't she run away?"

Nobody answered.

"So," the young woman continued, "when I heard *his* music... When I realised it was him, I had found my soulmate, and he was—oh, he is a kind man, clever, and sweet. I thought how rare it was. How lucky I was. Such a blessing, a miracle. So, forget about society's inane rules and these petty duplicities they do their best to teach us. I just... As I said, I threw myself at his feet. Said I would do anything, if he would have me."

The conversation then steered another way, but Darcy was livid. His attention was lost; he was feeling sick, nauseous, even. He rose and discreetly took his leave, his heart pounding, his throat tight.

He stayed alone all evening, locked in the study of his fashionable town house, reliving the weeks of his stay at Netherfield, seeing it all again. All those occasions where he and Elizabeth had been thrown together. He replayed the scenes through Elizabeth's eyes, what he had said to her, how he had behaved. What she saw of him, how he acted. How he had played it all wrong.

How he had met his soulmate, and she was kind, and clever, and sweet, and he had destroyed it all.

The miracle, the blessing—he had crushed it. Instead of throwing himself at Elizabeth's feet, he had scorned her, humiliated her. He had acted so wrongly all she could feel was disgust.

Darcy kept thinking all night. Of how he had met her, and had wanted to lead her to the church steps, and she had run away.

The sky was very blue, the desert was endless.

"Crossing the desert. As dream symbols go, this one is pretty easy to decipher, Mr Darcy."

Elizabeth was lost, walking in the dunes. But she was also having tea, seated in Pemberley's library, around a tiny mahogany table. *All this sand*, she thought. *Not good for the books.*

Mr Darcy was drinking tea; he was also walking faraway. The desert was so vast, they could walk for years and never meet again.

"This is your dream, Miss Bennet. I have never set foot in such a country, in such a climate."

Elizabeth smiled. "Whilst I, on the other hand, go to the desert every Thursday… East from Meryton, follow the lane for a mile, turn right after old Peter's cottage, the dunes are south."

"No, you are right." Darcy closed his eyes. "This is indeed mine. This—these images—comes from an illustration in a children's book I loved, when I was a boy, staying at the Matlocks' house for the summer. I remember it well. My uncle's school room, full of treasures. Light and dust."

Elizabeth was still walking. "Maybe we are both lost."

"I am waiting for you," he whispered. "Do you

know?"

∞ ∞ ∞

Darcy and Elizabeth met again. Not in the desert, but in town.

And not in dreamland but in the actual, mortifying light of reality.

Bingley and Jane had rented a house in London for six weeks. They wanted to enjoy the Season, and Elizabeth and Mary were to accompany them. Lydia had protested and cried against the unfairness of their choice, and if it had been up to Mrs Bennet, her youngest daughter would have been sent instead of Mary to parade in every elegant drawing room of the capital.

But fortunately, the decision was Mr and Mrs Bingley's to make, and Jane was adamant. She would not take Lydia, but Elizabeth and Mary, the two eldest sisters, as was right.

"Your music has been strong for almost a year," Jane whispered discreetly to Elizabeth, a day before their departure. "Travelling will do you good. Maybe you will meet your soulmate in a London ballroom."

Elizabeth smiled and felt wretched. She had never confided in her sister. She had never told

Jane about...Mr Darcy and the related disaster. Maybe she would, but—no, not now. The disappointment was still too strong.

As it happened, Elizabeth *did* meet her soulmate in a London ballroom.

Mary Bennet, the third of the five Bennet sisters, had at first turned up her nose at what London had to offer. But once in town, alone with Jane and Elizabeth and without the younger siblings to incessantly mock her lack of beauty and spirits, it became obvious that Mary was not so much spiteful as scared out of her wits. Knowing she was not as beautiful as Jane, and not as clever as Elizabeth, poor Mary wanted to reject the town before it could reject her.

The kindness of Jane, who had now more time to take care of Mary, and felt it her duty to do so, worked wonders on the terrified girl. The new Mrs Bingley wisely decided that instead of throwing Mary directly into the shark infested waters of dinners and balls, she would start by showing her diffident sister what she was interested in. Mary liked music and knowledge; thus, the three sisters went to musical exhibitions, visited churches, museums, and bookshops. And if on the way in, or on the way back, they stopped to glance at fabric for a new, more fetching dress for Mary, or bought new gloves to adorn her, it could be attributed to a happy coincidence, and not to discreet and efficient planning.

And when Mary met a group of young ladies who called themselves the Theology Associates, the young girl thought that she had found a dozen soulmates, if not her own.

The Theology Associates met every Saturday to discuss religion and philosophy. The girls, encouraged by Jane, soon became great friends and saw each other outside their regular philosophical rendezvous. Jane took them shopping. So, each time Mary went out with one of her sisters or her new friends, she came back with some new religious insights for her mind, and some new ornaments for her body. Dressed in silk, in colours that suited her, her hair done by Jane's personal maid, Mary slowly blossomed.

Elizabeth witnessed Mary's transformation with the sinking sensation she had been as guilty as the rest of her family in neglecting her sister. She had never paid any attention to

Mary. To be truthful, Elizabeth had thought her middle sister quite the fool—in this, Elizabeth had been influenced by her father who, she realised now with the distance London brought, had treated his younger daughters in quite a shameful, neglectful way. But that was no excuse. Elizabeth, who deemed herself clever, who wanted to do good, who fancied she imitated Jane in her benevolence, was guilty of judging too quickly, of judging on appearance, of not opening her heart to someone—her own sister!—who craved affection.

Yes, Elizabeth was duly ashamed.

She would not continue to sin, though. She had been neglectful, but would be no more. She now was careful to talk to Mary, to confide in her and hear her confidences in return, to draw her cautious sister into amusing debates. Elizabeth accompanied Mary to the Theology Associates meetings, to free Jane from some of her responsibilities, but also because she found that lively discussions of informed minds always were thought-provoking, even on the driest of subjects.

Thus, Elizabeth was the first to notice Mary's growing friendship with a Miss Hayes, the clever, educated daughter of a barrister, and thought this new intimacy an excellent thing. Miss Hayes was religious, and very well read, but she was also not averse to frivolous distractions and had not in her heart the strength to resist the charms of a pretty dress.

Thus, Mary now had a companion for her amusements. She agreed—if Miss Hayes would come with her—to attend her very first London ball.

∞∞∞

It was almost ten and the ballroom was glittering with candlelight. Jane was dancing with her husband and the line was long. Elizabeth had already been invited twice to join the set and had enjoyed the exercise thoroughly, but she now found herself in a parlour with Mary and Miss Hayes—a rose had been almost torn off a shoe, and some rearrangement was needed.

Elizabeth was kneeling before her sister, working on the silk flower; she did not hear the door opening, nor realise someone had entered the small room. "Dear Mary, do not move," Elizabeth was saying, trying to avoid disaster, while Miss Hayes watched the proceedings with interest.

Steps resonated behind her. Elizabeth turned —and saw Mr Darcy.

They both paled. Elizabeth rose with a sinking feeling of panic.

"Mr Darcy," she said in a strangled voice.

He bowed, she curtseyed. "Mr Darcy," Elizabeth repeated, her tone still strained. Every rhythm in her was fast, the rhythm of her heart, the rhythm of the soulmate music—screaming in her soul—how could she have ever doubted—

That Darcy was—that he was...

"You already know my sister Mary," Elizabeth heroically uttered. "And this is Miss Hayes, her friend, from..."

Mr Darcy bowed again and left.

Elizabeth stood petrified for a few seconds. Fortunately, the other girls did not notice her distress.

"Well, that gentleman was quite rude," Miss Hayes commented, with more amusement than dismay.

Mary shrugged. "It is his way—back in Hertfordshire also. I think Mr Darcy does not like surprises much."

Elizabeth's melody was so loud her heart was pounding. The beautiful oak slatted floor was melting, there was sand underneath, or maybe water.

"Mr Darcy does not like surprises?" Miss Hayes repeated. "How is meeting people in a drawing room, during a ball, a surprise? That was wilful disrespect, there is no trying to excuse it."

"I disagree," Mary said, with surprising determination. "Meeting someone you know from elsewhere, in such an unexpected manner, when you were not prepared for it… And you are supposed to find just the right thing to say, and comport yourself just as you ought, while really, your mind is blank, because—because you were not ready. It might be easy for you, or for Lizzy, but may not be for all of us."

"You take the charitable, Christian interpretation, Mary," was Miss Hayes's answer, "and it is very fair of you, but…" The two young ladies began to discuss religion, as they always ended up doing. Any other day, Elizabeth would have been amused, but now she could not follow. She was too shaken.

"Shall we get back to the dance?" she proposed with forced cheer.

Mary protested. "You should go, Elizabeth. But mayhap Miss Hayes and I could stay here?"

Elizabeth shook her head. "Oh no. I am not abandoning two young ladies without a chaperone, in such a place, to be preyed upon by so-called Christian gentlemen," she said, trying for her habitual light tone, and not being entirely successful.

The truth was, Elizabeth was feeling too sick —she was still in shock. It was better if the two young ladies found themselves in Jane's capable hands. She was soon able to lead the girls to Mr and Mrs Bingley, then, free of her charges, Elizabeth could at last step away and take a quick look around the ballroom.

The place was vast and crowded. Her inner music was ear-shattering; she could not even hear the orchestra. Mr Darcy was nowhere to be seen.

Soon she was asked to dance by a young man of her acquaintance and had to shake her discomfort. Mr Edward Ferrars was not the handsomest gentleman, but he had a nice smile, and was always scrupulously polite. They followed the music dutifully, Elizabeth trying to be attentive. The dance seemed endless—Mr Ferrars, not being very talkative, did nothing to distract her from her turmoil. When the dance was over, Elizabeth was escorted back near the bowl of punch, and Mr Ferrars—feeling rightly he might be unwelcome—left her alone after all the required politeness.

A minute passed—

Mr Darcy walked directly to Elizabeth.

"Miss Bennet," he said, bowing again.

"Mr Darcy," Elizabeth answered, with another curtsey.

"I am quite ashamed of my conduct a few moments ago. Please apologise to Miss Mary and to Miss…and her friend."

"Yes. Yes, sir. I—I shall," was Elizabeth's not quite coherent answer.

Silence.

Mr Darcy started again, "Please do not believe I wished to be deliberately discourteous. I was— I was not…" A new pause. "Seeing you again," he said at last, in a quiet tone, "I found myself quite bereft of words."

Elizabeth's eyes were lowered; she knew she was blushing. Darcy was looking away, somewhere in the direction of the elegant windows. Another bow and he was gone; Elizabeth could not enjoy the rest of the ball.

All night, she wandered on the sand.

When she woke up, she wondered if Darcy had too.

∞∞∞

Four weeks later, their time in London was over; Elizabeth was back at home. Her existence continued, as comfortable, as lonely, as empty as before.

'Empty' was a new adjective. She had never considered her life as such before. And how could she deem herself lonely, with two parents and three sisters at home? Still, Elizabeth could not quite shake the feeling.

Mary had also undergone an essential change. It was her turn now, after Jane, to blush at the turn of a phrase, or to look conscious when reading a love poem. It happened that Miss Hayes was her soulmate after all; the two girls had compared inner melodies and found out the truth.

This turn of events was not much of a surprise, but Miss Hayes was not rich and neither was Mary. As they were also quite young, the families had decided it was better to wait; there was some expectation of a wealthy aunt in the Hayes family, and maybe Jane could convince her husband to help the two young women in a year or two, if their financial situation was unchanged. But Mary had now earned the right to be melancholic and interesting. She could stare, lost in thought, onto the horizon—although, despite her morose airs, Elizabeth was certain her sister was really quite happy. Mary wrote long letters and was answered—whether it was only the fine points of theology the two young ladies talked about at such length, we shall leave to the reader to decide. The two young ladies were not officially betrothed, so trading letters was somewhat irregular, but Mr Bennet did not care, and Mrs Bennet had certainly never been a slave to the rules of propriety.

So, you met your soulmate. You revealed your music. You lived happily ever after.

Quite a simple process, Elizabeth thought.

For everyone but for her.

His music was still playing.

Steadfast and faraway.

The Dashwood sisters visited Meryton a

second time. Elizabeth was glad to set eyes on Elinor again; the serious, melancholy young woman had been, after all, on Elizabeth's list of possible soulmates a few months hence. But she could not but compare her state of mind now to her feelings a few months prior.

How light, how bright, how hopeful life had seemed at the time—and how dreary today.

When Elizabeth caught herself in the midst of those depressing reflections, she quickly checked herself. She would not be *that* woman —the one who complained endlessly when life did not turn out exactly the way she wished. No, Elizabeth was a happy creature; she *would* be happy. Only, even the weather seemed to turn against her—grey and oppressive skies stifling the horizon the afternoon she found herself taking a long walk alone in Elinor Dashwood's company.

Elizabeth had gone outside with no intention in mind. But Elinor's silence and Elizabeth's own private musings led her towards a very impulsive decision.

"Miss Dashwood," Elizabeth said unexpectedly, "I have a proposition, which am I afraid might come as a shock, or even upset you."

Elinor smiled. "My sensibilities are not so

delicate, Miss Bennet, as to be very easily offended. I have been the recipient of some quite astonishing confidences, I assure you, and here I am still, safe of body and sound of mind."

"Ah," Elizabeth smiled, "but you always seem so proper. One is afraid of uttering an immoral notion before you, Miss Dashwood, for fear of being judged and found dearly wanting."

"If the proposition is really immoral," Elinor said seriously, "I do not wish to hear it. But I would be surprised if such was the case. I rather suspect, Miss Bennet, that you are playing with the truth to increase my curiosity."

Elizabeth smiled. "I see you know me well. But in all earnestness my idea could be considered wicked by some, although I disagree with their judgment. Would you still care to hear my thoughts?"

Elinor stopped walking. Her expression was as ever prudent. "I am listening."

"I...cannot marry my soulmate," Elizabeth explained. "I have known this for a while; but I also recently came to the realisation that I did not wish to live alone, nor do I want to be single all my life. This is a recent discovery, but a legitimate one, I fear."

Elinor just nodded. Elizabeth continued. "I still hope I shall fall passionately in love—

with someone who is not my soulmate. I still wish to attain happiness despite the cruel tricks of destiny. But if love doesn't come for me... and if you... In truth, I do not know what your situation is, Miss Dashwood. But if it is similar to mine, we might strike a pact. I really admire your character—your sense, your moral strength—and I believe we would do very well together. What do you say we decide to get married, at twenty-eight, perhaps, if by that time, our hearts are still unattached? We would not be rich, but I think we could get by, and be content."

A pause, before Elinor spoke at last. "My soulmate is engaged to another," she said.

"I—I am sorry to hear it."

Elinor began to walk again. Elizabeth kept at her side, and for a while, both women were deep in thought.

"When you say your proposition might be seen as immoral, Miss Bennet, I suppose it is because some still consider non-soulmate unions to be unethical...despite how common they are?"

Elizabeth nodded. "Indeed, but it is not the only matter. In the country, where superstition and prejudice are still rampant, the union of two women would be tolerated by the local population only if their bond was sanctioned by God—if they were soulmates. So...if we decided to marry, I would suggest we lie, and pretend that we are."

"The union of two *poor* women would be hardly tolerated, you mean, Miss Bennet. Strange how the marriage of two rich females, soulmates or not, never raises any protest."

"Ah, but the rich live in London—they are eccentric and faraway—and they have the means to retaliate," Elizabeth said lightly. "So, Miss Dashwood, what say you? Shall we fight the Fates and decide our own happiness, even if the Erinyes have decided we do not deserve any?"

Elinor Dashwood walked for a while, reflecting. "Your plan is sound, Miss Bennet. In your idea there is a streak of independence, of rebellion against destiny, that I can only admire. But admire from afar, I am sorry to say. I am not a rebel. This plan is right for your character, Miss Bennet, it is not for mine."

Elizabeth just nodded. She would never insist on such a delicate topic. Besides, if she was disappointed, it was an intellectual disappointment. Elizabeth's feelings were not engaged. She had just wanted to...to act, to find a solution, any solution. Elinor was right: Elizabeth's spirit was rebelling, against soulmates, against bonds, against women's lack of choices in society.

"Perhaps I am wrong," Elinor mused, after a while. "Perhaps my spirit revolts too—perhaps I long for independence. But if this longing is true, there is another one stronger. I believe in love. And I still love—I still love *him*. I cannot in truth attach myself to you, or to anyone, Miss Bennet, when my faith and my heart so wholly belong to another."

A pause. "I feel," Elinor continued, "that the existence of the soulmates' bond changes the way we see the world... It changes us. Some say the soulmate music is proof of the existence of God, of His will. I believe so, but I also believe..." She shook her head. "The soulmate music is proof of the importance of love. It is our permission to look for it, to wait for it. It is our permission to be romantics. And I shall be. I shall wait. I shall believe, and hope, always."

Elizabeth nodded, feeling strangely wistful.

Then it began to rain, and the two women hastened home.

Two months passed.

Elizabeth's aunt and uncle invited her on a

trip.

Mr and Mrs Gardiner had always been close to Elizabeth's heart. Mr Gardiner was Mrs Bennet's brother; his wife, Madelyne, was beautiful, elegant, and better still, wise and affectionate. The Gardiners were soulmates, and Elizabeth had long looked to their affectionate union as the model her own parents could not offer her.

As Edward Gardiner and his wife loved their nieces, Jane and Elizabeth especially, they were frequent visitors at Longbourn, and, as the years passed, Elizabeth and Madelyne Gardiner had struck up as warm a friendship as was possible, considering their differences in age and situation. So, the Gardiners' invitation, as sudden as it was, was much welcome. Elizabeth's uncle and aunt had recently decided to go north for three whole weeks to enjoy the beauty of those regions, and they asked Elizabeth to join them on their journey. Their niece gladly accepted—in any circumstances, this was a scheme to make her happy, but in her current state of mind, the distraction was even more welcome.

Indeed, Elizabeth was glad to see the Gardiners arrive at Longbourn to fetch her. She was even gladder when the *adieux* to her family were over, their trunks set in the coach, the horses ready, and Elizabeth had gladly climbed inside and slid over to sit next to her aunt on the comfortable seat.

Then the strangeness began.

In all appearances, the Gardiners and Elizabeth were a merry party. In the inns, on the road, Elizabeth was friendly and cheerful, joking with her uncle, conversing with her aunt.

Inside, her soulmate music called.

The phenomenon had started on the first day of her trip—as soon as the horses set off. Going north. Going to *him*.

In Elizabeth's heart, the melody tensed, or reacted—she could not find the right words to define the bizarre impression. Each time the horses moved north, in the right direction, her music swelled. The song weakened whenever the carriage took a detour, or when their party stopped to rest at an inn. But each time they were back on the right road (north, north, north!), here the melody was again, gnawing at Elizabeth like an animal.

The soulmate song had never stopped, whether Elizabeth was in London, at home, or even when she was talking to Elinor. It was always part of Elizabeth's mental landscape, like a distant beast, somewhere in the forest. You cannot see it, but you know it is there, you feel its presence, you hear it growling.

But now—now the phenomenon was different. Stronger, odder.

It did not make sense. Yes, Mr Darcy's estate was north, but the gentleman himself was in London; Elizabeth knew it from Darcy's latest letter to Bingley. *He is not up there*, Elizabeth repeated silently, talking to the music, trying to reason with it as if it was a wild creature. *He is not north, he is in town, we are not going to see him, this has nothing to do with him.*

The music did not listen.

**

Pemberley was north.

Pemberley was Mr Darcy's estate, his family's estate, the work of generations. As the Gardiner party edged closer, Elizabeth felt the call of Darcy's home. The music wanted her to go to Pemberley. Screeching, as they moved away. Beseeching, as they travelled closer.

Or maybe, Elizabeth thought, after a sleepless night, maybe it was her all along. Maybe she wanted to see Pemberley (she wanted to see *him*, the notes sang) and the music reacted to her hidden desires. Or maybe Colonel Fitzwilliam was right and soulmate melodies were more powerful, more unfathomable than humans believed. Maybe there was some bizarre force at work, or maybe—oh, Elizabeth's head hurt.

She was not superstitious but could not help but wonder whether the Fates were in play. After a while, everything steered them towards Pemberley. The good roads were leading that way, the others were flooded. When a horse fell lame, they had to steer northeast—the right direction—to get another one. They received a letter: Madelyne Gardiner's dearest cousin was back in Lambton, a village very near Darcy's property, just at the edge of the Pemberley estate. Suddenly, Elizabeth's aunt wished more than anything to go and see her friend.

"Pemberley? The family is away for the summer," the servant said to the Gardiners, when they had settled at the inn at Lambton. "Mr Darcy is in London, I believe. You really should go and visit! It is such a magnificent estate."

Darcy was away. Elizabeth could go. They could visit Pemberley indeed, and not meet him.

At Pemberley Darcy was absent, but he was everywhere.

He was in the voice of Mrs Reynolds, the housekeeper, when she led Mr and Mrs Gardiner around the house, proud of how beautiful the estate was, proud of the Darcy family, proud of her master.

"Mr Darcy's father was an excellent man," Mrs Reynolds said, "and his son will be just like him —as affable to the poor..."

"I have never known a cross word from him in my life..."

"Fitzwilliam was always the sweetest-tempered, most generous-hearted boy in the world..."

Darcy was in the grounds, in their melancholic beauty. He was in the serene, grave, elegant architecture, he was in the sun that drifted through the windows, like a possibility of light. He was in the pianoforte Mrs Reynolds said he had gifted to his young sister Georgiana, he was everywhere, and Elizabeth began to rewrite the past.

She had disliked Darcy from the start...but could she trust herself, or her first impressions? She had been wrong about Wickham, after all; she had been wrong about Mary. Jane herself had said, a few times, that Elizabeth tended to decide early on an opinion, and refuse to budge from it afterwards.

"I am happy you chose to love me, Lizzy," Jane had even joked one day. "I shudder to think how my life would be, if you had decided otherwise."

"Jane, it could never have happened," Elizabeth had replied. And really it was impossible; Elizabeth would never have been blind to her eldest sister's many qualities. But—except when it came to Jane—Elizabeth's wilful character had often led her to make mistakes. In Darcy's case, had she been doomed to blindness also?

What if Darcy had been reserved, and not rude? No. Darcy had truly been rude to Elizabeth's family. Not to her though, not really, except once, at the very beginning.

But…what if he had been stern because he was grave? What if he had been cold because he was tense, or unhappy? What if…

Elizabeth was lost in thought, studying the portraits in Pemberley's main gallery, her aunt and uncle at her side, when she felt *his* presence. Through the music.

Darcy was coming to her.

He was close, Elizabeth *knew*. How could that be—when the servant had assured them Darcy was still in London? An assurance that was, in fact, partly untrue. "Mr Darcy and his sister are *en route* to Pemberley," Mrs Reynolds had asserted with confidence. "But they will not arrive before the morrow."

Despite them all, he was near. Elizabeth *knew*.

(A road, a horse, sun playing on the leaves.)

Getting nearer.

(The wind, the trees rustling, sparrows in the woods.)

This is crazy, Elizabeth thought. Delusions... But no—not delusions, *visions* of his approaching presence. Oh, but Darcy should not find her inside his home, looking at his portrait in the gallery, ogling his possessions. If he discovered Elizabeth at Pemberley, spying on him in his absence...

"I need some fresh air," she murmured to her aunt in the gallery. "I shall go outside for a moment."

Mrs Gardiner assented with a smile. Elizabeth almost ran down the stairs. A secondary door, a deep breath—she was outside.

(The horse, the sun, the lane. He was close.)

Darcy would soon be here. Elizabeth worked on her composure, preparing a few polite sentences to greet him. Her heart was beating fast—what would Darcy think of her? Coming into his house in his absence? But then why would his opinion matter? Elizabeth had never cared about his disapproval before—but before he was not...

Before, he was not her soulmate. He was not the man who had apologised at the ball, the man who haunted her dreams...

Before, he was not the owner of this gorgeous, well-maintained estate, a kind and generous master, influencing people's happiness for the best, when like so many others, he could ignore his duties, and leave despair and misery in his wake...

Elizabeth's feelings were still unsteady when Darcy arrived, alone, riding his fatigued steed. He glanced at her, seeming in no way surprised. "Peter!" he called, hailing a stable boy, who soon was away with the horse.

Then Darcy walked to her, perfectly attired and composed, if you ignored the dirt from the road.

A short bow. "Miss Bennet. I had a strong feeling... I thought... I knew I would find you here."

Elizabeth gave a quick glance around; they were alone. She curtseyed, then met his eyes as steadily as she could. "Mr Darcy. Yes. Yes. I —I felt—indeed I felt I would meet you, sir." With horror, she realised how her words may be interpreted, as though she had come to Pemberley on purpose, to seek him out, so she quickly stammered her carefully prepared explanation. She was on a trip, with her aunt and uncle, her aunt was born in the area, they wanted to visit the grounds. It was nothing but the truth but Elizabeth knew she did not make much sense—she was very red.

"Have you—" Darcy hesitated. Elizabeth envied the gentleman's composure; she felt, too acutely perhaps, the indignity of her situation. "Were you in the gallery, earlier? Looking at portraits?"

"Yes," Elizabeth breathed, turning crimson. So, whatever she had perceived, he had too.

Darcy paused, for the slightest moment. "Is there a chance...Miss Bennet, that you are here for me? Because you have—reconsidered your position?"

"No, sir," she answered, as quickly, as earnestly as he had asked. She could not meet his gaze. And maybe it was the wrong answer—was it? "No, we are here to visit..."

Her eyes were still cast downwards. "Well," Darcy said, after a while. "I had to ask."

A pause. "Would you accept my arm for a tour of the gardens then, Miss Bennet?" he said. "Or"—turning to the main house—"maybe you could introduce me to your friends?"

∞∞∞

An hour passed. Elizabeth thought Darcy acted now with a sort of polite, desperate resolution, that she did not know how to interpret. They took a long walk, the four of them; if Mr and Mrs Gardiner were surprised by Darcy's polite attentions, they hid it well, and were perfectly amiable. Then Darcy invited them all for tea, in the summer salon— a handsome room, but not the best, Mrs Reynolds explained. She begged their pardon —as they thought their master was only due tomorrow the household was still in the midst of preparations. The cook had to quickly whip up a batch of cakes, with delightful results.

Elizabeth had never loved her aunt and uncle more than during that afternoon. Their qualities she was used to, but their intelligence and excellent manners had never been more essential to her than today. The conversation with Mr Darcy had two points of entry: Mrs Gardiner being a native of the area, and Jane, their niece, being married to Mr Bingley, Darcy's closest friend. Helped by hot tea and pastries, those two subjects revealed themselves rich enough to sustain a lively discussion about customs, counties, and the absolute truth— that nobody in the room would deny—that Mr Bingley was the kindest, most generous man that ever existed.

In this discussion Elizabeth had no part; she could not utter a word. Darcy was civil, affable even—she would have said he seemed perfectly easy, except she knew him now, and was not fooled. She felt the tension in their music; she read it in a few glances Darcy discreetly gave her. He was noticing her silence, certainly, and could interpret it in the worst way. So, at last Elizabeth exerted herself to speak, talking about the beauties of the house, asking questions about Darcy's sister and their mutual friends. She thanked him for the tea, forcing herself to meet his eyes, her cheeks reddening with each word. Darcy answered immediately, they exchanged a few queries, even two or three opinions.

To think it had been so easy for Elizabeth to laughingly disagree with him before, while they were both staying at Netherfield. Now it was difficult to even form a full sentence in his presence.

Was Darcy disappointed in her? Was he finding her different from in his memory? Was he thanking God that she had refused him?

The next day, Darcy invited Mr Gardiner to fish with him. He introduced Elizabeth to his sister, Georgiana, and invited them all to dine at Pemberley the day after.

And the next. And the next. There was not a day of their stay in Lambton when Elizabeth and the Gardiners did not see Darcy, or his sister, or were not invited to a pleasant scheme on the grounds.

And it was only the five of them—Darcy and Georgiana, Mr and Mrs Gardiner, and Elizabeth. Their party had often been larger in the summer, Darcy explained; Mr Bingley and his sisters were frequent guests. But this year was different. Caroline Bingley was still staying with her friend in town, and Mr Bingley was, of course, at Netherfield with his new wife.

At the Lambton Inn, Elizabeth received a letter from Jane with news of home. Life went on as usual in the Bennet family, everyone in excellent health. Lydia was still discontented that she had not been allowed to go to Brighton or to London, but Jane had invited her to Netherfield for two weeks, and all was peaceful—or at least as peaceful as it could be.

∞ ∞ ∞

"Would you consider altering your plans, Mrs Gardiner?" Darcy asked on the fifth day, after another pleasant outing. "You could leave the inn and come to stay at Pemberley...for another week mayhap? I know your intentions were set and there were a few places you intended to visit, but with Miss Bennet and Georgiana becoming such fast friends, I feel we could have quite a pleasant time together."

Mrs Gardiner smiled and expressed how flattered she was by the invitation, but she would have to talk to her husband, of course.

∞ ∞ ∞

"Do you wish to stay, Elizabeth? At Pemberley?" Mrs Gardiner asked discreetly, that very evening at the inn.

Elizabeth did not remember the answer she gave. It must have been very jumbled; she could not look her aunt in the eyes. And that night Mr and Mrs Gardiner had a long discussion, to which Elizabeth was not privy.

Elizabeth knew that her aunt and uncle changing their travel plans was an important decision, with financial consequences. The Gardiners had reserved nights in advance in a few different inns, and some of the money could not be reclaimed.

But the Gardiners were not blind, and Darcy's attentions towards Elizabeth were too marked to be ignored. Elizabeth's aunt must have convinced her husband that the possibility of their niece finding a husband—and such a husband—was more important than the loss of a few pounds. The likelihood of a soulmate bond between Darcy and Elizabeth must also have been broached, but Elizabeth's aunt was too well educated to ask her niece directly, and Elizabeth was grateful for her discretion.

Thus, Mr Darcy's invitation was accepted the next morning.

Those days at Pemberley were exhilarating and golden. The weather was particularly hot, to the point that leaves were burning under the pitiless rays, and took shades of copper, as though autumn had decided to visit early. Despite her youth, Georgiana was the lady of the house. To her fell the task of organising meals, outings, and distractions for their three unexpected guests. Having rooms prepared at the last minute, planning meals, and entertaining their party could be considered a daunting task for a girl of barely sixteen, but Georgiana had help from her brother and from her companion, Mrs Annesley, a pleasing, well-mannered woman.

The recipients of her efforts were easy to please and happy with anything the young lady decided.

"As long as you allow my uncle to fish again and me to walk in your beautiful grounds, Miss Darcy, we shall be very satisfied indeed," Elizabeth said at the breakfast table, before asking whether Georgiana would accompany her that very morning for a stroll around the lake. Darcy was following the conversation, a cup of coffee in his hand; he was to visit tenants, then the whole party was to picnic together when he came back. Mr and Mrs Gardiner wanted to spend the morning in Lambton; Mrs Annesley was busy.

Elizabeth still felt Darcy's eyes on her when she and Georgiana said their joyous adieux to those assembled and left for their walk.

Outside, the air was already warm. A haze crept across the surface of the lake; some slight breeze played among the trees. They walked fast, and soon Georgiana's cheeks were pink from exertion. She did not go out as often as Elizabeth, but today the young girl clearly enjoyed the unexpected freedom of wandering freely, without a fixed goal. Darcy's sister must lead quite an elegant, sheltered existence, Elizabeth thought, to be made so happy by such an innocent pleasure. Thus, after half an hour of exploration and enthusiastic conversation, she was seized by a sudden worry.

"Will your brother disapprove, Miss Darcy, that we went a little wild? We did not stay in the lanes. We wandered in the park, even jumped from a stile... As we were spotted by an undergardener, we shall not be able to deny our crime. Will Mr Darcy be very displeased, do you think?"

"Oh no!" was Georgiana's spontaneous reaction. "Quite the opposite, really." The girl was a little out of breath, and they resumed a more normal pace, strolling along a well-kept path as respectable young ladies should. "My brother believes I am too shy, too reserved. Of course, he does not express it, not in such clear terms, but I know he would be happier if I made friends at school and invited them here for outings and games. I feel he worries I do not have any fun. But I...I am not always at ease with strangers, or even with people I know well,"

Georgiana added, turning bright red.

Elizabeth nodded. "You are reserved, Miss Darcy. My sister Mary shares the same trait. Even Jane—Mrs Bingley, my eldest sister—was diffident when she was younger."

"You have so many sisters. So many dear, close friends. I would like to meet them all."

But Elizabeth's thoughts were not on her sisters. "I suppose Mr Darcy is quite reserved himself."

"He is. Perhaps that is why he feels I should not be."

"Ah, you make quite the pair," Elizabeth commented, eyes shining with amusement. "He worries about you—he is a kind brother then," she added, a quiet truth more than a question.

It seemed important somehow. If Darcy's music was part of Elizabeth's soul, if she was to hear it always, even from afar, she had to be sure of the melody's worth and beauty.

Georgiana was happy to reassure her companion, without knowing, perhaps, how essential the reassurance was. Elizabeth felt quietly content, listening to Mr Darcy's praise— to her soulmate's praise—while the sun played on the water.

Walking back, changing their clothes, it was time for the picnic, Pemberley style, so really not a picnic at all. A beautiful, sturdy, wooden table had been carried outside and set under a tree, at the shifting frontier between shade and sun. The chairs, also brought from the main house, were of the utmost comfort, the linen and cutlery of discreet elegance; delicious wine was poured into crystal glasses as soon as the guests were seated.

Light was shining through the leaves. The conversation was serene; Mr and Mrs Gardiner related the good time they had had in the company of their friends, which led to memories from twenty years ago, followed by interesting anecdotes about the county. Georgiana was still exhilarated from her walk and found everything interesting. Elizabeth had a sudden, startling realisation.

She was happy.

Elizabeth was happy to be in the company of her aunt and uncle who she loved so much. She was happy to be seated beside Georgiana, to whom she was beginning to feel a protective kind of tenderness. She was happy about Mr Darcy's presence; she was happy to know that to him, her voice was always welcome, as proved by the discreet smile that sometimes played on his lips when she was talking.

She was happy when he did look at her sometimes, answering in his calm, serious voice when the conversation called for sobriety, or with a light dancing in his eyes, if Elizabeth was being mischievous. She was happy that fate had brought them together, for this meal, under the venerable oak. Darcy was talking; Elizabeth raised her gaze to him, and maybe her realisation, her gratefulness was apparent on her face, because for a second there he could not avert his eyes—and she felt something had been offered, and shared.

Afterwards, the afternoon was quiet. Once rested and dressed in suitable attire for the second part of the day, Elizabeth wandered downstairs, not wanting to let such gorgeous weather go to waste. Maybe she could find a book in the drawing room and read it in the garden.

Mr Darcy was present when she entered the room. He was standing, deep in thought, but turned and greeted her with a smile, and Elizabeth found it again, this sensation of contentment—the feeling was as easy and golden as the leaves outside.

She smiled back and explained her query.

"A book?" Darcy repeated. "Well, I do not believe you have seen the library yet, Miss Bennet. Shall we go and see it?"

She nodded, and for a second the silence grew heavy. After a pause, Darcy gestured to the door, then led her up the stairs.

Because—see, the query was not innocent. Elizabeth had been to Pemberley's library before. Many times, with Darcy.

At night.

Yes, those were dreams…her meetings there, with Darcy, the books, the beach, the desert and the tea. Indeed, Elizabeth now remembered her visions of a year or so ago, when she was reading in Netherfield's library and thought she could sense Darcy's presence—when she saw him, walking among his shelves at Pemberley. At the time, she had believed the impression a fancy, but she knew better now. Those were shared experiences, soulmates' visions—already.

They had never, not even once, alluded to those strange moments. But they both knew—and now Darcy led Elizabeth there, to this secret place they shared.

As if it was a test of some kind.

Pemberley seemed to grow darker as they

were walking into the depths of the mansion. No words were spoken before Darcy opened the library door and, with a small bow, bid Elizabeth to enter.

She stopped breathing. Because yes—she knew this place intimately. Every detail was familiar. The sunlight, dancing through the dust beside the high windows, the elevated ceiling, the dark oak floor, the shelves, the ladders. The room was silent; Darcy entered behind her, but he did not utter a word—for a moment Elizabeth wondered whether the scene was real.

She had been prepared, rationally, to find the place familiar. She remembered the conversation with Colonel Fitzwilliam at Rosings Park about shared visions. But it was one thing to be acquainted with a theory and quite another to have proof. To walk into dreamland, to see with your own eyes...

...that magic was real.

Elizabeth stepped into the centre of the room. Here was the small mahogany table, where they had taken tea—in the dream. Darcy was standing not far from the door, observing her, his expression unreadable. But he must be wondering also—pondering whether Elizabeth had really been there, had lived it too. Thinking that maybe those were not only his dreams, his delusions.

Elizabeth turned to him, wanting to reassure him, to give proof—but it was such a personal subject, it was impossible to speak of it directly.

The silence seemed to stretch on forever.

"It is a good thing," she said at last, "that the sand did not get into the cups."

Darcy did not react. Or at least Elizabeth did not see him react. His face was still a mask of stone, but in a moment he had crossed the room and was at her side—and for a heartbeat Elizabeth wondered whether he was going to… She could not move; she felt Darcy at the verge of—doing something rash—but then he walked away towards the shelves.

Somewhere, four bells rang. Darcy had regained his countenance. He summoned a servant and ordered tea; he ordered the tray to be set on the mahogany table—another silent, discreet proof of their mutual experience. Once the man was dismissed, Darcy invited Elizabeth to take a seat; it was rather strange, the two of them alone in the vast, silent room, maybe even a little improper, certainly a bizarre choice at least.

But Elizabeth would not have missed this moment for the world. Her concerns were soon dismissed, drowned by the noise of the sea—the sound of the waves, in the distance. Of course,

Pemberley was nowhere near the coast, and the ocean growled in her mind only; Darcy must hear it too, mustn't he? The ocean, this was theirs too. She poured the tea into the elegant, blue, porcelain cups—different from those in the dream. Darcy was looking at her hands, then his gaze met hers again. Elizabeth asked if he took sugar or milk, then handed him his cup; their fingers did not brush, but it was impossible not to think that it was a gesture she might do often, if she were his wife. If they were married, she might serve him coffee in the morning, tea in the evening. And then, once alone, at night... But the idea led to dangerous considerations, and Elizabeth had to talk to distract herself, or be lost in contemplations unworthy of a lady.

She asked about the cups, and their hue of special, deep blue. Darcy's answer led to a conversation about China, an uncle who had sailed there when he was young and had come back full of stories. The conversation was slow, it felt private, although the content was anything but. They only spoke of travels, real and imaginary, of great noble ships, of the ocean. Twenty minutes passed before Elizabeth decided it was time to leave—staying longer would really begin to flirt with impropriety. She made her smiling excuses and stood up. Darcy walked her downstairs, also in silence, but Elizabeth did not really mind.

Georgiana was waiting for them at the pianoforte. Soon, Mr and Mrs Gardiner were back from another visit, delighted with their day, and it was time to retire and dress for the evening. Dinner was friendly, cheerful, and interesting; Elizabeth's soul music was singing, low and steadfast and just for her.

The letter from Longbourn arrived the next morning.

The news from Elizabeth's home was distressing. Lieutenant Wickham had come to stay in Meryton again. Somehow, he had renewed contact with Lydia. Somehow, he had established some correspondence with the young girl, and somehow, he had convinced her to elope in his company.

Lydia had disappeared one night from her room at Netherfield, leaving a letter. Saying that she and Wickham were gone to Scotland, where they were to be married...but initial enquiries led the family to believe the young couple had gone to London instead.

At Pemberley, no one believed Wickham had ever intended marriage. It was clear enough to Elizabeth, from her previous encounters with the officer, that the lieutenant was not the kind to fall in love. He was only after pleasure and money, and he might get the first with Lydia, but the second he would not obtain. Like all the Bennet sisters, Lydia had a very meagre dowry, which meant Wickham had no incentive to wed her. No, he had left with Lydia with one intention only, to satisfy his own pleasure. He had lied to her about his intentions and must be now somewhere in London with the young girl, hidden in a sordid room, with no plan but the vague idea to abandon Lydia to her fate when he tired of her.

Mr and Mrs Gardiner were worldly enough to have the same opinion, and Darcy, it seemed, had no trust in his childhood friend at all. They all gathered in the breakfast parlour to discuss the next steps. Elizabeth asked Darcy whether he wanted to keep Georgiana in the room—maybe Darcy's sister was a little young to hear about such events. But Darcy only looked at Georgiana, said the news was about Wickham, and asked if she wanted to leave. Something passed between brother and sister, a message that Elizabeth did not know how to interpret. Georgiana decided to stay and listen.

She went a little pale when she understood the events but did not comment.

Thanks to the Bingleys' sense of discretion,

Lydia's situation was not yet hopeless. Mr Bingley, surprisingly perhaps, kept a cool head in times of crisis. After Lydia's flight, he had asked Jane not to utter a word of her sister's disappearance. They swore the chambermaids to silence and called Mr Bennet to Netherfield. There, Lydia's father was discreetly apprised of the events. They all agreed that it was best to keep Lydia's folly a secret as long as possible, especially from her mother.

If Lydia had vanished when she was living at Longbourn still, Mrs Bennet, in her distress, would have spread the news far and wide. But at Netherfield, there was maybe a chance yet to quell the rumours. It was still possible, maybe, to reclaim Lydia discreetly.

Mr and Mrs Bingley had told the members of the household who did not know the truth that Lydia had gone to London on a visit. The lie would not hold long, though, and Mr Bennet and Mr Bingley had written to beg for the Gardiners' help to find their niece in town.

"I know where Wickham hides when he is in town," Darcy said. "I am acquainted with many of his friends. I shall come and help."

Part Three

The next morning, they were to London.

The contrast was striking.

The weather was still unbearably hot. After impeccable linens, delicious meals, and lazy strolls in the park, they were now stuck in the stifling interior of a coach, shaken by the bumps of the road. A long ride, and after all the seductions of wealth, Elizabeth was thrown abruptly back into dire reality.

And it was a wonder to realise that in the company of a certain gentleman, this reality was not so unpleasant after all.

Elizabeth's thoughts were very naturally on Lydia, on her sister's health and wellbeing—

on the very real consequences the young girl's conduct could have on the reputation of the Bennet family. But Elizabeth would also not have been human if she had not been affected by her soulmate's presence during their ordeal.

Darcy was here with them, riding beside the carriage. In her aunt and uncle's ready acceptance of the gentleman's help, Elizabeth could read their belief that Darcy and their niece had at the very least an understanding or were even already discreetly engaged.

Engaged they were not... But Darcy's presence in a time of crisis was as wonderful as it was unexpected, Elizabeth thought. It was even better to have him at her side now than during those flawless days at Pemberley. It meant more, it showed more.

Especially because, despite Darcy's formidable financial means, their trip was in no way flawless. There was a shortage of food in the first inn they stopped at. The Gardiners and Elizabeth had to share a very small room in another, then there was a difficulty with the horses. Those obstacles were easily remedied, or were not difficult to bear, but the third day was gruelling. The heat had broken at last, replaced by a pouring, tepid rain. It battered the roads, and all of Darcy's fortune could not change the weather—their trip turned out to be most uncomfortable.

It was also extremely intimate.

In the carriage, first. When the rain first started, Darcy had to forego his horse and join them inside. Mrs Gardiner, Elizabeth, and their maid were on one seat, Mr Gardiner and Darcy facing them on the other. Five people in the same small space, even with all the comforts of a modern vehicle, could not escape the hazards of proximity. Darcy sat facing Elizabeth, their knees often colliding—'brushing' would have been too weak a term.

Hours passed; the rain did not subside. The horses were tired and progressed with difficulty on the muddy road. They were all exhausted, the inn still far away. Mr and Mrs Gardiner dozed off. Elizabeth fell in and out of sleep; each time she opened her eyes Darcy was right there, in front of her, so close. Not looking at her but gazing out of the window.

Sometimes he closed his eyes, although Elizabeth did not believe he was sleeping. It felt like they were stuck in an interlude of time. Despite the downpour, some heat still remained; the weather was hinting of storms, tension in the air.

Elizabeth's slumber was restless. "Are you comfortable, Miss Bennet?" Darcy asked when she opened her eyes, in a hushed voice, so as not to wake up the others.

Elizabeth answered that she was well and thanked him with all her heart for his assistance —and his carriage. The short conversation was formal, and felt like a lie, or at least like a glinting surface with hidden depths inside.

Darcy could not, Elizabeth thought, be unaffected by their proximity either.

Could he?

Time passed. The carriage had not made much progress. She fell asleep again—and suddenly found herself in Pemberley's library, a blue teacup in her hand. Darcy was looking at her with passion in his eyes; the elegant mahogany table was shaken by the bumps of the road, rain was falling on the books, then there was a noise, some shouting, people talking.

They both woke up with a start; they were at the inn at last.

The sun had set long ago. The establishment was full. They were not the only travellers late and hungry because of the weather and the state of the roads. Their room, although reserved in advance, had been given to strangers; food was scarce, everybody was cold, everyone's feet were wet. Tempers were brittle.

But not in their small party. Mr and Mrs Gardiner had not always been wealthy; they had suffered worse difficulties in life than some delay in a trip. They stayed perfectly philosophical, and Elizabeth discovered that her soulmate was a very practical man. If Fitzwilliam Darcy managed, without exasperation, the thousands of daily difficulties of a huge estate, a crowded inn was not big enough a problem to discomfit him. He stayed calm and efficient. The poor servants at the inn were quite overcome, trying to do their jobs as best they could despite being treated like enemies by dissatisfied patrons. Elizabeth kept silent during Darcy's negotiations, despite being secretly very ready to trade her future and meagre inheritance for a hot beverage of any kind.

At last reason and money prevailed. After two interminable hours they found themselves seated at a table in the common area with tea, bread, butter, and the happy knowledge rooms were being prepared for them.

They had a pleasant time on the narrow, wobbly benches, surrounded by sweaty and noisy travellers. Nothing reconciles one with life more than food and hot, steaming tea, and now that beds were guaranteed, they could enjoy their unexpected adventure.

Elizabeth could not but imagine how awful the same hours could have been if she had been with her parents. To her shame, she could picture it all. Mrs Bennet wailing in the common room, loudly criticising the inn's servants; Mr Bennet making sarcastic remarks but being totally unhelpful otherwise. If Elizabeth had been thankful for her uncle and aunt's evenness of temper before, she was even more so now, and included Darcy in her silent gratefulness. What a horrible experience it would have been to see her soulmate yelling at people, insulting innkeepers just because he could. Instead, he had quietly resolved the situation. She smiled at him for no apparent reason—a large, beautiful, grateful smile above her cup of tea. Mr and Mrs Gardiner's attention was elsewhere.

Darcy smiled back.

Their eyes stayed locked for a fraction of a second too long, before Mrs Gardiner turned to them and began to converse again.

"If I had known that I just had to arrange for bread and tea to make you smile like this, Miss Bennet, I would have provided them more often at Pemberley," Darcy said, eyes shining, at the bottom of the narrow stairs.

Servants and trunks were going up and down, the small hall was still overflowing with irritated travellers.

"And butter, sir," Elizabeth replied in a low voice. "Please do not forget the butter."

"Who would have known ladies were so easy to please? I should write a treatise. 'Of the hidden benefits of tea', it would be called."

"This is what Olympe de Gouges said, sir, before she was guillotined. That women are rational creatures—and no man would believe her. We are best pleased by rational means. So, when we are cold, we prefer hot tea to cold diamonds. Although," Elizabeth added, her eyes dancing, "the reason diamonds are so popular is that we can always sell them."

"To buy tea."

"Exactly."

"Now I am thinking I could put diamonds into your cup, Miss Bennet, but there seem to be inherent risks to the method, at least if you are not forewarned. Indeed—"

They were interrupted—their beds were ready at last. Elizabeth could not help smiling all the way up. She kept her good humour when sequestered with her aunt in the tiny space which, Elizabeth was pretty sure, was a hastily disguised closet. The innkeeper had only succeeded in finding two rooms; Mr Darcy and Mr Gardiner were sharing one, the ladies the other.

It was a strange night. Her aunt's presence in such close quarters felt odd—Elizabeth missed Jane and wished she could confide in her sister. The inn was loud, even late at night, people going in and out. Due to the lack of options, travellers were gathered in the common room; some tried to sleep, some drank and chanted rowdy songs instead, the rather vulgar lyrics fortunately drowned out by the howls of the bad weather.

Elizabeth slept in short bursts, twenty minutes here, half an hour there. In her dreams she found herself in the coach, with Darcy— together on the road, while the rain was falling hard.

Once in London, and safe in the Gardiners' home, Elizabeth could only think of Lydia. The more time passed, the more her sister was in real, physical danger. More things could be lost than her virtue. Elizabeth tried to reason with herself—surely Wickham was not weary of Lydia yet? Surely, he was still being attentive to her; he had not thrown her out on the street? Elizabeth's sister being abandoned by her lover, left in desperate circumstances, was a very real possibility.

Not now, not *yet*, Elizabeth hoped. But in a few weeks... In a few days...

They had to find her soon.

Elizabeth was to stay in town with her uncle and aunt. Then, if Lydia was retrieved, the two sisters could travel back to Longbourn together, as though nothing was amiss, as though Lydia had spent all this time in town in Elizabeth's company. The young girl's disappearance was still, through some miracle, a secret. Jane and her husband were appreciated enough by their servants, it seemed, that the few who knew the truth had not yet betrayed it.

Elizabeth just hoped it would last.

The search for Wickham began. Mr Gardiner hired two men to track him down. Elizabeth saw one of them briefly in the hall—he seemed dangerous and cunning, which, she supposed, was just the thing.

"These...'gentlemen' are experts in finding adulterous women, or wives fleeing their violent husbands, and dragging them home by force," Mrs Gardiner explained to her niece in a low voice.

Elizabeth shivered. Women had no rights, even against a savage, sometimes murderous spouse. If they fled, 'fellas' were hired to return them to more violence, sometimes to their death. As wives, they had no recourse.

What soulmate music had those women believed in, which got them shackled to such a master?

Mr Gardiner also looked in person for his wayward niece. Mr Darcy was searching too, following leads. He came for luncheon every day in the Gardiners' home, to make his report. Elizabeth rarely intervened, she just listened to the two gentlemen and Mrs Gardiner talking strategy, but she always thanked Darcy for his help, just before he left.

Darcy smiled at her then—it was their moment, the two of them, every afternoon. A few private seconds in the deserted hallway before Darcy went out into London's streets again. The serene voices of the Gardiners in the dining room, to their left. The bustle of town, like a fog, to their right. Nothing except a few words and a smile were ever shared, but those instants became essential to Elizabeth's day.

With the music, of course. Hers, his. Still here —always here—especially at night.

Mr Bennet's arrival was delayed for two more days. Mr Gardiner did not comment, but Elizabeth was deeply ashamed. Her mother, so unreliable one could not reveal to her the disappearance of her own daughter lest she tell the whole world and seal the poor girl's fate. Her father, who could not even arrive in a timely manner when his child's life was at stake. Those were sobering reflections. Add to this Lydia's thoughtless actions, and it was enough to make Elizabeth's think, for a rather unpleasant moment, that maybe Darcy had been right when he first met her—that she, or at least her family, were far beneath him.

Fortunately, these sombre thoughts were interrupted the next day by Darcy staying a little longer after his usual meal and discreetly asking Elizabeth whether he could have a word with her in private.

She started. Darcy added quickly, "Not for..." His voice faltered, before he said, "This is about Georgiana."

Elizabeth nodded, and after a polite, "Of course, sir," she led him into a small drawing room, which was often the children's domain when there were no guests and they were allowed to come down. Now they were with their nurse, and all was silent. Mr Gardiner had gone up to his study; Mrs Gardiner was preparing to wander out for some necessary visits. Her uncle and aunt would not have objected to her *tête-à-tête* with Mr Darcy anyway, Elizabeth thought, providing the door was left open and servants could go in and out at any time. They still thought Elizabeth and Darcy betrothed, and the gentleman's constant presence only strengthened their belief.

Elizabeth asked for more coffee—it was also a way to ensure at least one servant would enter the room during their discussion to vouch for their perfect behaviour. Then she asked Mr Darcy to take a seat before choosing a sofa not so far from him.

"Your father is arriving this evening, I believe," the gentleman started. At Elizabeth's sign of acquiescence, Darcy continued, "There is some information I wished to share with him, but I would like to tell you first, Miss Bennet. So, you will hear it from me," he added, and Elizabeth nodded again, her face serious.

Darcy then explained how Wickham's actions concerning Lydia were not entirely a surprise. The story was long, and Elizabeth did not wonder about Darcy not sharing the secret before, it touched on such private matters.

Wickham and Darcy had been close friends as boys, this she already knew. George Wickham was the son of the late Mr Darcy's steward. But, Darcy explained, as a young man Wickham turned quite wild, and went to London. There he spent his money while pretending to study law—squandering his inheritance before asking for more—this was all reckless but could be forgiven.

Till Wickham came back and tried to seduce Georgiana, who was, at the time, barely fifteen.

Wickham and Georgiana would have run away together, they would be married today, Wickham continuing his irresponsible behaviour and gleefully spending Georgiana's large dowry, if Darcy had not found them the day before the planned elopement. Georgiana had confided everything to her brother—Wickham had fled again, leaving Darcy's sister's safe and sound, but with a broken heart.

Elizabeth heard the story with a sinking feeling.

The fact that Wickham was a heartless man, ready to prey on young girls, was not news. But if Wickham thought he was worthy of a Georgiana Darcy with thirty thousand pounds, what were the chances that he would condescend to lead poor Lydia to the altar, when Elizabeth's sister had a meagre one thousand to offer? No, the youngest Bennet sister would be discarded soon.

This certainly did not bode well for the results of their search, Elizabeth told Darcy with accents of desperation in her voice. It was the first time her distress was made evident to the gentleman. Elizabeth had tried, and succeeded, to keep up a brave front since the news arrived; she did not want to add to everyone else's burden. But now, Darcy saw it all. Her reaction was nonsensical, Elizabeth knew. The situation had not changed in essence, just… The idea that Wickham was even more of a villain than she had thought was staggering.

"Lydia is lost," she whispered, her face pale, her hands trembling. Darcy drew his chair closer; he raised his hand as if to touch her, on the arm maybe, then he stopped—it was all he could do, all he was allowed to do. It was even too much, the gentleman must have realised, because when the steps of a servant carrying the coffee tray resonated in the hallway, Darcy stood up and retreated to the fireplace.

Too late. Yes, too late. Elizabeth's heart was beating, the music roaring in her ears; what had been calm, sleeping, denied between them, was ignited again. How could she not have seen it—their bond—how could she not have understood, all those months ago, in Netherfield's music room?

At the time she had felt the storm raging, the grey of the skies, although there was no storm and no clouds; now the tempest was back—yes, while she was sitting in the luminous drawing room of this modern London townhouse, while an old servant was carefully setting down the coffee cups on the ornamented table. There was, mayhap, nothing more mundane, nothing less romantic than this scene; still Elizabeth felt the wind blowing and the sea raging, her consciousness so mindful of Darcy's presence, of his awareness of her. The thunder, the ocean, those were his too, she thought, he must be feeling them also, as if they were again in the same place—together—together inside the room, and together on a wild shore. Suddenly she had this fierce desire to stand, to walk across the room and embrace him—it was a very strong urge, very...carnal, was the word Elizabeth would find later, reflecting in shame on the incident in the shadows of her room. She wanted to touch, she wanted to feel, it was an old, primal longing, from before manners and morals; an animal desire from a mythical past where men and women could act freely, could love and sin when their music called. The servant was still in the room, arranging the cream jug; a few moments had passed only, but it seemed like an eternity.

Elizabeth stood, and politely enough, she

asked the servant to leave.

She saw the man gave her a quick, discreet look of surprise. He obeyed though, and the door was left conspicuously open—what a mistake, Elizabeth thought, after all her efforts to make this conversation as respectable as possible. If she had just waited a few moments more, the servant would have gone on his own, but it seemed those subtleties did not matter any more. It was a gift, from her to Darcy, this slight impropriety on her part, showing the trust she had in him. She met his gaze and saw the gentleman's wonder; then he nodded and crossed the room again to take his place in a nearby armchair.

"I have something to tell you also, sir," Elizabeth said, eyes lowered. He nodded again. She hesitated for a second; the information was only slightly relevant to the subject at hand, and if she wanted to keep it a secret, she could—but here also, it was a gift.

Darcy had shared a private tale that gave Elizabeth the power to hurt him; she could do the same. She could not cross the room and embrace him, she could not put her lips on his and—did it really exist, that mythical time of humans' innocence, when Eve heard Adam's music and walked to him naked, and gave all of herself of her own free will?

But humanity had sinned; Adam and Eve had fallen. This path of absolute trust was closed to Elizabeth—though she could give him...she could give Darcy a morsel of her past, a piece of that same trust, and hope he understood.

"I almost came to harm myself, also at the hands of Mr Wickham," she started, and told Darcy the story. Six months ago, the dark, stifling, music room at Longbourn. Elizabeth playing the pianoforte. Her musical trap, Mr Wickham's reaction. What happened afterwards —the man's hands on her, his insults, Mrs Hill's timely arrival. Elizabeth did not share the exact details but she said enough for Darcy to get a clear picture of the events.

His face turned pale, as was Elizabeth's when he had told Georgiana's story. But this was the only perceivable change. Then Darcy rose again and stood immobile for a moment, looking towards the window. He was angry, deathly angry, Elizabeth could tell, even though she did not know how to account for her certainty. It was not the music betraying the gentleman's feelings, because the melody had suddenly stopped, entirely vanished, like it had disappeared on Elizabeth's arrival at Rosings. Darcy was stifling their song—cancelling it— because he did not want Elizabeth to hear the depth of his ire, or for other reasons she could not fathom? Elizabeth was taken aback by the strength of will it revealed—smothering your inner song—she could not do it, she could not see herself even trying.

Darcy took a few steps about the room. The universe was still dreadfully silent. For a moment, Elizabeth wondered whether she had miscalculated. Maybe Darcy now saw her as tainted by her experience, as...dirty. But no—it could not be—such a reaction was not worthy of the man she was beginning to know—

But then, 'fellas' like those hired by Mr Gardiner were at this very moment hunting women who had thought they knew...

Mr Darcy sat down at last.

"I felt it," he said, and the soul music was back. Elizabeth's heart sang again, and Darcy's eyes met hers. "I knew some harm had befallen you— I sensed it in the music at the time..."

It was the first time since Darcy's proposal that they had spoken openly of their bond. "I tried to ask you, Miss Bennet, during the wedding breakfast for Bingley and your sister, do you remember? I asked you if something had happened at Longbourn, but you insisted that all was well..."

Oh. "I did not— I apologise, sir. I did not understand, at the time."

"There is nothing to apologise for. Why would you have confided in me? You did not even consider me a friend."

"True." Elizabeth gave a tense smile. "But still. To think that I prided myself on being observant."

"If I had been clearer earlier…" Darcy began. But he did not continue; the silence grew thick between them. Then the housekeeper herself entered the room, in all appearances to ask whether they needed more coffee. Clearly, the servants had been talking, and the kind and loyal woman wanted to verify all was well with Mrs Gardiner's niece. She was reassured, it seemed, by the normalcy of the scene she walked in on.

When she was gone, Darcy spoke again. About more practical topics: he explained where he was going that afternoon, in his search for Wickham.

He was visiting a Mrs Younge, he said. Elizabeth listened and wished him luck; after a few minutes Mr Darcy said goodbye, and politely took his leave.

That night, the music stopped again.

The London bells had just chimed midnight. Elizabeth was turning fitfully in her bed, replaying the conversation from the afternoon, thinking about her past choices. At first, she was too lost in her own doubts to feel the sudden disappearance of the soulmates' melody, and when she noticed at last, she would not worry, not right away. After all, Darcy had already shown he could control the notes. He had done it at least twice, a few hours ago even. Maybe he was sleeping. It was true, the music had been a constant before, and did not stop when Darcy fell into a slumber—but soul music varied so.

Anyway, she was tired, and fell into a fitful sleep.

In the morning, the music had not come back.

Unease was settling. Of course, Darcy could still be stifling his melody on purpose, but…why would he? It took much out of him; Elizabeth remembered how tired and drawn he had been at Rosings Park, how ill he looked, when he had stopped his song to play that cruel game on her. And even then he could not totally erase it, some notes did escape.

Now there was nothing.

The sun was bright, the sky was blue. Mr and

Mrs Gardiner's children wanted to go to the park. Elizabeth accompanied the maids, she ran and played with her young cousins. They were so happy. People were talking and laughing under the trees. Such a beautiful day.

Still no music.

Darcy did not come for luncheon.

"Wasn't our favourite guest supposed to partake of this roast with us today?" Mrs Gardiner said, with a knowing smile towards Elizabeth. "I ordered beef just for him."

"Yes, Darcy was definitely supposed to come and eat today," Mr Gardiner confirmed with less subtlety. "He likes the rosemary potatoes. I suppose he was delayed."

Darcy did not arrive for coffee either, and no news came in the afternoon.

Never had Elizabeth felt so restrained by her womanly nature, or the laws of polite society. Sending a message to an unmarried gentleman to ask if he was well was out of the question, nor could she ask a servant to go to Darcy's house to see whether he had made it home safely. She could not even acknowledge her fears. It would mean saying her music had stopped, which meant revealing she heard such a melody in the first place—it was such an intimate subject— she could not talk of it to strangers, could she? Especially without Darcy's express permission?

Maybe she was being too rigid. Her uncle and aunt were not strangers, and they already believed Elizabeth and Darcy engaged; they even suspected they were soulmates. But again, engaged they were not, and Elizabeth revealing the existence of the music now was tantamount to forcing the gentleman to marry her after his reappearance, whatever Darcy's present wishes were on the subject.

Unless, of course, he was dead already.

He could not be. Could he?

Elizabeth's father had at last made it to London. Elizabeth asked to be received in the study and told Mr Bennet and Mr Gardiner that she was very worried about Mr Darcy's absence. He had gone to see a Mrs Younge, Elizabeth explained, before adding that Darcy had said his visit was to be a dangerous one.

It was untrue—Darcy had mentioned nothing of the sort. But Elizabeth found the lie necessary to raise her father and uncle's awareness of the danger. The two gentlemen were untroubled at first, but they agreed to send a message to

Darcy's house.

An answer came from the housekeeper, explaining that their master had not come home last night, that nobody knew where he was, and that they were all extremely worried.

Time passed again.

There was no action Elizabeth could take. She was not connected officially to Darcy in any way. She was a woman, with no independence, power, or money.

No music still.

He is dead.

Is he?

The Matlock family had been warned. They were the ones looking for Darcy now, and—that was all. The Earl of Matlock had no reason to keep them apprised of the results of their search. Mr Gardiner had a short meeting with the earl, to talk of Darcy's quest for Lydia, to mention Mrs Younge's name, but after that it was out of their hands.

No, the Matlock family did not have any reasons to forward news. They did not know that someone was eagerly waiting, that Elizabeth—

Darcy was dead.

He must be, it was the only explanation.

Two days now. Not even Darcy could stifle the melody for so long.

∞ ∞ ∞

The most horrendous thing was that life was still going on.

The Gardiners' children were still playing, asking Cousin Elizabeth to join in their games. The sky was still unmercifully blue. Servants were cheerful; everyone was busy. The quest for Lydia was ongoing. Now that he had made it to London, Mr Bennet was active, and grim. Mr Gardiner helped, but he had his business to take care of, a wife and three children to maintain. He spoke with energy of his affairs, as he should. His life was full.

Mrs Gardiner knew or suspected Elizabeth's distress, but her niece had not confirmed or denied anything—habits of discretion died hard.

"You know you can always talk to me, Lizzy, if something is weighing on your heart," her aunt had said on the first day of Darcy's disappearance. Then she had been most attentive, but still Elizabeth had not spoken—it was irrational, how she held onto her pain, her gnawing anguish for herself.

Maybe if she told nobody the music had stopped, it would not be true.

How had Charlotte survived it?

Elizabeth jolted awake.

Notes.

A phrase of melody. Very dim, broken.

The night was dark. For an instant she could not breathe. Was it—was it true? Or her imagination?

She tried to focus.

A new musical phrase, then another. No, it was not her fancy, the music came and went. The notes swam up to her consciousness (to the surface of the sea) before disappearing again.

Elizabeth could not sleep. Darcy was alive—alive! This was proof, but was he very ill? Or dying? In terrible agony? Or perhaps he had been retrieved, he was saved, back at Matlock House, healing. And nobody had sent the Gardiners a message, because—well, why would they?

Elizabeth had to rise, to pace the room. Somewhere, the clock struck one; dawn was still far away. Again, she was powerless, she could not do or ask anything before morning—the music fell silent again. Elizabeth was going crazy; truly, if this went on too long she would go mad, they would have to lock her in her bedchamber and hide her from all polite society, like the unfortunate woman from a town near Meryton, who was secretly held captive by her father in a spare room for twenty years—

The music came back—then vanished again.

Elizabeth kept pacing. Then she went to the window to gaze out at the deserted street. Sometimes a lone shadow could be seen, hurrying along the pavement, going...where? Back to whom? Maybe a servant would stop at their door, carrying a message. If Darcy had been found, if he had been carried back home, maybe he would ask for Elizabeth to be informed, but... It did not fit with the music, with the long moments of silence, with the broken notes. No, this was not someone who was well or getting better, this was someone who was slowly dy—
No! Elizabeth refused to see it, to accept it. She prayed for a while, for Darcy's safe return, for his

life; she knelt next to the bed, then fell asleep, like this, on her knees, her head leaning against the sturdy frame.

(crimson—the sofa—the strange feel of velvet —unpleasant smells—unpleasant taste—pain— blood—the floor would have creaked, if he had walked on it—the metal child, with his bow— noise—music—someone, far away, was crying—or laughing—women, laughing)

Elizabeth woke up.

Outside, it was light.

She was the first down for breakfast and this time, she could not contain herself. "Aunt," she asked, when Madelyne Gardiner came back up from some business with the servants, "any news from Mr Darcy's house?"

"Yes, indeed," Mrs Gardiner answered, her face grave. There would be no good tidings there. "They have not... Mr Darcy has not been found yet."

Elizabeth did not answer.

"I was wondering, so I sent Tom," her aunt continued, her eyes set on her niece with affectionate understanding. "But no, no news still."

Elizabeth drank her coffee.

She ate well. She would need strength, for what she had in mind.

"I am going at Travers'. I need new gloves," Elizabeth announced an hour later. Mr Bennet had departed early that morning for a short trip. There had been some sightings at a country inn of a young brunette who might have been Lydia, accompanied by a man who might have been George Wickham. On the road to Scotland. If true, it would be good news, because Scotland was where young couples fled to get married. Elizabeth could not quite believe it though, and her father did not either, although of course, he must follow the lead.

But no. They could pretend, they could fake hope, but deep down, they knew. Lydia was in London, somewhere. Lost.

And so was Darcy.

"New gloves at Travers's, Lizzy?" Mrs Gardiner repeated distractedly. The children had come down and prepared themselves for their daily outings, and despite the competence of their nurse, Mrs Gardiner liked to keep a watchful eye on the proceedings. "Good idea—and please, tell me if they have received the green wool we talked about, will you?"

"Yes, Aunt."

This was maybe too brief an answer for the spirited Elizabeth, and Mrs Gardiner gave her a concerned look. "Are you all right, my dear?" she added in a low voice, and they both knew there was much unsaid there.

"I am, thank you," Elizabeth answered politely, putting on her own worn gloves.

"You will take Molly with you, of course?"

"Of course."

Elizabeth had hoped to go alone, to avoid more deceit, but it was not to be. She smiled amiably when the young servant appeared on the steps, clad in her best coat, looking happy to go for a walk and escape some boring job. Ten minutes later they were at Travers's, the London streets as busy as ever. Elizabeth entered the shop with Molly in tow, and after some perusing, she asked the innocent girl to go and have a look at the back to see whether she could find any pleasant trinkets for the children.

As soon as Molly was out of sight, Elizabeth stepped out of the shop, hailed a hack chaise, and was gone.

The clocks had not even struck eleven.

∞ ∞ ∞

Darcy's cousin Colonel Richard Fitzwilliam was not an easy man to locate, at least for a young lady with no male relations to help her.

Elizabeth first thought the officer would be staying at Matlock House, with his parents, and that he would come to her, if she sent up a note about Darcy. But it was not to be; the young boy who enquired under the promise of the few coins came back to tell her the colonel was not with his family, but 'at the barracks'. More enquiries revealed this information to be a mistake also; in fact, the colonel was staying for a few days in a building rented especially for officers, in the southern part of town.

The street was hardly respectable; Elizabeth supposed that was the point, if the officers in question wanted to—how would Elizabeth's father put it? If the officers wanted to freely intermingle with the local female population without family supervision.

Maybe Colonel Fitzwilliam was also in a disreputable part of town because he was looking for Darcy—one could only hope. Anyway, it was a good four hours later that Elizabeth found herself at last in the corridors of an old Elizabethan building, in dire need of some repairs. A young ensign was taking the sun on the steps. She asked him about the colonel, and he directed her inside. Elizabeth made her way to the third floor, following his instructions. There she had to repeat her query, to someone who looked like a sergeant, and someone who may have been another officer in civilian clothes.

The whole place smelt faintly of beer and dirt. The two men answered Elizabeth's questions, but with much laughing and leering, followed by some very pointed remarks. Elizabeth ignored it all, she knew the risks she had decided to take. She silently made her way forward, to another hall with four other soldiers, and to a small table where Darcy's cousin was writing a letter, her walk accompanied by the two officers' whistles and comments all the way.

Colonel Fitzwilliam's expression, when he recognised her, was wary. Elizabeth could not blame him. She knew how bad it looked for an unaccompanied young lady to show up unannounced in such a place. And the colonel was not a relation, not even a friend.

"Miss Bennet," he said, his voice all prudence. Polite, with a hint of disapproval. "To what do I owe the extremely surprising pleasure of your visit?" was the next sentence. Behind her one of the men snickered, the other ogling her without subtlety.

"I know where Darcy is." She spoke without hesitation, conscious that tarrying would only lose time, or would get her politely thrown out. "Or at least," she added in a lower voice, "I can see where. I can *see* it," she repeated, a discreet emphasis on the 'see', looking right into the colonel's eyes, silently willing him to understand.

"Oh," said the colonel. Then, "*Oh*."

"Yes."

"Will you follow me?" Colonel Fitzwilliam said then, after a slight pause. He led Elizabeth towards what seemed to be a small and dirty drawing room, leaving the door wide open.

"Philip," he ordered one of the men, "find Barton. Tell him I have *respectable* company," he added with a glare at the two officers from earlier who kept staring at Elizabeth. "Ask for some tea, and I would like to get it before Michaelmas, this time." Another dark look got rid of everyone, and Elizabeth sat down on a chair which had also seen better days.

"My apartments are much more comfortable," the colonel added with a look in the direction of another hall, "but that would hardly be proper. So…" he said, then paused, studying Elizabeth.

Silence fell. She felt she was being assessed —as an ally or as threat—analysed, judged, and classified. This version of the colonel was very different from the one who had gallantly conversed with her in Lady Catherine de Bourgh's luxurious dining room. For the first time, Elizabeth had the thought that Colonel Fitzwilliam was a dangerous man—dangerous to his enemies, and to Darcy's, hopefully.

"Miss Bennet, what do you see?" he asked, finally.

Elizabeth briefly described her visions of the night. Colonel Fitzwilliam listened in silence. "You are sure it was him?"

"I am."

"Soulmates, then. That is why he wanted to help your sister. You are the woman Darcy proposed to? You refused him?"

"Yes, sir."

The colonel just nodded, as if specifics were unimportant, before he asked, "Can you tell me more details about your vision? I need a thorough description of the place but also— any general impression, any intuition you had during this shared experience."

"Shared? Do you think Mr Darcy felt my presence?"

"If the vision was true, yes, there is a fair chance he did—although, it depends on his condition. Did you perceive distress? Is he injured? Wounded?"

"I do not know," Elizabeth answered sadly. "I could not see him, just his surroundings... I heard the music—barely." She explained how incoherent the melody had been; Colonel Fitzwilliam did not receive the news with satisfaction.

She then tried to do as the officer had asked and focused on describing what she saw.

"I was in London... Mr Darcy was...we were still in London," she began. "I cannot explain my certainty. Maybe it was the noise coming from the street."

"If Darcy knew he was in town, his understanding could have coloured your impression," Colonel Fitzwilliam said. "As I—as I said during that meal we had together, our army has done a lot of experiments."

"And you have been involved in those, Colonel?"

"Quite."

Elizabeth nodded, then attempted to put words to the confused sensations of the previous night. "He was lying on a red sofa, very red, velvet, and quite worn down. I did not see him…but I—I *was* him, I was lying there, perceiving my environment, and it was clear in my mind I was a prisoner in a…" Elizabeth searched for the right words to use. "Mr Darcy was in a house of pleasure," she said finally. Colonel Fitzwilliam did not comment, his eyes not leaving Elizabeth. "On the second floor," she added, because she just knew. "There was… there is…a cellar—not in the vision, but he had been dragged there before—there was blood. Somehow. His blood, or someone else's…"

"Can you tell me more? About the place?"

"Only the decoration. The—Mr Darcy had been left alone—because he was grievously injured, I suppose, and could not escape. There was no, er, female company, no company of any kind, really. The *décor* was gold and red, in many shades, with a crimson, worn out wallpaper…lilies, like the emblem of the French monarchy. But again, this was in London, I am sure of it. There was also a golden Cupid…and some sort of bronze statue nearby, showing, um…"

Elizabeth blushed.

"Every detail is important, Miss Bennet." Colonel Fitzwilliam gave a discreet smile. "I have friends who…who would be familiar enough with the interiors of these places. They can help us find the right location."

Elizabeth nodded, then tried to recall more. "The statue of a faun, Colonel. The creature was quite naked, locked in an amorous embrace with one...no, two nymphs, who—who thought clothes hardly necessary in such an endeavour. The statue was... There was an attempt to paint it—to paint very *particular* places—in garish colours."

Colonel Fitzwilliam gave another small, tense smile, and suddenly Elizabeth remembered, "The window was open."

"What could you see?"

"The street—no, not the street... It was night. Buildings. A low one, very old, with a pointed roof... Behind it, a church, mayhap."

"Could you draw it?"

Then came a lot of waiting.

As Elizabeth had hoped, Colonel Fitzwilliam had already been, in fact, searching for his cousin. Men came and went, asking questions; the colonel directed the enquiries, giving orders, sometimes asking Elizabeth to repeat what she had seen, or making her draw the church again on a different piece of paper. The images were then given to different groups, looking into the most probable locations.

Elizabeth had sent a message to her father, saying she was safe, in respectable company, and following a lead about Lydia. Mr Bennet, Mr and Mrs Gardiner must be going crazy, she thought, looking for her all over the place—her father must be sick with worry. But she could not say more, lest they came to angrily fetch her... Then she would not be able to help.

The afternoon turned golden, and Elizabeth feared she might have to spend the night here. How could that be managed, she wondered, but answers came suddenly, from an unexpected source: Colonel Fitzwilliam's older brother the viscount, the heir and eldest son of the Earl of Matlock.

The viscount had been summoned by his brother, it seemed. He arrived around five, in sumptuous clothes that did not fit the surroundings. The man let himself fall into a chair with an exaggerated yawn, glanced at Elizabeth with curiosity—but he did not ask, or even address a word to her, and Colonel Fitzwilliam scrupulously avoided any introductions.

"Yeah," was the first thing the viscount said, after crossing his satin clad legs, and before his brother even asked a question. "The faun—quite garish, but that is Marie for you. *Aux Délices. Aux Délices de Marie,* the place's official name."

"Are you sure?" Colonel Fitzwilliam asked.

"I recognised the statue from Barton's portrayal. And there are not many whorehouses that big—if we trust your depiction, at least."

Elizabeth could not help but wince at such crude language, but Colonel Fitzwilliam just nodded and began preparations. He wanted his best men with him, but they were still searching and would take an hour to come back. Two new soldiers joined the group, and the colonel and his brother gathered them in another room, probably to talk tactics and give orders not fit for Elizabeth's delicate ears.

Ten minutes later, the viscount came back into the room to partake of some stale tea and questionable biscuits.

"What is happening?" Elizabeth could not help but ask.

"Cousin Darcy went looking for a little country slut who ran away with a rake," the viscount explained. "Now we think the girl might have been sold to Marie. Darcy has followed the trail, I am guessing. He found the *Délices*—Marie's place —and…something happened there, something happened to him… We still do not know what."

The viscount's voice was calm, his tone crisp, contradicting Elizabeth's first impression. She was very ready to despise the man, if only for what his thorough knowledge of places like *Aux Délices* revealed. But the intelligence in his eyes made her rethink her opinion. Like his brother, Colonel Fitzwilliam, this was someone who could surprise you—and who you might not wish to have as an enemy.

The viscount studied Elizabeth for a moment.

"And who are you?"

"A...friend of Darcy."

"One has to appreciate the pause before the word 'friend'."

"Shut up, Percy," Colonel Fitzwilliam said, entering the room. "This young *lady* is, in truth, a friend of Darcy, no pause necessary. And we do not want her reputation harmed, do you understand?"

It might be too late for that, Elizabeth thought, and maybe the viscount believed the same thing, because a nuance of irony danced in his eyes, but he made no other remark.

"Barton, at last," the colonel said, when a tall, thin man with a resolute face entered the room. "We are leaving. Take the pills and the whole apparatus, just in case."

Soon, they were in the street. The viscount, his purse in hand, distributed money to the group of eight sturdy men. Then he walked away with them, towards the horses, Elizabeth supposed, while Colonel Fitzwilliam was handing her into a carriage. Barton sat near the coachman.

They were going to Marie's. Elizabeth was needed to see if it was the right place, and, she supposed, in case she should have a new vision, or glean more information from her bond.

Night had fallen. The coach's advance was slow. London's streets were dark and noisy.

"This is not good for you, Miss Bennet," Colonel Fitzwilliam said, after a while.

"No."

She had entered a lair of soldiers all alone, and now she was following one to a *whorehouse*.

And so many people had seen her face already.

She should have worn a veil, she realised. Really, she should not have entered the officers' building without it, but she had left in such haste—her thoughts only on Darcy—she had not been planning ahead. Elizabeth took her kerchief now, and tried to transform it into a makeshift covering for when she would be out of the carriage, but—too little, too late.

"This is why I could not tell my family I was coming to see you, Colonel," Elizabeth finally explained. "They would have ordered me to go and talk to your father—to the earl. But his lordship would not have believed me, not about the soulmates' dream, maybe not even about the bond. I would have convinced him, I believe, after a while; still, hours, days would have passed...and my vision would have been dismissed as womanly fancy. You were the only one who would understand the importance of the images I saw, sir—and the necessity of acting quickly."

Colonel Fitzwilliam just nodded.

"And of course," Elizabeth added, "my father would never have let me go to"—she paused —"where you intend to take me now—he would quite forbid me to go."

"And rightly so. But I am a selfish man, and I want to save my cousin more than I want to protect your name."

"A man's life is more important."

"I hope you do not doubt, Miss Bennet, that when we find him, Darcy will not hesitate for a moment to—" Colonel Fitzwilliam paused and looked away.

I hope you do not doubt that when we find

him, Darcy will not hesitate for a moment to marry you, despite the harm done to your reputation… Certainly, that was the thought Colonel Fitzwilliam wanted to convey. But what were the odds of finding Darcy alive, really?

And then Elizabeth realised.

"The music is stronger," she said. "It—it has not been interrupted for a while."

Colonel Fitzwilliam's face was determined.

"Good."

∞∞∞

Aux Délices de Marie was the right place, but Darcy was not there.

Blood stained the sofa upstairs. Elizabeth could not avert her eyes. On the right, the statue, with the faun and the naked ladies. On the left, a golden Cupid with his arrows, pointing at emptiness.

Darcy had been here. In this room. Hurt. Bleeding on the crimson cushions.

Dreaming of Elizabeth, as she dreamed of him.

Stay alive, we are looking for you, was Elizabeth's irrational plea, sent into the void.

A soldier had been left to protect her; downstairs, Colonel Fitzwilliam and his men were...conversing with Marie.

"You were right," the colonel told Elizabeth a few minutes later, leading her outside and then to the carriage again. "Darcy came here, following your sister's trail. Wickham must have sold Lydia—Miss Lydia—to this house, we do not know the details yet. Darcy tried to reclaim her, but Marie's main protector is in league with dangerous people. The discussion went awry and Darcy was shot. They would have killed him, I believe," the colonel said, meeting Elizabeth's eyes, "if they had not realised how important he was, and what ransom they could obtain. They left him there, injured, for hours. Then they took him away."

"Where? Do you know? What about my sister?"

"Sent to another of Marie's properties a few hours ago. That is where we are going now, hoping we shall find Darcy also."

"But...there have not been any demands, have there? For money? For Mr Darcy's life? No ransom note has arrived at Matlock House?"

"No."

"Why?"

"I do not know, Miss Bennet."

This was not a good sign. The music was still present though, hesitant but real, weak but steadfast in Elizabeth's mind as she held on to hope. Because of traffic, the ride was again not as quick as they would have wished it to be, and when they arrived at last at Marie's warehouse, as this second location was called, the colonel's men, on foot, had preceded them.

To Elizabeth's frustration, she soon realised that the battle had been won—or lost, depending on how you wanted to see it—without her.

Lydia had been found and sent to the Gardiners' house in the viscount's carriage. Nobody had even thought of waiting a few minutes so Elizabeth could see her sister. Nor could she obtain any information on Lydia's wellbeing; to be frank the men did not care about either of the two women at all.

They had no time for the Bennet family's concerns. They were here for Darcy.

Except Darcy was still nowhere to be found.

Time passed. Elizabeth stayed in the carriage —feeling as if she was going slightly crazy. Colonel Fitzwilliam, the viscount, and the soldiers had disappeared inside the building. It was a big, ancient structure, in a better state than the one she had found the officers in.

The moon was out. Somewhere, a clock rang eleven. Light played inside Marie's building; behind the windows, shadows were moving. Elizabeth could not hear anything—she could not stop thinking of Lydia. What may have happened to her, what reception would her sister have at the Gardiners' home.

Staying in this vehicle was senseless, was it not? Now that Lydia had been retrieved, Elizabeth should be at home, by her sister's side, with her father and her uncle and aunt. She should not stay here, waiting for who knew what...and suddenly Elizabeth was of half a mind to just walk away, to go back to her family despite the dangers of such a late hour. She could hail a hack chaise again, direct it to Cheapside. Pay one of the colonel's soldiers to come with her, to protect her—yes, she really should— but then Colonel Fitzwilliam stepped out of the building, Barton in tow.

"Darcy is not here," the colonel explained. "He should be, but— We lost his trail."

All thoughts of leaving abruptly vanished.

"How can I help?"

Colonel Fitzwilliam studied Elizabeth for a moment. "Can you fall asleep?"

Elizabeth hesitated. "Hoping for another shared dream?"

"That is the idea, yes."

"Here, in the carriage? Perhaps I could, but...it will take...it might take some time. To find sleep, I mean."

"On that matter," Colonel Fitzwilliam began. He turned to Barton. "The pills."

The man handed his officer a leather satchel. Then, with a nod from the colonel, he walked away while Darcy's cousin stepped inside the carriage again.

"You want to make me sleep," Elizabeth said, looking at the pills in the colonel's hand; there was also a flask, with water, or maybe tea. "Is this laudanum?"

"The main substance is a derivative of opium, yes—mixed with other, different ingredients. I am afraid I am forbidden to tell you more, Miss Bennet."

"This is connected to the...army experiments."

"Indeed. This particular drug has already been tested; it is often used by our spies with impressive results. But the process is dangerous, and this is why I need your agreement beforehand. You will—well, you will be drugged, Miss Bennet. As if you were drunk, but with other, more powerful effects. It should help though, help tremendously with the connection to your—to my cousin. This is what we use," Colonel Fitzwilliam added after a pause, "with soulmates. Couples. Our agents, sent to obtain information behind enemy lines."

"Charlotte was right," Elizabeth whispered, distantly amused. Then, "What are the risks?"

"Madness, in some rare cases. To my knowledge, it has happened only once, at least after the drug was perfected. But it did happen. And we had two cases of strokes... You are young and healthy, so I assume it should not be a problem. I would not ask, Miss Bennet, if I was not desperate to find Darcy quickly. Still no ransom note has been received. It seems to me that with each hour we lose, tragedy looms closer."

"I—yes." Elizabeth shivered. "Give me the drug."

∞∞∞

The effects started slowly. Elizabeth swallowed the pills with what was rather coarse and bitter tea. For a few minutes afterwards she thought nothing would happen.

"If we find Darcy thanks to this, I pray I shall be sent to Spain on the front lines for a while," Colonel Fitzwilliam stated with dark amusement. "Darcy will not be happy I used his soulmate as an experimental subject."

Elizabeth answered—something clever—except she did not. It was the strangest sensation, the impression that she was outside her own head, that she could see the words she wanted to speak, hanging in the air, except she had not spoken them. "Miss Bennet?" Colonel Fitzwilliam was saying, somewhere. "The process has started. Take deep, long breaths. Sometimes, the subjects forget to breathe."

"What a reassuring thought," she commented. Except, again, she did not actually speak—the music was so very loud.

Her soulmate's melody. And—no, it was not that loud, it was just...*there*, playing inside the carriage, strong and beautiful, like Elizabeth was in the front row of seats at an orchestra. Everyone could hear her music now, even Colonel Fitzwilliam, Elizabeth thought, except when she concentrated on Darcy's cousin, she realised he was looking at her with a serious air, waiting. Likely he did not hear anything, it was just her.

"I—the drug is working, I believe," she murmured, Colonel Fitzwilliam nodded, then put two fingers on her naked wrist.

"Do not be offended, it is—the touch, it is to remind you of...where real things are. Now, listen to me, Miss Bennet. I want you to follow my instructions pr—"

The next word must have been 'precisely'. Elizabeth would never know, or hear the instructions, because suddenly she was elsewhere.

"No," Darcy said. "Do not come here, Elizabeth. Too much blood. This is not for you—not for your eyes."

The process had not been gradual. Or to be exact, there had been no process. Elizabeth was just—not in the carriage anymore. Darcy was in a tunnel, a large ochre one, with stalagmites and strange carvings, like something from a tale, from a dream—and of course, a dream it was. Darcy was standing tall, he was not wounded —although he was, Elizabeth knew, in truth he had been shot, but in Elizabeth's mind's eye he was safe and sound, wearing the same clothes as he had been when she had last seen him. So, the vision was a lie. She did not see the real surroundings, she imagined Darcy as she wished he was—but still—the *bond* was real.

It *was* Darcy talking to her, his presence, his mind…

A gunshot. Another one. Someone yelled. Shouts. Someone was running. Maybe Darcy, except, in the vision, he—

"Go away, Elizabeth. I…I love you, but you should not see this."

Another gunshot.

"Colonel!" Elizabeth cried, and with that word she was back in the carriage; Darcy's cousin was holding her wrist tightly, like he wanted to drag her back. He looked very worried, but Elizabeth felt sane—not mad yet, she decided. "Colonel, there is a fight… Guns! Darcy is in a cellar, in a sort of underground passage. I do not see the place as it really appears, but—"

"A fight, here? In Marie's building?"

"Yes, here, here," Elizabeth answered without thinking—she just knew. Darcy was close. Without thinking she stepped out of the carriage, looking at the house, at the neighbouring buildings in the darkened, dirty street. *Here*, somewhere. *Please, please…*

"Why don't we hear the gunshots?" she whispered. Her head hurt. The music was still playing, she could—she could grab the notes and let them carry her, like a river.

"It may not have been—what you see may not have been chronologically accurate, Miss Bennet."

"Chronologically?"

"What you saw... The guns... It may have happened a while ago. Did Darcy say something?"

Elizabeth blushed violently—but no... Certainly, the whole experience had been distorted by her own desires. What she thought Darcy had said—maybe it did not happen...

Her migraine was getting worse. They were walking, she suddenly realised, towards Marie's building. Colonel Fitzwilliam was leading her forward, holding her arm. He was tense, the world was fuzzy and strange.

"It sounded like a violent scene. Mr Darcy did not wish me to witness it."

"We have to find him," Colonel Fitzwilliam said, his voice more anxious than she had ever heard. They were inside the house now, Barton and the men searching the dark, dirty rooms, while terrified looking women scantily dressed were huddling in the corners. Four disreputable looking fellas had their faces bloodied and their hands tied to a pipe. This was not a house of pleasure, Elizabeth realised. It was more—yes, a warehouse, where thugs slept, where they kept young women before sending them God knows where.

Her migraine was getting worse. Colonel Fitzwilliam was giving orders. The men scattered. Cellars were being searched; Elizabeth was losing all notion of time.

"The drug is, er, still acting on me," she explained to the colonel, as he led her into the darkest confines of the building. "I feel like I am...maybe...sinking?"

"Yes. The process is only beginning, I fear. While you are still with us, Miss Bennet," and this sounded ominous, "look around you. Feel the—the atmosphere of the place, try to tell me whether anything seems familiar. This is a very old building and a very old street. There are —one would say catacombs, I suppose. Hidden passages below the streets. Tunnels, from darker times in history. The entrances are sometimes very well concealed."

Indeed, human beings could be very creative when it came to hiding from authorities, soldiers, and taxes—the ironic thought was Elizabeth's, but it was never actually uttered. She felt split, like the idea was floating in the first part of her mind while the other one was occupied by—

Darcy was behind her, holding her, his hands around her waist. She leaned back, her head resting on his chest. The cave was beautiful now, copper and silver. Treasures—all illusions, of course.

"Where are you?" she whispered. "How do I get here? Downstairs, with you?"

"Too much blood, my love. I took his gun, but —I fear the infection is... I have no wish for you to witness my death."

I am not alone, she wanted to say, *there is help*, but somehow she just thought of asking again, "How did you come here?"

"They dragged me through the courtya—"

"Miss Bennet!" Someone was shaking her—the colonel. She came back to her senses on an old, dingy armchair. The room was dark and dusty, lit by the pale glow of the moon.

"...yard!" she breathed. "They dragged Darcy through the courtyard..." She could hardly form words, but she could see... "Steps. Wood. Wine bottles, kegs, oak kegs. Smell like—cherry..."

"Here?" the colonel asked, and how... What... The armchair had disappeared, Elizabeth was standing in a musty cellar, staring at wine bottles. How did she—when? One moment she was sitting, and the next... It seemed minutes had just vanished, from her time, from her life.

Had they gone through the courtyard already, then down underground?

She could not—remember…

"Miss Bennet," Colonel Fitzwilliam repeated, because he had already addressed her twice at least. "Are we in the right place? Are you hearing me?"

"No. I mean, yes. Sorry, Colonel, I…" She took a deep breath and looked around. "Indeed, Mr Darcy went through—this door, here." They stepped into another small cellar, and you would expect a secret passage to reveal itself behind a mahogany bookshelf, with mysterious engravings—not so here. The secret, sturdy trap door was concealed under a heap of coal, as all trap doors in history generally were. But this coal had been very recently shovelled away…

A ladder, and at last, they went down into the treasure cave, and there…

…there were the men, and there were the guns, and there was Darcy.

Elizabeth would learn, much later, what had really happened. How Darcy had been shot early by Marie's associates, left to bleed on the sofa while a first faction decided to ask for a ransom. How he had been brought to this building thereafter... But a second faction—composed of wiser men, mayhap—decided that ransoming a high member of the gentry would be folly, a way to sign their death warrant... And Darcy's wound had begun to turn bad, so the only way was to kill him right now, this second faction advocated. In short, the men disagreed—some of them were drunk, some of them were scared; then they learned about the colonel's men raiding Marie's main house. Panic rose; they decided to lead Darcy into their underground hideout. His fate had not entirely been decided, but it was clear that the intention of half of them at least was to end it here and to bury the body...

But Darcy had stolen a pistol while the men were arguing, and he...

But no, Elizabeth did not know all of this yet. She was just aware that at last, they were in the right place—Darcy's presence, very near —she began to run—Colonel Fitzwilliam called after her—but he did not grab her arm because —shots, resounding around—one so close—her ears ringing...

Elizabeth was lost in the music.

What she saw was not real, she knew. *Phantasmagoria*. Metaphors. She was running in the Minotaur's labyrinth, an illusory maze of choices and perils, ancient carvings on the walls from the beginning of time, and all of it was fake, her mind interpreting facts, her soul music desperately looking for symbols in a place which in truth must be a series of smelly, half abandoned tunnels and cellars, littered with the rot of centuries... But she saw none of it, she only understood, dimly, that Darcy must be on the run, Marie's fellas hunting him...

...or now fighting Colonel Fitzwilliam's men instead...

Darcy's presence. Like a beacon at the centre of the labyrinth. A left turn, a right, she stepped on what must have been bodies, but in her world were statues, marble recumbents, and at last...

"Elizabeth," he said.

That—that was real.

Strong arms held her.

"Oh my God," Darcy's voice said, holding her so close. Taking the Lord's name in vain, was the crazy thought that crossed her mind—

Shots.

Someone had found them. And, oh God (taking the Lord's name in vain) she might have been the one to lead them to him.

In the world of symbols, Darcy pushed her away, drew his own gun, and fired—

Everything went blank.

∞ ∞ ∞

Elizabeth was standing in a white void.

The world was music. People were notes. Whirlwinds of songs, and Elizabeth could hear them all—Darcy's and the thugs' and Colonel Fitzwilliam's and his men's and Marie's captives' and—

—*there was no good and evil.*

—Elizabeth understood, understood them all, swept into the intimacy, the deep truth of their songs, why they were there fighting and what had led them here and—beauty and pain, killers and prostitutes and...

—just music, and she knew them all now, their tragedies and their faults, their broken hopes and the agony, screaming in the dark...

—streets now, lost souls and houses and churches and secrets, cold and warmth, misery and...

joy...

—her aunt and uncle, her father, and Lydia and the servants in the house and...

—smoke and work and despair and ambition and help me, please, help, and…

—every soul in the country screaming of loneliness and love, yearning for hope and…

—Jane?

Can you hear me? Jane?

Too late; Elizabeth's awareness jumped again —

—deserts and ice and cities and human grief and bliss…

∞∞∞

—encompassing…

—everyone

∞∞∞

and…

∞∞∞

"For Christ's sake, I am telling you, she is fine!

The final stages of the drug…"

"…her nose…bleeding all over her face! Damn it, why don't you—"

"I swear to God, Darcy, you will shut up, and let the doctor…"

∞∞∞

Elizabeth came back to her senses by increments. The first time, she was still in Marie's building, in the old, dingy armchair, in the moonlit room. Alone. No, not alone. A young soldier was keeping guard; the one who had been enjoying the sun on the steps of the officers' house, an eternity ago.

As soon as he saw her open her eyes, he handed her a glass of water.

"The colonel said you should drink a lot, ma'am. To wash the medicine away. No, please drink more than that. Respectfully, he said, Colonel Fitzwilliam said, I should force you to—"

Where was—

"They washed your face, you had a terrible nosebleed… No, ma'am, you should drink…"

"Mr Darcy?" she asked, as soon as she swallowed some more of the tepid water. Her throat was parched indeed, and she could hardly speak.

"He is badly injured, ma'am. The doctor—and the, er, his—his cousin? His other cousin? The viscount, they've taken him home."

Home.

She should not be here *still*, Elizabeth thought vaguely—it was difficult to focus. If Darcy was safe, or at least out of immediate danger, then she was just a woman, alone for no reason in a… In a less than respectable place. She tried to rise but her legs were too weak.

She had to go home…

Elizabeth, Darcy said.

I am here, she answered.

Darcy did not hear her. Or did he?

The music was playing… No. *Music* was playing, all the music.

The white world and its siren song. The ocean, where you could be lost, and never come back.

She dived under.

The next time Elizabeth woke again was in the carriage in the company of Colonel Fitzwilliam. They were going—somewhere. When Darcy's cousin saw her regain consciousness, he handed her a flask; inside was some cold tea. Elizabeth drank it all in silence, trying to make sense of her surroundings.

"Mr Darcy?" she asked again.

"The doctor saw to Darcy's wounds before he was carried home, Miss Bennet," Colonel Fitzwilliam answered. "It looked worse than it was. The man is—optimistic, as much as those people can be. They always avoid anything that sounds like a certain diagnosis, have you noticed? They would be too terrified to be proved wrong and lose their reputation..."

Elizabeth tried to follow the music again, but she had lost *him*, lost the tenuous connection.

Maybe she had done all this for nothing, and Darcy would die. And she would be like Charlotte, with an empty space in her soul—

Stop. She had done all she could; she could not help him now. *Home.* She had to think of herself, of Lydia, of her father. "I must go back," she croaked, her voice still weak. Colonel Fitzwilliam handed her the flask; she swallowed more cold tea.

"Indeed, you must. I believe I have found a solution to save you, Miss Bennet. Or—I apologise, that sounded very dramatic. I meant, I have found a solution to help with the damage done to your reputation." Elizabeth tried to listen, but her mind was still floating. "To be honest," the colonel continued, "I hoped Darcy would be found in a better state, and you could both come back to your uncle's house together as engaged soulmates. Or even that we would go and see a reverend right away, wave the 'soulmates in peril' exception, and get you two married before dawn. But as such a simple solution is not to be…"

Colonel Fitzwilliam paused, except—he did not. Elizabeth had lost her grasp on reality again. She sank into darkness, and when she came to, the carriage had stopped in front of a very, very elegant house.

"…in such cases indeed…" The colonel was speaking to someone.

An elegant feminine voice resonated.

"Richard, really. You had better have an excellent explanation for—I mean, at such an hour—I cannot believe… Merciful heavens, who is this young woman?"

"Miss Bennet," the colonel said, "let me introduce you to my mother, the Countess of

Matlock."

∞∞∞

It should be the other way round, Elizabeth had thought. Considering the difference of age and rank, she should have been the one to be introduced to the countess. Which was a strange fact to obsess about, especially considering that Elizabeth had dropped again into a hazy state; she was huddled in a corner of the coach, eyes closed, floating.

The coach was trudging through the night in the city's obscure streets. Elizabeth must have appeared to her companions as if she were unconscious, or sleeping.

"Come on Richard, she is a nobody! Do you know I sent Darcy to visit the most connected young ladies I could find? Your cousin has such great prospects, he should not find himself helplessly bound to this..."

The Countess of Matlock's voice trailed away. Elizabeth's eyes stayed closed.

"Mother, they are betrothed. Miss Bennet is Darcy's soulmate."

"Are we sure that is the truth? We cannot be sure that is the truth. Come on, darling, you know how these things go. Young women, they lie! Upstart social climbers, who would do anything…"

Elizabeth should say something, protest. She could not; maybe it was all a dream.

"Mother, I can vouch myself that their bond is true. She found him through his music. I already told you…" Colonel Fitzwilliam's voice was lost for a while, whispered explanations in the countess's ear. Elizabeth vaguely wondered whether the colonel had told his mother more than he ought about the soulmate military procedures. About the experiments. He should protect the king's secrets, but—mothers and their sons… These ideas were faraway, floating, in a universe of wonders.

"Still," the countess said, "her uncle is in *trade*."

"Darcy is dearly attached to Miss Bennet, Mother. He will want his wife to have access to the best society, and he will need female help—he will need *your* help to introduce his young, naïve bride to the best circles. Who else would he ask, but you? Mama, come on. You are the only one with the necessary connections, the only one with the diplomatic talent to accomplish this *tour de force*…"

"If he lives," the countess answered primly.

"Yes. If he lives, Mother, he will marry her, be sure of it. His soulmate. She compromised her reputation to save him... What do you think a man like Darcy will do?"

The countess let out a dramatic, exasperated sigh.

"So," Colonel Fitzwilliam started again, "whatever your opinions are on the matter, we have to act as though this marriage is an inevitability. Which, personally, I am all in favour of. Miss Bennet is very amiable, and she acted right, she really did. An honourable and brave woman—doesn't that more than mitigate her dubious parentage?"

Another sigh. Clearly, the countess was hardly convinced of her son's dangerous liberal views about individuals' worthiness.

Yes, Elizabeth was slowly waking up.

"You and your ideas, Richard, darling... So, what do you—in the meantime, what do you want me to say to *these* people?"

"Miss Bennet's father will be present, Mother, with Mr and Mrs Gardiner... They are Miss Bennet's uncle and aunt. You have to be thoroughly amiable. You have to make them so happy—amazed, incredulous—that the Countess of Matlock is visiting them in this informal manner just before dawn. So amazed that they won't— You understand, Mother, you spent all day and night with Miss Bennet, searching for Darcy. You did not leave her side for a second. You were so dreadfully worried for your dear nephew, but comforted to be in the company of Darcy's anguished soulmate and *betrothed*… You understand what I am getting at? You have to charm them so thoroughly that they will forget to ask the details of what exactly happened tonight."

"You mean, you hope they will not ask about the whorehouse."

"Mother, I am shocked." Colonel Fitzwilliam's voice was perfectly serene. "Mayhap, let us not utter that particular word in front of Miss Bennet's family?"

"Richard, if these people are not fools they will wonder why, if everything was so very respectable, Miss Bennet fled their home secretly without her maid and gave absolutely no word of her whereabouts afterwards."

"Yes. Well. There, indeed, lies the difficulty."

As most plans go, the success of this one was

ambiguous.

The Countess of Matlock played her role superbly. In fact, despite the drugs lingering in her blood and the awkwardness of the situation, Elizabeth quite admired the theatrics of the moment. Richard's mother was clearly enjoying herself, and if she had not been born a countess, her career on the stage would have been a resounding success. But her audience was wary. The Gardiners and Mr Bennet were polite. Politely distant, really. Even cold.

Fortunately, the countess was too lost in her performance to notice.

Then Elizabeth was sent to bed, and Colonel Fitzwilliam was summoned to the study by Elizabeth's father and uncle to have 'a talk'.

The next morning, the colonel and the countess long gone, Elizabeth told the entire truth to her father. Yes, every detail—she hid nothing. She gave her reasons for her escape; she explained where and how she met Colonel Fitzwilliam; she explained the nature of Marie's houses; she spoke about the drugs and the very late arrival of Colonel Fitzwilliam's mother in the proceedings.

Do not believe, though, that all Colonel Fitzwilliam's elaborate construction of lies had been for naught. On the contrary, the Countess of Matlock's tale was extremely valuable. It was to be the official version, for servants, for society. The lie would even be told, Elizabeth's supposed, to her own mother.

But she wanted her father to know the truth.

Chances were, the respectable version of the story would not be entirely believed, but the important part was, there was such a story to tell. Gossip was inevitable, but without the Countess of Matlock's endorsement, it would have been social death for Elizabeth. Now, there would be only talk—not proof. The difference to her, and to her family, was staggering.

Social death except, of course, if she became Mrs Darcy.

But Darcy had never felt so very far away.

He was alive, the soul music was playing. But now that Elizabeth was back home, prisoner of a rather unpleasant family interaction, the reality of her soulmate, of Darcy—of what they had shared in the treasure cave—it all felt like a fantasy.

Like, well…like a dream, from which she was now awakened.

Everything was greyer in the light of day.

Elizabeth was allowed to keep Lydia's company. Or shall we say, Elizabeth was encouraged to keep Lydia's company; in fact, she was practically confined to her sister's chambers.

The two 'bad' Bennet girls, Elizabeth thought with a streak of rebelliousness. Punished and hidden in the attic.

It was not an attic, of course, but the vast and pleasant guest bedroom of the Gardiners' house. And Elizabeth was not as much punished as treated coldly by her uncle and aunt when she ventured out. The Gardiners had listened to her story in silence; then they had asked a few questions, that was all. Now, Elizabeth's uncle hardly spoke to her, and Elizabeth's aunt was scrupulously polite.

It was sad but not unexpected. Elizabeth had lost their trust. Her friendship, her closeness with her aunt, was now a thing of the past. Madelyne Gardiner had seen her niece willingly escape her home. Elizabeth had lied to her, to their servant, she had put the Gardiners in the terrible situation of thinking they had lost the young lady who had been entrusted to their care —and all of this, they believed, could have been avoided if Elizabeth had been frank with them.

It was too much to ask of their friendship to survive the strain. It was the price, Elizabeth thought. The price she had to pay for finding her sister and her soulmate.

Elizabeth was also beginning to fear that this price would include her father's affection, and that—that would be a tragedy. When she had first arrived at the Gardiners' house that night, with the countess and the colonel at her side, Mr Bennet had been at first pale with relief; he had to sit down when Elizabeth entered the room. The second daughter given back to him that night—his hands were trembling. When everyone was gone, though, and Elizabeth had told him everything the next morning, Mr Bennet became pale again—this time with anger. Anger directed at her—at Elizabeth—at her lies.

Mr Bennet was not the kind of man who yelled, so he just left the room, retreated to Mr Gardiner's study, and pointedly ignored his erstwhile favourite daughter for the next two weeks.

Two weeks! It can seem such a short while. But Elizabeth's situation was dire. No news from Darcy. No, that was unfair... The Gardiners received a message from Colonel Fitzwilliam, saying that his cousin was doing better.

But...this strange, distanced feeling that her soulmate was just an illusion. The palpable disapproval of her family, the clear resentment of her father. And maybe there were also some drugs left in Elizabeth's blood, adding to the discomfort.

But then, there was Lydia.

And there, Elizabeth could be useful. And there, she *knew* she had been useful. The umbrage of her father, uncle, and aunt could be understood; they felt Elizabeth had betrayed them for a man...and mayhap, this was a reasonable interpretation of the facts. But it was also thanks to Elizabeth that Lydia had been returned to them.

In this Elizabeth had acted right, she could be *sure* of it, and the certainty was a balm.

But there also lay another worry. Had Elizabeth really saved Lydia, or had her sister suffered too much, in spirit and otherwise, to really come back to them?

It was difficult to judge. At first, Lydia did not say anything. She woke up, she ate the breakfast Mrs Gardiner brought up; Elizabeth and her aunt, allies in these moments at least, strived to make the young girl speak, to learn what had happened, but Lydia would not answer their enquiries. Whatever grudge Mrs Gardiner was holding against Elizabeth, she was still a kind woman, and she really tried to reassure and comfort her younger niece, hoping to gain her confidence. But Lydia would not talk. And soon enough Mrs Gardiner was taken again by family concerns, her own children, her husband's business, preparing for her guests' departure —because of course, Mr Bennet wanted his daughters back in Hertfordshire with him.

Thus, after a while, Elizabeth and Lydia were mostly left alone in the vast, beautiful bedroom, with only London's distant bustle as company.

"This is not my fault," were Lydia first words, on the third evening. She had sat up in bed; Elizabeth put down the book she was unsuccessfully trying to read.

Lydia looked so stubborn, like a vexed child. "Not my fault," she repeated.

If Elizabeth had been Jane, she would have answered, instantly, "Of course it is not, dear," but Elizabeth was not all tenderness and sisterly subjectivity. She still had a rational mind. And it was Lydia's fault, was it not? The young girl should never have followed Wickham.

But...

"What happened, my dear?" Elizabeth said, taking Lydia's hand. "Can you tell me?"

"He said—Wickham said—that I was his soulmate. He was not entirely certain at first, but then he told me, 'I am ready to be convinced', because he was so in love with me—he said. So, I played my secret music on the Lucases' pianoforte while I was staying with Maria. And Wickham said—when I played, he recognised it —it was *his* melody...his soul melody. He told me. It was proof, you see?"

Elizabeth closed her eyes. "But Lydia... Remember, Liddy, I told you—I told you that this method was a common trap. Used by men to— to seduce the innocent. I told you how the same thing almost happened to me..."

When Wickham had behaved so badly with her in Longbourn's music room, Elizabeth had told her sisters half the story. She wanted to warn them, but she had not named Wickham as the culprit; she had just said the guilty party was 'an officer'. She had downplayed the whole encounter, because—

Because that was what Elizabeth and her father had decided at the time, to hide what had happened, to protect Elizabeth's reputation. And now, because of this foolish decision, both her reputation and Lydia's were in ashes anyway.

"But it was not the same, Lizzy! Wickham loved me! He really thought I was his soulmate.

He swore…"

Lydia, hardly sixteen, had fallen into the trap. It was such a tragedy, and in Elizabeth's mind, they played, the melodies she heard, the music of the girls in Marie's houses, the notes dancing in her mind. But a memory now, but such a clear one.

Lives and destinies twisted by hardship, bad luck, and a terrible lack of love.

But it was so luminous an experience that Elizabeth could not talk about it now. She could not think about it now. It was too big for her to comprehend, honestly.

Still. Souls lost.

And *no*, Lydia would not suffer the fate of those girls, broken and alone. Their music, screaming regrets and bitterness. Begging for help, no one coming. No heroes, no Darcy to save them.

Elizabeth sat down on the bed and slowly took her sister's hand in hers. "You lacked prudence, dear Lydia," she stated after reflection. "But is it a wonder, at your age? And I certainly lacked caution myself in my latest actions."

Lydia softened, and Elizabeth wondered if behind all her bravado, her sister had not been dreadfully afraid of her friends' reactions. "We both did wrong, Lydia, in our family's eyes. But I swear, I shall not abandon you. I shall help you in whatever way I can—"

"Do you know where—where George is? Wickham?" Lydia asked.

"No, we—we do not."

"He sold me. To that house."

"I know, Liddy. We think—Colonel Fitzwilliam believes that Wickham fled. That he left the country when he realised Darcy had been abducted and that the army was involved in his search."

"Marie," Lydia whispered. "She is not really French, you know. She is just pretending. Her accent is not even right." Elizabeth nodded, amused despite herself. "So, she, er," Lydia continued, "she gave me to those men. On the first night. Before Mr Darcy arrived. Before you found me... There were three—three men," Lydia explained, meeting her sister's gaze with fear more than shame, and a clear challenge.

This is what happened, Lydia's gaze said. *This is what happened to me, and I cannot change it. Now despise me if you dare.*

And mayhap the old Elizabeth would have reacted with horror and spite. Perhaps the old Elizabeth would have shamed Lydia, her fallen sister. Lydia had been inconsiderate *once*, so she should be blamed for all the following consequences, the old Elizabeth would have judged.

But—not now. Now Elizabeth could not, in all conscience, react the same way. Not after glimpsing into the abyss. And not when she had taken such inconsiderate risks herself. She had hazarded her safety and reputation for love, like Lydia had.

"Imagine," Mr Bennet had said, with an unexpected, cold rage, in Mr Gardiner's study, when Elizabeth had told him all. "Imagine if Colonel Fitzwilliam had not been an honourable man. You were alone, Elizabeth, in a house full of soldiers. Can you imagine what could have happened? In fact—are you lying to me? Did it happen, Elizabeth?"

"No!"

But it had happened to Lydia. Because Colonel Fitzwilliam had honour but Wickham had none. Because Lydia had trusted the wrong man. Elizabeth had taken risks and escaped unscathed. Her sister...

Elizabeth held Lydia's hand tighter. "We will support and help each other, Liddy, I swear. If Father casts us off, we shall go and live in that little house in the woods, just the two of us. Do you remember, how we used to play there, near the Joneses' farmhouse?"

Lydia's voice was very small. "We shall eat wild raspberries and grow turnips?"

"Indeed! We shall grow the best turnips in Hertfordshire, and become very rich, and they will all be jealous."

More likely, if their father forsook them, Lydia and Elizabeth would throw themselves on Jane and Bingley's kindness; they would live at Netherfield or in a nearby cottage on Bingley's purse. But even if starvation in the woods was not a likely outcome, it was an unpleasant thought, to imagine themselves cast out. *It will not happen,* Elizabeth decided, trying to quell her fears. Elizabeth, after all, was not fallen, and it was in the interest of the Bennet family to hide what had happened to Lydia.

Most likely, there would be no public estrangement. Just a terrible, terrible coldness; in truth, Elizabeth felt cold already, despite the fire and her perfectly adequate clothes. And Darcy—there was no Darcy—of course there was but... Elizabeth had never felt so alone.

Six days later, they were in a carriage bound for Longbourn. But when at last they arrived home, after a tense ride with their sullen father, only Mr Bennet stepped out. The coach started forward again, Lydia and Elizabeth still inside it, to deposit the two young ladies on the elegant steps of Netherfield.

Jane was there, waiting. She greeted Lydia first —the young girl was the one who had most suffered. She expressed how very welcome her younger sister was. And at last, when Lydia stepped, rather happily, into the beautiful hall, Jane walked to Elizabeth and tenderly embraced her.

"You were right, Elizabeth," Jane whispered. "You were right to act such. And brave, so brave. I am so proud of you."

The tension of the last days quickly dissolved, and Elizabeth fell sobbing into her sister's arms.

That night, Lydia went to bed early. The girl was exhausted. Elizabeth also suspected Lydia felt safe at last; she felt loved again in Jane's care, accepted as she had not been in the Gardiners' home, or in the company of her father. When the girl was escorted upstairs, and the three others were left alone in the drawing room after supper, Charles Bingley raised his glass of port towards Elizabeth.

"To my heroic sister Lizzy, who saved my dear friend!" he said. "Darcy would be dead without you. I shall never be able to thank you enough —when I think of him shot by those ruffians, his body thrown into the Thames, or left in that putrid cellar to die— You know, I hope, that you and Lydia will be always, always be welcome in my home, Lizzy. Seriously—well, I am all seriousness, for once. Colonel Fitzwilliam told us all in his letter. Elizabeth, you acted like a modern Amazon."

"I am flattered to be compared to Hippolyta, who would not be?" Elizabeth answered, smiling. "But the Amazons' attire is so unsophisticated; I shall not wish to be always clad in warriors' clothes. I want to keep my silk dress, my green muslin, and my ivory slippers."

"You will regret your decision when you ride towards the enemy on your warhorse, shooting your bow," was Charles Bingley's answer, before Jane, always the practical one, added:

"Father will come around, Lizzy. He knows his reaction is unreasonable—that you are not at fault. Except, of course, in hiding your purpose from him."

"I had to."

"I know, and I understand. I believe, in fact, that our father's anger is directly proportionate to the affection he has for you. You are his beloved daughter, his favourite. And suddenly you were gone, willingly. He thought you were dead or in—in dear Lydia's situation—and the anger and the pain were so high, they did not disappear when he found you unscathed. He is still... The wave of emotion has not subsided. But subside it will, and then he will miss your presence dearly."

"I certainly hope so."

"Oh, and by the way, Elizabeth," Bingley started again, "in his last letter, two days ago— no, yesterday... No—it was the missive I received this morning, I believe—Darcy asked if he would be welcome here, at Netherfield? He specifically wanted me to ask you whether his presence would be welcome—knowing you would be staying here..."

Elizabeth's heart skipped a beat. She put down her glass and pretended to study the piece of embroidery she was supposed to be working on. For a moment, the music was loud, so loud, pounding in her ears—for a moment she could not breathe.

"Yes," she answered, after a while. The silence had been too long, she knew. She forced herself to raise her eyes and look at her brother-in-law.

"Yes—Mr Darcy would be very welcome."

∞ ∞ ∞

"You chose not to tell me, Lizzy," Jane said, her gaze serious. "And I understand. It was also Mr Darcy's secret, and not yours to tell."

"You mean, Jane, that I chose to keep secret the fact that we were—that Mr Darcy and I are soulmates."

The two sisters were in Elizabeth's room, still clothed, both sitting on the bed. Holding their knees, in this relaxed and trusting position they often had chosen when Jane was still a maiden, and they were sharing a bedroom in their childhood home.

"Yes."

Elizabeth smiled. "You understand my reluctance to tell you, *but...* Your next sentence will start with a 'but', I suppose?"

Jane blushed and laughed.

"*But,* Lizzy... There is selfishness in me, some unjust pride—because I am a little hurt by your lack of confidence. Not much," Jane said hurriedly, taking her sister's hand in hers, as if afraid she had been too harsh. "Not much, I swear, but—if you had spoken of your bond with Mr Darcy, you know I would have kept your secret?"

"Oh, dear Jane, I know!" Elizabeth sighed and let her head drop onto her sister's shoulder. "Of course, I know. As it is, you had to learn the truth through one of our father's angry letters, I suppose?"

"Exactly so. It was quite the shocking revelation, to be honest. Charles and I learned all in one missive. That you had run away and were back the next morning with Lydia, that Mr Darcy was your soulmate, that he was grievously injured... That you had spent the night in a—you know. The Countess of Matlock lied about it, and we were supposed to smile and nod and pretend the lie was real. Papa was so furious..." Jane hesitated, then smiled. "Charles was horrified at first, learning his closest friend was injured. But you are acquainted with his happy disposition. The next day, he was thinking that of course Mr Darcy would soon be perfectly well, and how wonderful it would be when you, my dearest sister, would be married to his dearest friend. He already rejoices, imagining the four of us living close by, dining together twice a week..."

Elizabeth was thoughtful for a moment.

"I did not confide in you, Janey, because at first, the idea of Mr Darcy being my soulmate was horrendous. I did not want to think of him, and when I did it was with pain and shame. I did not want the bond to exist. If I had told you, the whole business would have become much too real."

Jane nodded. "I also believe, Elizabeth, that you knew perfectly well I would have been the voice of reason. I would have told you that the prejudice you held against Mr Darcy was unjust, and that through the bond, the heavens were telling you to give him a chance. And you did not wish to hear my admonitions."

Elizabeth looked away. "Perhaps."

The two sisters were silent for a while. Then Jane smiled and squeezed her sister's hand with great affection. "But he will soon be here—Mr Darcy, I mean. So…"

There was a question there, but Jane saw Elizabeth's deep blush; she smiled and changed the subject.

"Lydia," Elizabeth whispered, entering her sister's room the next day, just before dinner. Mrs Goulding and her mother-in-law were to come and eat with them. The Gouldings were old friends and neighbours of the Bennets; they had resided in Meryton for generations.

It was almost dark in Lydia's room—the curtains already drawn. Too early, Elizabeth thought.

The young girl was standing near the table, staring at a particularly gorgeous dress. The garment had originally been Jane's and had been altered for Lydia. Bingley had money, he liked to spoil his wife, and Jane's sisters benefited from it in an indirect manner.

Lydia should have been excited. Instead, she was looking at the sumptuous silk—a deep blue to perfectly compliment her brown eyes—and just seemed lost.

"You were rather silent this afternoon at tea, dear," Elizabeth said. "Is anything the matter?"

Anything the matter, on top of all the horrendous things Lydia had lived through? But they had not spoken about it again—that was the English way, you buried the ugly truths and hoped they would just disappear.

There had also been, for a few days, the fear that it would be impossible for Lydia to stay at Netherfield—that it would be impossible for her to hide her shame... In short, her two eldest sisters had wondered what they should do if it turned out that Lydia was with child. This had, fortunately, turned out not to be the case.

"Nothing is the matter. I am well, Lizzy. Is this not a pretty gown?"

"It is lovely," was Elizabeth's sincere answer. "Are you going to wear it tonight?"

"Mayhap I should... What if I stayed here this evening, Lizzy, though? Do you think Mrs Nicholls would bring me a tray?"

This was not like Lydia at all. "Of course, dear. She will be happy to do so. But are you sure you do not want to eat with us? We shall be a merry party, and it will do you good."

'A merry party' was an exaggeration, certainly. Mrs Goulding was not the greatest wit, and her mother-in-law loved to share mean but somehow still uninteresting gossip. Lydia used to love company though, and Elizabeth believed some conversation would cheer her sister up.

Lydia did not respond. She caressed the blue silk longingly for a moment.

"This dress is a lie, is it not?" the young girl said after a while. "I am—I am tainted, and everyone knows it. Not the Gouldings, but... The fact that you, and Jane, and Charles, are treating me normally, that I dine with you all, it is a lie, yes? Make-believe, to pretend my reputation and yours, Lizzy, have not been thoroughly destroyed. But the servants know. We are all performing roles, like—like in a play."

Elizabeth sat on the bed, hesitating, before deciding to tell the truth.

"You are right, it is partly a lie, Lydia. But it is a well-kept one. At Netherfield, half of the servants are not even aware you ran away. They thought you went to London, and that I joined you there. Then we both came back...and that is the end of the story. Mama knows nothing, remember? Nor anybody in Meryton."

"But what do people know in London?"

Ah, that was another matter. Elizabeth sighed.

"Well...our uncle and aunt will keep our secret, of course. To the servants there it was said... It was explained you made a mistake and went away with a friend, a *lady* friend— to have an adventure and travel together. And... and somehow, you were found out, and brought home, before you could get into too much mischief."

"I was brought home—on the same night you saved Mr Darcy and came back with the countess?"

"Well." The story did not make much sense. "Yes."

And so many people knew the truth, about Lydia and—Marie's house. The Matlock family. The soldiers. Darcy's servants, certainly.

Lydia made a face. "Will anyone believe such a tale?"

"Maybe not. And even if it were true, people would still talk and speculate. But as Father said, we have an official story to rely on, that is the important part. A story that will seem more authentic if Mr and Mrs Bingley of Netherfield —if all your friends are still treating you as a respectable young lady."

"Instead of sending me to a farm somewhere."

"Instead of sending you to a farm somewhere. The message it conveys, when you dine with us downstairs, is that despite a few thoughtless decisions, you are still...that your innocence... that nothing really bad happened."

"But something did. And when someone wants to marry me, they will know. They will ask around and there will be gossip. Bad gossip."

Elizabeth could not argue; it was true. She was preparing an answer about true affection surmounting all obstacles when Lydia started again. "Though—my soulmate is still out there, yes?"

"They are. You still hear your music?"

"I do. It has not varied, despite…everything." Lydia's expression was tense. "My soulmate, he… It was not Wickham."

"It was certainly not Wickham, dear Liddy. You know he lied to you, do you not?"

"I—I do… I do know, in theory, but… My soulmate is not Wickham," Lydia repeated, as if the reality of the statement was just sinking in. "My soulmate is still out there. And I shall tell them the truth, and they will love me anyway," she claimed, with all the idealism of a sixteen year old. Elizabeth did not contradict her, and who knew?

Maybe it was true.

Lydia put on her blue dress.

And if she was rather quiet at dinner, there was a still a spark of hope in her eyes.

Mr Darcy was to arrive a week later. He would have been there earlier, Elizabeth learned from Bingley, but his doctor would not let him leave, and there were some family matters he had to take care of.

Elizabeth waited. The week passed.

∞∞∞

Mr Darcy's return to Netherfield was not a momentous occasion.

The gentleman arrived half a day before he was expected, so no one was waiting for him. Jane was visiting her parents at Longbourn, still hoping to foster a reconciliation between her father and her sisters. The housekeeper, Mrs Nicholls, was upstairs preparing Mr Darcy's apartment, and there had been some scuffle in the kitchen which had caught most of the servants' attention, so some of them did not even hear the carriage approaching. On arrival, Mr Darcy's valet jumped from his high seat and walked directly towards the servants' entrance, an entrance he knew well, having spent more than four months at Netherfield a year ago.

Mr Darcy himself was quite familiar with the place; he climbed up the front steps with such a nervous energy one would have thought he had never been injured. The door was opened by a footman, the gentleman ushered in directly... just at the moment Charles Bingley was walking down the stairs and Elizabeth, for an unrelated reason, was stepping out of the music room.

The three of them started with surprise.

Bingley was the first to recover his wits, and he walked to his friend with great delight.

"Darcy! What a joy to see you! How do you feel—not too exhausted by your trip, I hope… Are you well? Are you still in pain? How is the shoulder?" He did not leave his guest time to answer—anyway Darcy's gaze was fixed on Elizabeth, who could not seem to move. "Jane is still away," Bingley continued directly, "so you will have to wait before being greeted officially by the lady of the house. Till she is back you will have to content yourself with me—and my two beautiful sisters—Lizzy, here you are, and where has Lydia got to?"

Elizabeth had regained her countenance. She dropped a curtsey in Mr Darcy's direction. The gesture, too formal for such a close friend of the family, betrayed her unease, an idea which made her blush deeply. "Lydia is practising in the— she is playing the harp," she answered, before meeting, at last, the eyes of the newly arrived gentleman.

"Mr Darcy, how do you do?"

"How do you do, Miss Bennet?" was Mr Darcy's very proper answer. A painfully awkward silence ensued. Elizabeth saw Mr Bingley hesitate, prepare a sentence, and perhaps think the better of it. It was clear in Elizabeth's mind that her kind brother-in-law had almost joked about betrothals or alluded to soulmates.

But Jane must have told her husband to be discreet while the situation was not yet resolved, because after a few seconds, Bingley said, "I shall show you to your room, Darcy, not that you do not know the way. Lizzy, do you think you can take Jane's role, pretend to be mistress of Netherfield and order tea for the three of us? Our guest must be in want of some refreshment."

"I trust I shall find myself equal to the task, Mr Bingley," Elizabeth said pleasantly, but her heart was beating wildly. She was relieved when the two men disappeared up the stairs, except on the highest step, Mr Darcy turned to glance at her—she thought. She could hardly be sure—it was dark above. Maybe he had. A quick glance, mayhap? She ordered tea, with enough food to comfort the weariest traveller—was Darcy still in pain? He must be, less than two months after his injury. *He should not have come*, she thought —of course she was very, very happy he had, but enduring the discomforts of a carriage bumping at the mere caprice of the road, in his weakened state, it was folly... His friends must have told him it was folly.

But travelled he had. Darcy was here, at Netherfield. Elizabeth asked for the tea to be laid out in the blue saloon—she was alone in the room, the gentlemen were not back yet. She rearranged the plates and the flowers three times before the door opened. Her heart jumped; Lydia stepped into the room, saying, "I so hate the harp. Is there cake?" There was, but Lydia had to wait.

Elizabeth's soulmate music was louder, beating faster. Or was it her own heart going wild—or both. The door opened again, and at last the gentlemen entered.

There followed a perfectly normal conversation around a perfectly normal tea. Bingley was cheerful as ever, asking Darcy about his recovery. He would also, Elizabeth believed, have congratulated his friend on 'his heroic deeds'—that was the expression Mr Bingley used when they spoke of what happened in London. But there were servants present and the subject was avoided.

In fact, Elizabeth realised, the reason Mr Bingley and Mr Darcy had taken so long to come down was, surely, that they had discussed 'the events' in private. Bingley must have been, as he generally was, effusive with his praise—but enough speculation. Now, here they were, the four of them, in the well-lit, comfortable parlour, the sun shining outside. Alive, Darcy was alive, in the same room as Elizabeth, drinking tea—there were hours in London where this would have been considered a dream.

Elizabeth passed sandwiches and biscuits around—despite the miracle it was, the scene looked pleasant and ordinary. Darcy and Bingley on a sofa, Elizabeth and Lydia on another, complimenting tartlets or asking about the state of the roads...and no one talking about the fact that two of the people in the room were soulmates. Soulmates, but not betrothed—*yet*, her treacherous heart was whispering. Nor was it possible to ask Mr Darcy why he had come —and now new subjects were being broached, the reparations Mr Bingley was overseeing on his land, news of Charlotte and Mr Collins. Ten, twenty minutes passed, in this safe, but maddening conversation—then Elizabeth dared to look directly at Mr Darcy...

Her music swelled—or was it his? Elizabeth fought to keep her emotions in check, feeling that the mere variation in her notes would betray her feelings. Soon, the music was serene again, but Darcy must have felt, must have heard the change in the melody. She dared a new glance—some indescribable emotion was playing on his face. Elizabeth went back to studying her tea. She felt his eyes on her for a while—and then Jane was back; the moment dissolved in cheerful salutations and discussion of the practical matters of Mr Darcy's stay.

Darcy and Bingley went out to tour the estate, and soon enough it was time to get dressed and go down for dinner.

Lydia refused to eat with them. This time Elizabeth did not insist—being in Mr Darcy's presence might have brought up some painful associations.

Elizabeth took great pains with her attire. She wanted to look beautiful, but in a casual way. As if—of course one would dress carefully for a new guest, but she did not want to seem… Would 'eager' be the right word in those circumstances? Then she had to laugh at her own ridiculousness. If this was the worst of her problems at this moment—choosing her gown, instead of trying to save her sister from a dreadful fate, or knowing her soulmate was dying alone in a sordid cellar—yes, this was a good problem to have.

The dinner was, as Elizabeth had anticipated, a moment of joy. Or, perhaps, it was a moment of joy for Jane and Bingley, and a private, euphoric one for Darcy and Elizabeth.

Nothing of import was said though, not that night. But Jane was all smiles—she felt

Elizabeth's quiet contentment and hopes, and her husband's open satisfaction at having, as he said, 'his favourite people' with him. In a strange reversal of roles, Darcy took his share of the conversation, while Elizabeth was mostly silent.

Her soulmate across from her at the table. Their melody quietly playing. For a brief moment, she was not at Netherfield any more, but in the carriage, in the rain, Darcy looking at her.

Then Bingley asked for some roast, and she was back.

At night, the music was wild.

Elizabeth could not sleep. She was cold—she was hot. Her skin felt sensitive, like her whole body hurt. She opened the window to let the air in. It was brisk—English nights always were, but the chill did not calm her. Her cheeks were burning, she felt the desire to—she did not know what exactly—but oh Lord, that music.

Mr Darcy was staying in the guest wing, Elizabeth in a bedroom in the family wing. But Netherfield was not that large a place; the two rooms were not even that far—

Good Lord, what was she thinking?

Walking in the silent corridor, in her cream-coloured nightgown…

There would be a tempest outside, like in a novel. But at least in those stories there was a sorcerer involved, or a heart wrenching mystery to unravel. The beautiful heroine with her hair undone had some respectable motivation for leaving her bedchamber at night, while Elizabeth…

She did not go anywhere, of course. Elizabeth Bennet was not a heroine in a novel; she was a gently bred young lady, who would never act so brazenly. But then she had a sudden thought…

What if *he* came to her?

The idea was unsettling; Elizabeth felt even warmer. The idea that Darcy could—it was not a pleasant thought. It was too bright, too powerful. Like something unreal, that could change her whole life, change who she was as a person. She wondered briefly if this was how Lydia had felt, when she had thrown herself into Wickham's power.

Still, what if—what if Darcy knocked discreetly at her door? At midnight? She would know it was him.

Would she open it?

Elizabeth feared—and maybe hoped—but of course, no. Mr Darcy would never.

Then she heard footsteps outside.

The music pounded in her heart, but nothing happened—nobody rapped at her door. She waited and waited, to finally fall into a fitful sleep.

It was like an explosion.

When Elizabeth went down for breakfast, Darcy was already there, looking perfectly respectable, nothing askew in his attire—but the tension was unbearable. The electric, unsettling energy of the night; the ocean, calling. Elizabeth ate poorly; when she took her leave, Darcy joined her in the hallway.

"Miss Bennet, would you walk with me?"

"Yes." Elizabeth could not answer politely; she could not even think straight.

Spencer, bonnet. Three minutes later they were outside.

A slight wind was blowing, shaking night rain from the leaves, but neither of them cared.

As soon as they were round the corner of the building, Darcy took Elizabeth's hands in his. "You will not, I hope, still resist what exists between us," he started. "Elizabeth, tell me, tell me, please, that I am not mistaken this time, that you feel this with me—" Emotion seemed to choke him; Elizabeth stood petrified, tongue tied —

"You are not mistaken," was her answer, at last, her voice raw as though she was forcing the words out, and so she was, wanting to bare her soul, fighting against the powerful bonds of society and education.

"In the cellar—in the cave," Darcy whispered, and it all came back—the labyrinth, the fear, the exhilaration, Darcy's arms embracing her, his whispered words in her ear. "I told you, Elizabeth. You know, you know I love you still—I love you always—I never stopped…"

Elizabeth was very red. "I did not know, but—I hoped," she whispered. "I hoped, passionately—" Darcy held her closer; she dared to look at him.

"God," he whispered, and all of a sudden, his lips were on hers; it was not a short kiss, it was not a chaste one either. Elizabeth was swept away, gone—

(A wild shore, waves crashing, savage—)

…and there was the characteristic and

unwelcome noise of a carriage on the gravel walk; guests coming for a morning visit. Darcy did not hesitate, seizing Elizabeth's hand again, he resolutely led her away. They walked at a fast pace towards a thick shrubbery, then, sure they were out of view, they stopped—their eyes met, the next moment, she was in his embrace—

The kiss lasted for an instant—an eternity. Afterwards they stood immobile, holding hands, in silence. "I would have come to you earlier," Darcy whispered after a while. "I would have, as soon as I regained consciousness, but—"

"You were injured…"

"And even now—here—I was not…entirely sure of the welcome of my suit."

"After what we shared," she breathed, "how could you doubt?"

He hesitated, for hardly a second. "You saved my life, Elizabeth. You found me, you fought for me. But maybe your generous heart would have pushed you to rescue any friend of yours, if you knew you had the necessary information. It did not necessarily mean…"

"The way our spirits connected," she whispered. "The way I felt your presence… It might not have happened if—if I did not feel…"

"That is what I told myself," Darcy said, in a

low voice, "in the dark of the night, in Matlock House, when I was recovering. That is the belief that helped me, when the pain was keeping me awake. I hoped, I prayed I was right…"

"You were," was Elizabeth's whispered answer. Darcy lifted her gloved hand, and began to kiss her fingers, rather passionately; she closed her eyes, shifting closer…

"Miss?" came a disapproving voice.

It belonged to Thomas Davies, Netherfield's head gardener. The man also worked at Longbourn; he had known Elizabeth since infancy—a kind, honest man, who would have, just now, reduced them to cinders with the power of his scandalised glare. Elizabeth stepped aside, struggling to regain a respectable countenance. But she could not even find in herself the strength to be embarrassed—her heart was too full.

"Miss, guests have just arrived. The Lucas ladies, I reckon—I am sure Mrs Bingley would like your help to greet them *correctly*," the good man said, now concentrating his censure towards Darcy, as the evil seducer who had certainly led the innocent Miss Bennet astray. Mayhap, Elizabeth thought, the faithful servant was one of the select few who knew about Lydia's elopement, and would not let such an event happen again under his watch.

"Indeed, I should go back, thank you, Davies," she said amiably.

"I shall walk you to the house," Darcy said, offering his arm. Elizabeth took it, and they found their way back to the main entrance, Davies respectfully walking ten feet behind, steadfastly determined to protect Miss Bennet's virtue. But considering Lydia's late actions, and her own, Elizabeth felt she had no right to take offence.

It was getting colder; the wind was blowing. Netherfield Park was drowning in a thin, grey mist. Darcy did not utter a word; Elizabeth kept silent too, but as short as the stroll was, the brief walk back felt—*gratifying* or *pleasant* would have been weak, unexpressive words, and the English language was guilty of not creating more accurate terms. Darcy, so close. Their arms touching. His presence, the knowledge of his rushed and passionate words, the euphoria of their brief, stolen embraces. The swiftness of the revelation, the unreality of the whole event—it made for a heady, potent sensation.

Elizabeth would notice later, thinking back to these moments—and oh, how often she would come back to them, with a secret, powerful joy —how her soulmate melody had been discreet, a whisper almost. As if they were on a ship, and the orchestra was hiding below deck. The musicians were still playing, but they had chosen to make themselves scarce, because this instant was *theirs*, she thought—Elizabeth and Darcy's. Their words, their kiss. It did not matter, she felt, at this moment, that they were soulmates—it should not matter. There was no unearthly power manipulating them. This was theirs and theirs alone.

Too soon, they were at the main door, the satisfied gardener vanishing among the well-tended bushes. Too soon, Darcy and Elizabeth entered Netherfield Hall, too soon they were divested of their attire by efficient but unwelcome servants. Too soon, after a last, serious look, Darcy disappeared towards the study. Elizabeth joined Jane and her guests, feeling that her heart would break from joy, and the musicians must have been sick of discretion, because her melody swelled again, accompanying each and every one of her steps.

After the guests were gone, the meal that followed should have been of the type to appease Elizabeth's spirits. Mr Harrison, Bingley's new steward, had been invited to join them. With him had come his young apprentice, a lawyer's nephew here to learn business. Cold meats with a side of irrigation, pies, investments, and unsatisfactory rooftops should do wonders to cool the ardour of youthful passion, but nothing could affect Elizabeth's happiness.

"We should talk," Darcy said discreetly afterwards. Bingley, Jane, and Harrison were debating the possibility of hiring new staff. "But not here."

They found the desired solitude in the winter parlour. On Jane's orders, the room had been made ready for the upcoming season. It was still deserted, and without fire; the air was very cold, but neither of the lovers was able to feel it.

Darcy took her right hand in his and drew her very close.

"There is an issue I wish to discuss with you," he said straight away. "This morning, you may have considered my conduct rather presumptuous..."

Elizabeth blushed and laughed. "Indeed, sir. Quite impudent."

"I am behaving," he said gravely, "as if we were betrothed already. While you have not given me your answer—to a question I have not asked. Elizabeth, would you do me the honour of becoming my wife?"

Elizabeth could not breathe—although, she

should of course have seen this coming.

"I—" she said, strangely embarrassed. "You cannot be in any real doubt of my answer."

"Ah, but I was not in doubt of your answer last time either. I would rather not make the same mistake twice."

"You are already holding my hand, sir. And my heart has been yours for a long time."

Silence prevailed. There was no other touch than the contact of their intertwined fingers—Darcy finally roused himself, saying, with a wry, warm smile, "I had better go and talk to your father now, with your permission."

She gave it, and he was gone directly.

After the first flush of exhilaration, Elizabeth began to worry about the reception waiting for Darcy at Longbourn, but her fears were for nothing. The gentleman came back safe and sound—and just in time for dinner. Darcy entered the drawing room with a discreet, soft smile, and answered Elizabeth's enquiring glance with a reassuring nod. She felt much relieved, although there was no rational reason for Mr Bennet to refuse his blessing to her marriage, and a lot of practical reasons to give it.

"Your father wants to see you tomorrow, Elizabeth," Darcy whispered while he was leading her to the dining room, and it was Elizabeth's turn to nod. "As for tonight... Will you allow me to share our joyous news?"

Her happy smile was the only answer he needed.

Darcy's announcement of their betrothal was not met with much surprise, but with much emotion. Jane was moved almost to tears. She rose from her chair and went to embrace her sister, while Bingley joyfully congratulated Darcy, saying, with the least menacing stance ever, that it was high time the issue was settled, and if Darcy had not proposed marriage, he would have been obligated as Elizabeth's brother-in-law to challenge him to a duel. Darcy did not seem very struck by the threat, and just said, with an inscrutable but affectionate look towards Elizabeth, that he would have acted much earlier, if it had been a possibility. Elizabeth blushed, but Bingley did not notice the silent exchange and explained again, cheerfully, and most sincerely, how glad he was and how he was certain Darcy and Elizabeth would make each other very happy.

There were no protestations on this subject. "Oh Lizzy," Jane said, pressing her sister's hand in hers, "this brings me so much contentment. I thought, with our guests, and at lunch, when you were so distracted— But then you did not tell me anything, so I did not presume…"

"Oh, I believe you did presume," Elizabeth said with a smile. "But you were too polite to ask."

"You cannot blame me, my dear Lizzy, for wishing you the best, and wanting you to know the same happiness as mine."

"No, I certainly cannot."

The evening continued in this merry manner, Bingley making plans for the future. He was, as Jane had predicted, imagining the four of them living quite close together, the cousins being raised under the affectionate supervision of both families—because of course he had already endowed the future Mr and Mrs Darcy with at least three children, to add to the three, or four, or five, he was supposed to have with Jane. Elizabeth turned scarlet when the subject was broached, and Jane had to smilingly remind her husband that this thread of conversation was not exactly respectable to have in front of her sister, who was still unwed.

It was then Bingley's turn to colour, and he apologised to Elizabeth. "See how this union seems perfect to me? I had you married already."

Darcy seemed a little embarrassed also, but

the conversation quickly turned to the plays and concerts the four of them would go and see in town when next they would visit—in much more propitious circumstances.

∞∞∞

"I loathe to be practical in such a situation, Lizzy," Jane said later that same evening, after joining Elizabeth in her bedchamber for a more intimate *causerie*. "But your engagement to Mr Darcy—it is also good for Lydia. Having two sisters married, and very respectably so, should stop most of the speculation."

Elizabeth was not so optimistic. "At the very least, it will ensure our sister is never abandoned, or left in dire financial circumstances," she replied.

They talked for some time of their sister's future, and how to coax Lydia to join them again for meals, which she had not done since Darcy's arrival. But for once, Elizabeth's thoughts could not stay long on the young girl's plight, she was too happy.

"Is it not a fortunate coincidence," Jane reflected with a radiant smile, "that we, two close sisters, should find our soulmates to be two best friends?"

Elizabeth could not help but laugh. "It certainly does make things easier."

"Or maybe it is not a coincidence at all," Jane continued, her gaze thoughtful. "Maybe it is destiny — maybe even an act of Heaven. Maybe our betrotheds were chosen as our soulmates *because* they were best friends, and it was always meant to happen so."

"I suppose I am to be the voice of reason, Jane, and see your interpretation as overly fanciful, but to be honest, after recent events, I do not know what reason is anymore."

In fact, Elizabeth's own fancy kept wandering —especially after Bingley's predictions at dinner. It was after a pause, and with some mortification of her own, that she finally asked her elder sister, "Jane, I know it is a private matter, and do not answer if—if you would not talk of it, but... As a maiden, and not united to Mr Darcy yet, I have, er, we have, visions, shared visions... We have seen ourselves in other locations, real or imaginary ones. You, er, did you experience this also? With Mr Bingley?"

Jane had a shy, lovely smile. "Indeed."

"When you are married, the—the *intimacy*, I assume, changes the relationship in profound ways. Those visions... Do you still have them, as —husband and wife?"

"We do," Jane answered, in a low voice. "It was surprising at first. Charles and I were always together in truth, so I wondered, why would the soul music need to bring us—together, but elsewhere? But the music did—does. It is like having this beautiful, hidden existence, in parallel to the real one. We have our secret places, where we go to find each other, whether Charles is at the other end of the county or even when we are, um, when we share the same bed... And then sometimes we are sent elsewhere, to new, fantastical locations, and I always ask myself—is my imagination strong enough to create such strange metaphors? Is Charles's?"

"Maybe," Elizabeth said with prudence. What she saw, what she heard when she was under the influence of the drugs, she was not ready to share yet, even with her sister. But she had given it a lot of thought. "Maybe it is not only your imagination at play. Mayhap there is a whole world out there... A universe of dreams, of... of shared phantasmagories that we all access, through the melody."

The concept seemed strange to Jane, and she took a moment to consider it.

"Like Aristotle's world of ideas?"

It was one of Mr Bennet's favourite notions from the famous Greek author.

Aristotle believed that all abstract concepts, mathematical and otherwise, lived in a sort of parallel plane, a shared universe, accessible to all humans if they were clever enough to access it.

"Indeed," said Elizabeth thoughtfully. "But instead of mathematical equations, it would be a world of imagination, or dreams, or—I—I do not know."

Jane shook her head. "Perhaps you are right," she said, but Elizabeth believed it was more polite acquiescence than real consideration of the topic. "There is also…" Jane hesitated, then blushed.

"In one of these dream places," she finally added, "Charles and I always are…" She stopped. "As we said at dinner, you are still unmarried, Lizzy, so I should not speak of it."

Elizabeth smiled. "Oh, but it is too late. My mind is already drawing conclusions."

"Lizzy," Jane said, laughing, but her cheeks were a little pink.

"May I safely say that in this place, you and Charles are constantly rediscovering the delights of your honeymoon?"

"Yes, quite," Jane said, now as scarlet as Elizabeth had been at dinner, and Elizabeth felt a renewed surge of affection for her elder sister, her kindness, and her constant delicacy. "But the thing is, Lizzy... Oh, I do not know quite how to explain. See, in this imaginary place, Charles and I do not change. I am still—physically, I am still as I was on the evening of my wedding day, to the necklace I was wearing, to the last pin in my hair. And Charles also, when I meet him there, he still has...this haircut he got especially for our wedding ceremony. He is still... His face is a little more youthful than it is now, though only ten months have passed. Time stands still. And see, what I think, what I hope..."

Elizabeth was listening, fascinated.

"I think, when twenty, thirty years have passed, Lizzy, Charles and I shall still be able to come back to this dream place. And we shall always be young in it. We shall always be able to feel— We shall never grow old, or at the very least, our love never will. Oh, I beg you, do not laugh at me, and at my ridiculous, romantic notions."

Elizabeth quickly took her sister's hand in hers. "On the contrary, this is...so beautiful. I am so glad for you, Jane," she added in a strained voice. "So happy that... Any other man than Mr Bingley, any other love than the one you described would have bitterly disappointed you. And you are so loyal, you never would have said. In an unequal marriage, you never would have showed any dissatisfaction, but I would have known. And then we both would have been dreadfully unhappy," Elizabeth added, with a laugh.

"It makes me even happier, Lizzy, to know that we did not have to compromise our ideals, and that destiny was so good to us."

The two sisters sat in companiable silence for a while. When Jane finally took her leave, she paused at the door and said, "Do you remember, the conversation we had ages ago, well before Charles came to live at Netherfield? We were talking about soulmates, and you were wondering whether I ever perceived your soul music— And…I told you the church quite forbade such a thought…"

"I remember."

"I heard you," Jane said in a low voice. "When you were in London, that fateful night. I was sleeping, and all of a sudden… Your melody was so strong, Lizzy, it woke me up, and I knew it was you. You were not scared, or at least it did not sound that way. It was…as if you were seeing stars. I—called for you, but you did not answer…"

"I heard you too," Elizabeth whispered, and it was not a lie.

∞ ∞ ∞

In the morning, Elizabeth set out to visit her father at Longbourn, as he had asked. Darcy had told her that his visit had gone well; Mr Bennet had been polite, if not particularly warm, and after a short moment of reflection, he had agreed to his daughter's marriage. Elizabeth's anxiety grew on the way anyhow, but it was somewhat assuaged when she was greeted by her mother and her remaining sisters as if nothing particular had happened. And indeed, for Mrs Bennet, who had been living in perfect ignorance of the latest events, nothing had.

Elizabeth had not been home for more than three months. Mrs Bennet had visited Netherfied at least once a week, so she was rather indifferent to her daughter's return, except for chiding her for neglecting Longbourn and her younger sisters. To be fair, Mrs Bennet's grievance was justified, and Elizabeth had no way to answer it satisfactorily. The truth was, Elizabeth and Lydia's father had made it clear they were not welcome in their childhood home, but Elizabeth could not explain why, lest it betray the whole story.

In the drawing room, it felt as though time had stood still. Mrs Bennet soon forgot her second daughter's offences to complain about some servant's misbehaviour. Mary complained again that Elizabeth had not brought any new music sheets back from town, and Kitty bemoaned the lack of fashion plates. Elizabeth was half disappointed, half amused by the flaws of her family. She could only hope that she would do better with her future one—and oh, how novel, how delicious was this idea—her heart beat faster. Her melody answered, and for a moment, Darcy was standing right at her side.

Illusion, of course. But it made her stronger when a few minutes later, Elizabeth was introduced into Mr Bennet's study. She was ready for coldness, or even spite, so the restrained emotion on her father's face when he beheld her took her quite by surprise.

Mr Bennet did not greet her aloud; he gestured for her to sit. Elizabeth obeyed, and father and daughter looked at each other in silence. Mr Bennet's expression was a complicated one, as if he was looking for words, but not finding any.

Finally, he began, in a low voice.

"I am glad, Elizabeth. I cannot say I am a great friend of Mr Darcy still, but I was worried, so worried, that after your deplorable adventures in London, you—" He made a haphazard gesture, that Elizabeth easily interpreted.

"You thought it was over for me, Father. That my prospects were thoroughly ruined."

"Indeed. Not to say that you would have been necessarily unhappy," Mr Bennet continued with a weak, but wry smile. "I could imagine you living out your days at Netherfield, walking in the morning, reading in the afternoons, getting older, scaring Jane's friends at dinner with your sarcasm."

"That sounds much more like a description of your own fate, sir," Elizabeth could not help saying, and then wondered whether she had offended him.

Mr Bennet just shook his head. "Not an unpleasant destiny, but I wanted more for you." A pause. "So, that man is indeed your soulmate," he stated, after a few moments.

"Mr Darcy? Yes, he—" Elizabeth hesitated. "Did you believe he was not? Father, did you think I had been lying to you, all this time—about that night?"

"It was a possibility, yes," Mr Bennet declared with the utmost calm. "Lydia had already betrayed us all, having a secret affair with a rake. You could have been doing the same. I could believe that you had been entertaining some sort of...immoral relationship with Mr Darcy, Lizzy, and that you had thrown yourself into mortal peril to find him, compromising yourself and bringing shame upon all your family."

Elizabeth was horrified. "Father, I never—"

"How could I be sure of the truth? You had a soulmate and never told me. You could confide in me, on such important a matter. In fact, you ought to. As your father, I had the right to be apprised of such information, with such heavy consequences on your future life."

There was still anger in Mr Bennet's voice—hurt, even. Elizabeth was not convinced; she did not believe it was a father's prerogative to know the mysteries of his daughter's heart. But she would not argue with him now, not when she felt, at last, the possibility of a reconciliation.

Outside, a cold rain was falling. Making a sudden decision, she told him—she told him everything. From her early dislike of Mr Darcy to the gentleman's sudden proposal, her subsequent loneliness, their reunion at Pemberley. How, in the tense days after Lydia's elopement, her bond with Darcy had blossomed. And then the misery—the tragedy—of almost losing him.

Her father listened with the utmost attention. But if Elizabeth had hoped for a change of heart after her harrowing tale, she was disappointed.

"I do not know if we are fundamentally

different in nature, Lizzy," he said at last, "or if it is the difference of age and wisdom, but I still cannot condone your actions. You could have gone about the matter in a much more rational manner. You could have told the truth to your uncle, to me. You could have written a letter to Colonel Fitzwilliam exposing the situation."

"A letter? The colonel would not have believed me. Or he would have, but later, after exhausting all other avenues, after a visit to convince himself of my sincerity. Time was of the essence. It would have been… We would have been too late."

"I could have visited the colonel that very day and vouched for your sincerity."

Ah, but Elizabeth could not believe it. Her father would never have done so, or not quickly enough. Mr Bennet was not a man of action. His wit, his powers of observation, his philosophical stance were qualities certainly, but they did not speak of a character prone to diligence, or with a will to make quick decisions when a friend was in mortal danger.

But again, this was not something Elizabeth could say.

"Colonel Fitzwilliam believed my story *because* I had taken such risks to find him. I risked my reputation and myself, all for the sake of my soulmate. It made it easier for him to trust my intentions."

Mr Bennet sighed, then seemed deep in thought for a while.

"I did not know you had it in you to be quite so impulsive, Lizzy," he said finally. "But we could have this debate all day, without a chance of convincing each other—and I—I am tired. I missed you dreadfully, my child. I am beyond happy that despite all the odds, this has ended well for you. Because you are sincerely attached to Mr Darcy, are you? If you are not, then I would still not force you to marry him, despite everything."

Elizabeth blushed. "I am, Father. I—love him. I was surprised myself, when…when my affection turned out to be this strong, but…"

(Sand on the books, rain on the road, shots in the cellar.)

And for a second she was elsewhere. Pemberley library, the fire cosy and inviting. Darcy turned to her, smiling, his hair greyer, tiny lines around his eyes, and Elizabeth *knew*… The scene would happen many years in the future, after many happy years of marriage, after many children—after many rainy days, sunny afternoons, and a thousand proofs of love. Darcy held his hand out to her, and—

She was back.

Her father had not noticed her absence, or maybe there had been none. Maybe the visions happened in no time at all. Maybe time had other rules in this strange, foreign land.

"Now, you had better be happy, Lizzy," Mr Bennet said, emotion choking his voice. "That is an order. This is the only way to prove me wrong, you see? The only way to prove it was all worth it."

"Very well, Father. I will obey you, and prove it was."

∞∞∞

"Sometimes I cannot quite believe it," Darcy said, while they were walking, the next day, down a neglected avenue of large sycamores. "Sometimes I hardly believe, my dear Elizabeth, that you are here, at my side. That I have the right to—that all is settled between us."

Elizabeth did not speak immediately. Everything seemed soft and bright, their wordless connection, their music gently playing.

"Sometimes I hardly believe it either," she

finally answered. "I thought I might have lost my chance— When I changed my mind, about, er..."

"About me?"

"Yes. When I realised..." Elizabeth paused. She did not quite know when the shift happened. Sometime during their hurried and uncomfortable trip to London, mayhap? Or perhaps before, in the glow of Pemberley's summer days. "When I *knew*," Elizabeth continued, "should I have said—that the situation... That my feelings for you had changed? Would you have welcomed the news?"

"Would I," Darcy simply replied. Elizabeth did not need the surge of the music to comprehend his meaning.

She shook her head. "I should have spoken sooner. When I was staying with my aunt and uncle, and you were looking for Lydia—when you were coming for lunch every day. I should have told you then."

"Why didn't you?" he said, but the reproach was belied by the tenderness in his tone, and the swift kiss he brushed over her gloved fingers.

"I was not sure of my welcome. Is that not very cowardly of me? When you had been so brave, asking for my hand in Charlotte's house, when we hardly knew each other. How can you forgive my weakness when you have shown only strength?"

"I acted the fool the day I proposed, we both know it. Expecting you to marry me without a proper courtship. Expecting your easy acquiescence while I told you, most obnoxiously, of my perceived superiority... Do you know when I realised how wrong I had been?"

He then told Elizabeth about his brief flirtation, if it could even be called so, with the charming Miss Diana Stiles. About the conversation he had overheard. How he had realised his mistake, and the extent of what he might have lost because of his pride.

Elizabeth felt a twinge of fear, almost disorientation, when she realised Darcy could have wed another. She gave his hand a short squeeze.

"That lady was brave," she said. "Miss Stiles's friend, I mean. Confessing her feelings to her soulmate in a frank, direct way... I wish I had been able to act so. I blame my upbringing, really. No," Elizabeth added with a more sincere smile, "I blame England."

"England?"

"Indeed."

"For not opening your heart to me sooner?

Dear Elizabeth, how, may I ask, did His Majesty the King, or his excellence the Regent, fail to assist you in this endeavour?"

"The king is blameless, sir, of course. The guilt I place on our whole country and our education habits. We ladies are told to hide what we feel, never to been seen as forward, never to take the first step. Those principles are constantly repeated to us from infancy. The people we trust the most tell us every day that a conduct of restraint is necessary. Thus, when it becomes unnecessary, when the opposite, in fact, is required, these chains are difficult to shake."

"I would not deny," Darcy answered after some reflection, "that if you had told me my suit was not hopeless, during those tense days in London…it would have been of great comfort to me, especially when I was injured, in that dreadful room."

Elizabeth thought of the crimson sofa, the garish faun, the blood.

"I believed I would die, and all my thoughts were of you," Darcy continued, in a low voice. "You were very far away, and I had only regrets. And all of a sudden—there you were with me."

"I dreamt and saw you."

"You were sitting on the sofa, watching me, Elizabeth. So, I closed my eyes and permitted myself to drift. You stood up and walked to the window, do you remember? Watching the street? Studying the church? Then, later, much later perhaps—time was hazy—you looked at me and said, 'Stay alive. We will find you.' Or did I dream it?"

"No," she whispered. "You did not."

"Thus, you have nothing to reproach yourself for. You were with me. Even if we had not... understood each other before, you never left my side."

She took his hand in hers. "And now I never will."

A moment of perfect quiet followed. How many couples had she met, Elizabeth thought, whose relationship she had deeply misjudged? She would have seen them silent, and attributed their attitude to coldness or lack of affection. While inside, their hearts were singing. Lovers, married or not, married to others mayhap, walking to the same melody, living, like Jane and her husband, a clandestine life of passion in secret, hidden places.

Could she map this other world? It was a bizarre thought, and was there a connection between those dream locations? In this parallel world, would you meet others, if you went deep enough?

She quelled her crazy line of thought; they had serious subjects to broach. "Dear Fitzwilliam," she said at last, and felt the intimacy very daring.

Then she hesitated; the matter was grave indeed. "When we are wed... You will not, I believe, receive Lydia at Pemberley. Not with your sister...with Georgiana so young, and still unmarried."

Lydia's name was in danger of being publicly compromised, and furthermore, she was fallen, and Darcy knew it. Society, morality even, ruled that an unmarried young lady like Georgiana should never find herself in the same room as...such a 'creature' as Lydia, people would say, lest Darcy's sister be contaminated by her companion's sins.

"Despite Lydia's mistakes, and the terrible consequences that followed, I cannot forsake her," Elizabeth continued in a low voice. "I want to... I intend to help her, as much as I can. I will not abandon the connection. As my future husband," she said slowly, "I thought you should know."

Darcy was silent for a moment. They were still walking, the trees protective, the breeze playing its own chords.

"I knew the subject would be discussed

between us, and I have given it some consideration," he said at last. "Using my authority as a husband to ask you to sever such an affectionate relationship would be cruel and," he added with a smile, "knowing you, I do not believe it would go down well. But I also think — I cannot help but think… If Georgiana did not have a substantial dowry… If she was poor, and if she had left with him, with Wickham—would she find herself in Lydia's situation now?"

"If your sister had no dowry, Wickham would not have tried to seduce her."

"I wish I could be so sure. Revenge could have been his motivation. He could have convinced Georgiana to elope, promised her marriage, just to spite me. And then… Selling her, abandoning her to the same fate…"

Elizabeth shivered.

"Your sister and mine are in very different situations, it is true," Darcy stated. "But if Georgiana had lost…everything, and at such a young age, I would hope she would not be completely forsaken. I would hope she would still have some friends who would try and help her. Thus, Miss Lydia will be free to visit you at Pemberley. We will find a way to help your sister, Elizabeth." He held her hand tighter. "We will."

"Thank you," she said, her voice full of

emotion. What her gratitude was for, of all she had to choose from, she did not really know.

Silence prevailed for the rest of their walk. There was no touch other than the contact of their intertwined fingers, but their hearts were beating in the same rhythm.

Epilogue

Dream places.

An imaginary grove, somewhere in the mountains. Snowy slopes, biting wind, a huge blue sky, an encompassing view. In the little cave though, they were never cold, and quite naked on the furs. Jane had been right. There they never changed, never got old. It was a place they visited quite often.

"When the war is over, we could travel to Europe," Darcy said sometimes. "And search for this cave in truth. In the Alps, mayhap?"

"Or in Russia, far away," Elizabeth whispered, in bed, her arm around his naked body—this was a rather intimate situation. "There is a frozen lake nearby, don't you think?"

"Russia? It will be more difficult to find. But try we shall."

An old, beaten castle. It had known better days. Once it had been teeming with life—children running, elegant ladies wearing fur, tales of heroism sung in the great hall. Darcy and Elizabeth explored the deserted rooms, talked, smiled, admired the park through the broken windows, and knew that life would come back.

The coach. The rain.

The library.

The sea.

The desert.

A great vessel beaten by the storm. Maybe it would sink, maybe in an hour, maybe in a few moments, but each time they visited, the ship was still fighting, there was hope, and salt on their lips when they kissed.

"Sometimes I feel we visit the memories of other people," Darcy said. "And mayhap, they visit ours."

∞ ∞ ∞

It was almost a year later, during another walk, under different trees, that Elizabeth could at last fully open her heart to her husband.

Charles Bingley's happy predictions had come to pass. Six months after Mr and Mrs Darcy's wedding ceremony, Mr and Mrs Bingley had left Netherfield to purchase an estate close to their friends. Jane missed Elizabeth's company too much, and Bingley found that he would not miss Mrs Bennet's at all.

Furthermore, Lydia could not stay in Meryton. Despite her two elder sisters' marriages, tongues had begun to wag. How had the rumours spread? Perhaps when Mr and Mrs Gardiner had visited Longbourn, their servants had whispered about the events in London. Mayhap it was a disgruntled maid at Netherfield. Or maybe it was just folly to expect such a secret to be kept forever.

But the atmosphere in Meryton soon changed for the worse. Lydia was talked about, she was cut and sometimes subtly insulted in the streets of her home town. It was an untenable existence, and Jane and Bingley would not let it stand.

Moving to Derbyshire was the answer. There, Darcy's name held such importance that his friends and relations would never be disrespected.

At the Bingleys' new estate, Lydia was happy, or as happy as she could be after her bitter experience. But as subdued as she could be sometimes, there was still, in the young girl's spirits, a sturdy tendency for joy, an irrational confidence that all would be well.

Elizabeth could not blame this trait, as she suspected she shared it.

Lydia had not met her soulmate, but her music was clear and strong.

Maybe. Maybe, one day.

It had been a busy year, and such a happy one. After the wedding ceremony, the Darcys had made for London, and Elizabeth had spent three months being paraded around by the Countess of Matlock. It was her introduction into society, a society that Elizabeth found very similar to the one in Meryton, except with more diversity, more expensive candles, and fancier attire.

At last, the countess deemed the operation successful, and to her delight, Elizabeth was allowed to go back to the relative seclusion of Pemberley. Jane and Elizabeth could then take up their old habit of spending much of their free time together, and together also they travelled to stand with their sister Mary at her wedding to Miss Hayes—a wedding that had been made possible at last, thanks to Darcy's generosity.

Then she went back to Pemberley, and it seemed each day had the golden hue of summer.

And so it came that one morning Darcy and Elizabeth were walking under Pemberley's most venerable oaks, and Elizabeth felt her heart singing, for no other reason than she was in love, and her husband loved her back.

The old western lane where they had directed their steps was mostly abandoned. With its old chapel, and its centuries-old trees, it spoke of a time long past, with its own soulmates, tragedies, and bliss. It was their destination of choice that morning. First the sun on the gravel, the rose garden's elegant bushes, then the harmony of the lanes, and at last the stately calm of the massive trees. Their stroll ended on the gentle heights of the hill, where they turned back to a striking view of the house —a welcome sight, and the symbol of the life they were building together. This was also the time for heart-to-heart conversation, before the whirlwind of business and guests.

Thus, that very morning, Elizabeth could break their silence to say, without real transition or warning, "The problem, sir, is that I am unsure you are really my soulmate."

It was uttered with a smile. And as Darcy now knew his wife well, he could answer with perfect serenity.

"This statement would worry me much more, my dear Elizabeth, if we were not already married. And despite the recent scandals in London, I would advise you not to attempt divorce—it is a very cumbersome process."

"It would also be difficult to convince the judge of the absence of a bond, considering the dreams we share."

"Especially the new one, from last night."

Darcy spoke with a mix of tenderness and heat that made his wife blush.

"That one, also, yes." Elizabeth regained her countenance before adding, her eyes shining with mirth, "Thus, I take back my words. I should have said that mayhap you are not my *only* soulmate, Fitzwilliam."

Darcy seemed perfectly unperturbed. "Please proceed with your explanation. I am looking forward to hearing more."

Elizabeth nodded, her expression turning serious. "It is, in truth, a topic I meant to broach months ago, but I—it was an experience difficult to comprehend, and at first, I did not know quite how to share it."

Elizabeth then related to her husband all that had happened when she was under the influence of the army's drugs. She described how she fell in a universe of music—how she believed she could hear every human in the Lord's creation— the unworldly feeling that accompanied it.

It was a long tale; Darcy listened with great attention and asked several questions to better understand what his wife was trying to express.

"This is fascinating, of course, Elizabeth," he said at last. "But I do not believe it changes anything, not as it relates to our soulmate bond. You heard others, yes, but my music was the first and the strongest. And it is *ours*—we share the same melody. Thus," Darcy added with a smile, "I am sorry to say that I remain unconvinced. I shall consider myself *your* soulmate, and the only one. And if the Emperor of China came here and tried to claim you, saying you perceived his music and thus belonged to him, I would have to politely reject his pretentions. I refuse to share you—I am sorry if that discomfits you, my love."

"I shall have to get used to this sore state of reality. Indeed," she added, "it would be an exhausting existence, to be an emperor's soulmate. But more seriously, Fitzwilliam... The Church of England affirms that it is not possible to hear other people's music—only your soulmate's. While here I am, sure that this is a lie."

"I would not worry so much about the church's doctrine. Their edicts seem to change in direct relation to the politics of the day, or with their desire to please whoever is on the throne."

"But what of society?" Elizabeth said, her speech growing quite impassioned. "Our ranks. Our rules. Our education, differencing so cruelly between social classes and conducts. What I heard... Those strains of music... They were not identical, obviously. Each with its different melody, its unique personality. But there were no inferior or superior notes. There was not, in their songs, in their complexity or their worth, any difference between a duke or a servant, a maid or a fallen woman." Elizabeth took a shaky breath. "The way our society is set, it is all a lie. It is fake, Fitzwilliam. I feel this more strongly each day, since I have had a glimpse of the truth, of the reality behind appearances."

They had stopped walking. Darcy took his wife's hand in his. "You know, my love, that you can never speak this opinion aloud, except to me. You cannot say this even to your closest friends...even to Jane. Even now, in such modern times as ours, such a speech could be considered as rebellious—as Jacobin, revolutionary—and put you in terrible peril."

"I know. But tell me, Fitzwilliam, in all sincerity, what do you think? Is my opinion so horrendous to you? Or do you... Do you understand? Do you agree?"

Darcy took a long time before answering.

"I cannot say that I do, no. I respect your views, Elizabeth, but—I like the world as it is, I suppose. I like England, society as it is, even if I admit it might be because of my birth and the generosity of the Fates."

They resumed their walk. "Although…" the gentleman began after a while.

"Although…?"

"Two years ago, I would never… I would never have married you. I would have believed such a union to be beneath my station, as you know far too well. And before Georgiana's failed elopement, I would have condemned fallen women, as you said, without a second thought."

"You changed."

"I did."

Opinions were not set in stone, Elizabeth thought. She herself had altered so much, so quickly, sometimes it was hard to fathom.

And if she…*heard*, how many others did? Colonel Fitzwilliam must have tested his own drugs, certainly, as had others in his employ. Numerous people around the world must be doing similar experiments and arriving at the same conclusions.

One day, someone would talk.

There is much more to soulmate music that we humans know, and more than we probably will be able to ever discover.

One day, the world would change.

"I still see it, sometimes," Elizabeth whispered. "When I sleep. This other universe, this infinite whiteness. The melodies, I hear them all again. I do not know if it is but a memory of what I experienced, or if I have access now....to everyone. To this shared...to dreamland."

"Would you take me there? Make me listen? Show me?"

Elizabeth stopped. Their bond. The music, carrying them to strange places together. If doors were open to her, could she and Darcy both step...there? What would happen if they... crossed the desert, got out of the coach, stepped outside the cave, took control of the ship?

It was a scary, exhilarating thought.

"Maybe," she said, with a smile. "Maybe I could."

It started with a whisper.

A few notes. A short musical phrase.

It ended with a symphony.

———————

Postface

Dear Reader, thank you for reading "Who is Elizabeth Bennet's Soulmate?". I hope you've enjoyed the book.

As a bonus, a short Pride and Prejudice Variation, called "Colours."

Colours

Laura Moretti

Chapter One
Red

The world is grey.

When she wakes up at Pemberley in the morning, the sky is iron, the air is stifling, the walls are bleak. She gets dressed—well, her maid dresses her. Her maid is grey—well, the maid's eyes are grey, and she hardly talks. To be honest, Elizabeth hardly talks to the maid either.

Then Elizabeth goes down for breakfast, and the food has no taste. It is strange. Food tasted good before; she remembers how ravenous she was, at Longbourn, her childhood home, eating in the morning with her parents and noisy sisters. After a brisk walk, coffee tasted like luxury and strength, bread smelled like kitchen and laughter, butter and honey.

And there is butter and honey at Pemberley, of course. And much more—an elegant display of much more—but nothing feels real; everything seems to be drowned in grey tones. Maybe it is the season. February. February is a bad month—always. It is the month where people starve because winter provisions run out. It is the month where lovelorn maids hang themselves in the attic. It happened once—not at Longbourn but at Lucas Lodge; Elizabeth was only thirteen, but she understood.

February is the month where she is eating breakfast, at Pemberley, alone.

With three footmen and her husband. Who does not look at her. Or maybe he does. But she certainly does not look at him.

Though, nobody could say that Elizabeth Bennet (Darcy) is not always perfectly polite.

"Would you like some more coffee, Mr Darcy?" she asks, with a smile.

Of course, she must look at him now. "No, thank you," he answers.

She smiles again. Then she eats.

The world is grey beneath the windows' panes. The air is grey in the room. She can hardly breathe.

"I like red," she says. "I wonder where all the red has gone?"

She thinks her husband is looking at her. "It is

winter," he murmurs.

She just says, "I understand."

She finishes eating and goes back through the grey, silent halls of the grey, silent mansion.

"Elizabeth, you have changed," Jane said, when Elizabeth visited her, three months ago. Jane lives far away. She has a husband. Not Mr Bingley. Jane is with child.

Jane is far away.

Jane lives behind a wall of grey mist. Elizabeth cannot see her; she thought Jane could not see her either, but clearly she could. "Elizabeth, I think you are suffering from melancholy," Jane said.

She did not say, "You have a melancholic character." Elizabeth does not have a melancholic character. She did not have one before, at least.

Jane's voice makes 'melancholy' sound like an illness.

Maybe it is.

Elizabeth thinks about Jane's words, those words from three months ago, after breakfast, when she is back in her room. The room is grey. It is really not, of course. The colours of the walls were beautiful, Elizabeth seems to remember.

She wonders where all the colours have gone.

Maybe she lost some of the colours when her father died. Elizabeth was left with Jane, her mother wailing, and two sisters she despised. (Lydia is gone.) No, no, the word 'despised' is correct. Elizabeth despises her sisters—three of them at least—because she can see their mother in them.

But Jane was still there, and Jane makes everything better.

Then Jane gets married.

To a man she really does not love that much. But they are going to be thrown out of the house by their cousin, so, yes, Jane gets married.

The colours get a little dimmer.

Then there is the incident. Elizabeth's reputation is ruined, et cetera, you know the story; she has to marry Mr Darcy.

She does not want to marry him. But she must.

On their wedding night, they fight. He says marrying her is a degradation. That she is beneath him, in every way. Elizabeth should fight back, she should answer, but she does not. She does not have it in her any longer. She just sits on the bed while he berates her. Finally, he stops.

He waits for her answer.

"Very true," she says.

He just stares at her. She does not look at him.

Then they arrive at Pemberley. This huge, empty building, with nobody in it. Except her husband. And an army of servants.

Elizabeth despised her mother and her sisters. Now, her husband despises her.

How God must laugh.

It is on that day, Elizabeth's first day at Pemberley, taking a stroll in the empty park, where she does not meet anybody, that she realises the colours are all gone.

It has been ten months.

That day, after breakfast, Elizabeth visits the tenants. She talks to Mrs Reynolds. She does what she has to do.

Dinner. They eat, at the long, empty table. Elizabeth is very polite. She talks a little. She smiles. She does not know how to act otherwise. When he asks how she finds the soup, she says it is delicious and that they should thank the cook. She asks whether he has had a good day; her husband says it was a productive one. Elizabeth nods, and smiles, and says she is glad, and then her thoughts wander.

To nothing.

When she returns, he is staring at her. He is worried.

He is very worried.

It does something to her, that look. It pierces the fog for the duration of one beat of a heart.

Then it goes back to grey.

But still, at night, she wonders.

She remembers his look. It was a strange look. Worry, yes, but not only that. If she listened to her intuition, she would even think she saw something like despair.

Despair is strong. Despair is...not what Elizabeth expected. She lets her mind wander for a while, pondering. Then she decides she was wrong.

Two days pass.

Everything is still grey.

Elizabeth is breakfasting on Tuesday when her husband enters. He puts something near her plate.

Flowers.

They are very red. Deep red. Red like blood, red like velvet, red like beautiful mysteries lurking behind theatre curtains. The red is so strong she almost gasps.

She raises her eyes to him. "You said you missed red," her husband explains. "Those are from Lady Harden's hothouse. I rode there yesterday."

She does not say anything, just gazes at the flowers.

"I…I thought you might prefer poppies. I think I heard you once say how much you liked poppies, but they are impossible to find in February," he explains. "Well, maybe in London. I sent a letter. I shall have news, soon. Next week, I think."

She looks at him, her eyes sincere.

"Thank you," she whispers.

He does not say anything after that.

The footman goes to fetch a vase. Elizabeth drinks her coffee, eats her eggs, looking at the flowers the whole time.

"Do you want the flowers to be put in your room?" her husband asks, after she has finished.

"No!" she says, a little too quickly. Truth is, she hates her room. She cannot breathe in her room. She does not dislike the breakfast parlour. The parlour is nice, with high ceilings and large windows, opening—on the grey out of doors, but opening nevertheless.

"No," she repeats, smiling. "I like it here. I think I am going to stay and read in here today."

He gives her a wan smile and observes her for a moment. Then he nods, and leaves.

She wonders, for a fleeting moment, how he was before.

How he was before the death of his sister.

But mostly, she just looks at the flowers.

The world is grey, and red.

Chapter Two
The Merry Horrors Of War

There are guests tonight, and Colonel Fitzwilliam is staying for a while. To be exact, he has stayed for a while, and leaves tomorrow.

Dinner goes well. Elizabeth is the perfect hostess; she behaves well. She shows education and taste.

"What the hell happened to your wife?" asks Colonel Fitzwilliam, later, when the guests are gone, Elizabeth has retired for the night, and he is playing billiards with Darcy.

"What do you mean?" Darcy asks. (He knows very well what Fitzwilliam means.)

"She used to be so lively, at Rosings."

"Did you think her inadequate tonight?"

"No! For God's sake, Darcy, you know what I mean. It is like a candle has been snuffed."

"Yes," Darcy says slowly.

(That is all he says.)

The game continues.

Colonel Fitzwilliam is not the type to give up easily.

"Have you quarrelled?"

"It is a forced marriage, Richard. On both sides."

His cousin is having none of it. "Come on, Darcy, you liked her well enough at Rosings. I even thought… I even thought, for a moment there, you were going to propose."

"Well, I did not. And I ended up married to her regardless."

"You could have found a way out of it," Fitzwilliam says. "Could have paid the family."

Darcy does not answer. They keep playing.

Then suddenly he cannot pretend any longer.

"Lord, Richard," he whispers. "I do not know what to do."

His cousin nods. "Tell me what happened."

"Yes, we quarrelled. On our wedding night. I shouted at her, and she just…took it, Richard. I thought she would protest. Insult me back, even. She never seemed to lack spirit. But she just… She said I was right, and she just… She just took it."

"What did you say?"

"That she was beneath me."

"Always the charmer."

"And then… As you said. The fire is gone."

Darcy looks somewhere undefined, on the other side of the window maybe, but there is nothing on the other side of the windows. Just the night.

"Hmm." Fitzwilliam plays; he thinks. "I have seen that, with soldiers."

"Soldiers?"

"They are shocked, by...death, or a cannonball... Noise, blood, or the general merry horrors of war."

"She has not seen the merry horrors of war."

"I am not saying it is the same thing, just that they are similar phenomenon. What I mean, is... You did not kill her spirit with one fight. Something else happened. Several things, I bet. People... They are well, and suddenly— a series of events—things that would not affect someone else..."

Darcy thinks. About Elizabeth. Lydia's dishonouring the family, with that man—that sergeant, from the North. Their father's death. The family thrown out of their own house. Jane's departure.

Elizabeth torn from her friends, sent...here, with him.

"How do you... Those soldiers, did they get better?"

Fitzwilliam does not answer instantly. He plays.

"Some of them," he says, lightly. Too lightly.

"There are doctors, in London, you know."

They talk about doctors for a while. Then they talk about other topics. Family. Money. Women (for Fitzwilliam).

Then Fitzwilliam says, "I know something that helps."

"What?"

"Helping."

"I am not sure I follow."

"Helping others. That helps. Those soldiers, those who volunteered at hospitals, opened houses for the wounded, raised money—those are the ones who got better. But it does not have to be that complicated. Even helping one person, it—well—helps."

Darcy frowns. That hardly makes sense. And even if it did, whom is Elizabeth going to help? Nobody needs help round here. It is Pemberley. Everybody is well.

"So, what about you?" Fitzwilliam asks. "After, you know, everything. After...Georgie. How are you?"

"I am well," Darcy answers.

Chapter Three
Light Blue

The doctor comes. From London, very recommended, very expensive. Very sure of himself. When he comes, Darcy is not present. He should have been, but there has been some trouble with a mine, on another property.

The doctor listens to Elizabeth. They are alone, in the parlour, near her room. She tells him everything. She speaks about her night terrors, her fears. Then how those disappeared, suddenly. Leaving food with no taste, the view with no colours.

When Darcy comes back the next day, something is very wrong.

The footman will not look at him. A maid does look at him—with fear in her eyes—and almost flees. Mrs Reynolds appears. She is livid.

"I have to talk to you now, sir. It is imperative... sir," she whispers. She seems almost afraid.

"What is it?" Darcy asks as soon as they are alone.

"Sir, the doctor has come."

"Yes? What did he say?"

"Sir," Mrs Reynolds explains, not meeting his eyes, "Mrs Darcy is locked in a tiny closet upstairs, on the third floor, screaming."

"What?"

"He said—the doctor said—that Mrs Darcy was very ill. That she needed a shock, to 'restore' her brain, sir. He said that terror and hunger and… I refused to obey him, but Jenkins—Jenkins did not know what to do because you said to 'do all the doctor said', and the doctor imposed on him, I think, saying it was imperative, that you would be furious if there was disobedience and… But Mrs Darcy, she is not ill! She is not mad! She is a little melancholy sometimes, yes, but…"

"Where is she?"

When Darcy arrives on the third floor, yes, Elizabeth is screaming. He tries to open the closet, but the doctor has the key. He kicks the door down. Elizabeth throws herself into his arms, sobbing.

"Oh, please, please, please, get me out of there. Oh, please I am begging you…" He is dragging her into the light, and she is clutching his shirt (it is a light blue shirt) and trying to breathe. She begs, "Do not put me back in there. Oh God, do not put me back… I shall be happy. I swear I shall be happy, just do not put me back…"

"Never," he is whispering in her ear. "Never."

She is burying her face in his shirt (light blue shirt). "I swear," he breathes. "I swear to God. Never. That will never happen again."

The doctor is back the next day, with his assistants. He explains that Mrs Darcy should come with him, to his clinic, in London. Mrs Darcy is such a good case, a perfect case, he declares. He has a new method, with icy water and isolation and shocks—physical and of the mind. Elizabeth is there listening, and Mrs Reynolds is there listening, and the footmen are there listening, and some of the maids have gathered in the hall, and Darcy throws the doctor and the assistants out, politely, paying them their dues, saying thank you so much, but we do not require your services any longer. He walks them to the door then shakes the doctor's hand, keeping a straight face all along, and tells him in a very low voice, that only the doctor can hear, that if he ever comes back, he is going to kill him, chop up his body, and feed it to the dogs.

When Darcy comes up two hours later to see Elizabeth, she is herself again.

Bathed, dressed, her hair done.

Tense smile.

Perfectly composed.

"Mr Darcy," she says, "I apologise for my behaviour. It seems I lost a part of my rationality up there." She smiles and adds, "Never a good idea when you are trying to prove you are not crazy."

Darcy is not composed.

"I am so sorry I was not at home to prevent this. That man—that man is out of his mind. This will never happen again."

"Thank you. That is very reassuring. But of course," Elizabeth continues, extremely politely, her smile just this side of terrified, "this is what a husband would say to reassure his wife, to calm her before the men arrive the next morning to take her to Bedlam."

Darcy looks at her with dismay.

"Is that what you think is happening here?"

"I...do not know," says Elizabeth, in a light tone. "Is it?" Her smile disappears; she stands up and begins to pace the room. "You are trapped with a woman you do not esteem or want, Mr Darcy," she explains, her voice imperceptibly shaking, "and now, you are told she is not completely well. Would not 'the clinic' be a perfectly clean, acceptable way to get rid of an undesirable partner? And if I protest, if I panic," she says, with an edge of, well, panic in her voice, "it will be more proof that I am crazy."

"Elizabeth," he begins... And suddenly, all his wife's formality vanishes, only supplication and dread in her eyes, and he cannot think straight. "Dearest," he says, and she does not register it, she does not notice, for now. "I do not want to get rid of you. On my parents' grave, on Georgiana's memory, I will not do it. That man—those men—will never come back, I swear…"

She is listening. Her eyes are focused on his shirt again. Light blue. The shirt is the first thing she saw when he pulled her out of that dark closet. The light blue is what she was clasping when he took her in his arms, repeating words of reassurance.

She nods. She thanks him. She spends the whole night awake, haunted by vivid, terrifying dreams—no, by visions, worse than dreams, because dreams are unreal, and this is very real. People—women—undesirable wives or mistresses or fallen daughters are tortured in hell, yes, right now, labelled 'crazy', experimented upon, laughed at. Elizabeth has heard the stories, but they say—they say the reality is worse.

At least those visions are in colour.

The doctor does not come back.

After a while, she realises he never will.

The next day, and the next, and the next, she sees light blue everywhere. It is connected to him. To her husband. To his shirt. It is connected to 'dearest'—yes, she heard it, she just—noticed later. What a word to use.

Light blue is connected to her husband's

embrace, to his smell. To the intense emotion in his eyes when she looked at him with such gratefulness, after he pulled her out.

The sofa in the summer drawing room is blue. And there is a vase, with red flowers, on the table.

She sits down.

She looks around.

The world is grey, and red, and light blue.

Chapter Four: Silver

"Your alliance is a degradation."

"My family's expectations, the inferiority of your birth…"

It is not that she feels inferior. Or that she believes her alliance has been a degradation. She does not. She does not degrade herself, even in her own mind. No. It is the feeling that he does. That he is at her side, day after day, looking at her, feeling degraded.

That is where the grey comes from. Well, part of it.

"I am sorry if I speak out of turn," Mrs Reynolds says.

They are in the autumn parlour. They are drinking tea and going through all the weekly, necessary decisions.

"I just want to say, Mrs Darcy, from me and the servants, that we're so happy you are... I mean, we were so worried, when that doctor was here."

Mrs Darcy pales. For a moment, Mrs Reynolds thinks that she is going to say something sincere, for once, something personal, something that is not amiable and polite and sensible and pleasant, but the moment passes, and Mrs Darcy is composed again.

"Obviously, it was...a scary moment," she answers, smiling. "And not my finest, I fear, Mrs Reynolds."

"Madam, that man was out of his senses. And dangerous."

Mrs Darcy's smile becomes weaker.

"Mrs Darcy," Mrs Reynolds continues, "everybody appreciates you a lot here. You are always kind, calm, and generous. We all hold you in the highest esteem."

Mrs Darcy seems stunned. Like this is a complete surprise to her.

She smiles, a weak one, but yes, a real one. Her eyes glint. Maybe tears.

"Thank you, Mrs Reynolds," she whispers.

It means a lot. Thinking she is in a house full of allies. Not full of enemies, who would bear witness against her and send her to icy water and shocks. To oblivion. But then, she remembers, oblivion is off the table. Thanks to her husband.

She sees it often, that scene. She plays it in her mind. She is in his arms. He is whispering in her ear. She is clutching the shirt. (The light blue shirt.) He is…shivering with emotion, almost.

A strange man's embrace—no reason to affect her so.

She supposes it has been years since she touched another human being. No, not years. But long.

How long since he touched someone?

Mrs Reynolds is still talking. Elizabeth has missed a part.

"… and he was not like that before," Mrs Reynolds says. Elizabeth raises her head. She listens. "Oh, he was never the most talkative of boys, but he smiled a lot. He was always so kind. And he laughed, when he was a young man— with Mr Bingley and the colonel. They could be quite wild."

"Wild?" Elizabeth smiles—another real one. "My husband was wild?"

"No, I mean, forgive me, Mrs Darcy, that was badly expressed," Mrs Reynolds says, amused. "I mean, comparatively. But then, you know, his sister."

Elizabeth nods.

"We all thought, this fog will lift when he gets married," Mrs Reynolds continues. "And then you came, a pretty young bride… But clearly…"

Elizabeth wonders all day.

She wonders when they are eating luncheon, she and her husband, mostly in silence (polite, not unpleasant silence). She wonders when he is gone, all afternoon. He is taking care of his duties; she is taking care of hers.

Duties are like flies. They come, buzzing; Elizabeth swats them one by one. They are incessant. They are worthless. They make no sense.

But now the wondering is like a glue. Holding things together.

Mrs Reynolds said, "fog." She said, "We all thought the fog would lift."

Elizabeth wonders.

Fog?

What does the world of her husband look like?

Her word is grey—and red, and light blue. She looks at the red flowers in the vase. Her husband has an arrangement with Lady Harden's gardener now, and red flowers are brought regularly to Pemberley. They appear, like magic, in the rooms she walks into, like those fairy tales where flowers just blossom on the princess' steps, but of course she knows the process is much more complicated here. It is not magic, sadly. It is money.

But. But, there is thought. Behind the money. His thoughts.

She is writing letters, in the drawing room where she spends most of the time now, because the sofa is light blue. Light blue hums like a musical note.

Yes, what does the world of her husband look like? Is it foggy? Is it grey?

Does anything pierce the fog, ever?

Dinner. (She observes him. She is trying to guess the colours in his mind.)

There was despair in there, she remembers. (Black?)

Night comes.

It was a good day.

For a while, at the beginning, at Pemberley, when life was sinking into grey waters, she counted the bad days and the good days. The good days were when something good happened. Or something interesting. Or peculiar. Like a cup of good coffee. A visit where someone uttered a clever joke. Once, she woke early and saw the sun rise over the grounds, through her window, and it was magnificent. A silken drape of beauty thrown over the sky— that morning, she had tears in her eyes too.

But soon it seemed grey was all there was, so she stopped counting.

But today, the wondering. About him. It kept everything else at bay.

The next morning. Breakfast. Mostly in silence (polite, not unpleasant silence).

The next morning. Breakfast. Mostly in silence (polite, not unpleasant silence).

Nothing is happening. The grey is winning again.

∞ ∞ ∞

The next morning. Breakfast. Mostly in silence (polite, not unpleasant silence).

"Would you like to take a walk with me?" she asks. (After coffee.)

He says, "Yes."

She did not think before asking. If she had, she would not have asked. He has his flies to swat.

But soon they are out of doors, and she has her hand on his arm.

∞ ∞ ∞

She forgets everything. She just walks, in the beautiful, cold light of the morning. Feeling his warmth near hers.

They go far. The lake (almost white, reflecting the sky).

The lime trees, black, nude. Witches' fingers. Writing dark letters in the air.

The hills. The sky.

Everything white and silver.

She thinks about 'the inferiority of your birth' and 'the degradation' again, but not in a bad way.

Silver threads are connecting her to her

husband, she realises. One of the silver threads is the shared memory of that night, of what he said. It is always there, this thread, whatever happens. It does not matter the number of breakfasts they take together, the insults stay there, their shared knowledge of them connecting them.

But there are other threads.

One silver thread is flowers appearing wherever she goes.

One silver thread is her hand clutching that shirt (while he is shivering).

One silver thread is that she is wondering about him.

One silver thread is all those breakfasts together (after all).

One fragile, glimmering silver thread is that he said 'dearest'.

(What a word to say.)

The sky is huge. And endless. And silver.

Chapter Five
Mahogany

"When I came back into Hertfordshire," Darcy says, on one of their walks. "When I came back into Hertfordshire, the second time. I…"

He stops. She waits.

Crocuses are appearing in the fields around, piercing the frost. They are very yellow.

The rest of the sentence does not come. Elizabeth tries to guess. The problem is—she does not want to think about that time. Her childhood, yes. Her youth, yes. After the death of her father…no. It is all hidden in a fog regardless.

Around them, crocuses everywhere. Bright, violent yellow.

Egyptians revered them as a symbol of the return of the sun. (Her father explained it to her.)

Silence. Walking. Silver air, silver cold. Stunning winter dawn.

He changes the subject.

"That night, Elizabeth. Our wedding night. I…"

He hesitates, and she says, quickly, "I am not particularly keen to revisit the subject, sir."

He does not say anything after that.

Crocuses are beautiful but leave her with a taste of dread.

Not that subject. It would destroy everything.

He would apologise politely, coldly. Not really meaning it. Maybe he would speak a little more about how unsuitable she is (in a polite, reasonable way).

It would destroy everything, rip off all the delicate silver threads. Rip off 'dearest', and the blue shirt, and the tender smell of his skin.

No.

Of course, the unfinished conversation is a new thread connecting them.

A yellow one. Like the crocuses.

The day passes. It is not a pleasant one.

The yellow thread is pulsating. The other beautiful secret bonds (all delicacy and grace) are shattering—no, not shattering. Vanishing. No. Dimming. Disappearing from view like faraway stars erased by the glare of a blazing sun.

Elizabeth wants to retreat into the grey. Grey is safe.

She cannot.

In the grey she can rest.

She is restless.

Of course, their chambers are connected. She has her bedchamber (a grey one), her parlour (charcoal), and her dressing room (no particular colour). He has the same, she supposes. The two main rooms are connected by a door. Always closed, of course. She locked it after their wedding night, she supposes. She does not even remember doing it.

They both hear noise through the door, sometimes. Often. Steps. The floorboards creaking. The muffled sound of voices—his conversation with his valet, her conversation with her maid. (Those are rare. The maid is hard grey.)

It is night. Her maid is gone. She hesitates. On the other side of the door. Her chamber is grey, of course, as is the air, as is her future slumber.

She knocks lightly. She opens the door. She enters.

It is all golden and brown on the other side.

The fire is still burning, candles are lit, and the valet is folding garments. Her husband is sorting books on an oak sideboard. They both turn to look at her.

Mahogany tables, brown (maybe dark green) walls, golden light. A lot of books, scattered. Leather bindings, brown or dark red. Maroon drapes. The fire.

She wonders whether it is what the inside of her husband's soul looks like.

She is not moving. "James, can you leave us?" her husband says, in a casual, polite voice.

The valet vanishes.

∞∞∞

"How are you tonight, Elizabeth?" her husband says. "Do you want me to ring for some tea?" (In a casual, polite voice. Like his wife in his bedroom is an everyday occurrence.)

"Tea would be lovely, thank you," she says, smiling, and then she enters the room for real. (In a casual and polite way. Nobody will say that Elizabeth Bennet—Elizabeth Darcy—is not always perfectly polite.)

I wanted to say how much I enjoy our walks together, Mr Darcy. And I do hope that the slight unpleasantness of this morning will not prevent us from walking together again, is what she came here to say. With a light smile, to pretend the topic is less serious than it really is.

But now the words will not come out.

"This is a beautiful room," she says instead.

"I think so too," her husband answers. He is in his shirtsleeves, not completely undressed yet.

"It was my father's."

Elizabeth looks at the books. Memorises the titles. She looks at the mahogany table.

He looks at her.

Her hair prepared for bed. Under the dark-grey dressing gown, a sophisticated silk shift and a bed jacket. Off-white, both. Off-white feels intimate.

It feels true.

It fills him with despair.

She looks at the other table. Where the valet left the garments. "Oh, this is the light blue shirt," she says. Lightly.

Every artificial sentence of small talk she utters pains him a little more.

He feels like ending it all. No, he does not. A gentleman never would. A Christian never would. But he understands why people do it. When everything is meaningless, a shallow and cruel image of what it is supposed to be. When the fire is so near, it would warm you up, but you raise your hand to it, and the wind freezes your heart.

"You know," she says, "I have this silly idea…" She turns to him. She smiles. She walks to him.

He pays attention. Her tone is light again, breezy, but a little too breezy. Like she is going to say something important. "I have a…liking for… I notice…colours," she explains.

He nods. "I know you like red."

Now she is near him.

"Yes." Facing him. Very near. "And also," she says, "I like your blue shirt. Because you were wearing it when you freed me from that closet." She raises her hand.

No icy wind blows.

"When you opened the door, and I…"

She puts her hand on his chest.

He stops breathing.

She stops breathing.

Chapter Six
Circles

Darcy's world is made of concentric circles.

It is dark, mostly. Night. In his mind, the circles look like Celtic ruins, made of crude grey stones, on a grassy plain, dimly lit by the moon. It looks like Scotland, that he visited, with his parents, when he was very young. Scotland at night.

The first circle represents him. Ghosts live there. She does too.

The ghosts are his parents and Georgiana. She is Elizabeth, of course. She is a being of pale fire. Her hair is undone; she is wearing only a thin linen shift. It is a strange image, considering he has never seen her in such a state of undress. But that is how she was in his dreams, when he fell for her, at Netherfield—yes, it happened in Netherfield; afterwards, he just fell deeper.

The second circle. It is larger. There reside people he is responsible for. People living at Pemberley—on the estate, or connected to it. Bingley belongs there too, as does Colonel Fitzwilliam—Darcy is not responsible for Colonel Fitzwilliam, but his cousin sleeps there regardless. Circles are not always logical.

In the third circle lives his family. Darcy's cousins, uncles. Aunts. His duty is to respect them, to help them, to visit them. If something goes wrong, he must make it right. If he cannot, then the fault is his.

In the fourth circle moves a strange crowd, of people he is connected to somehow. He is not responsible for them, but he owes them courtesy, politeness. Efficient men with a profession—lawyers, merchants, barristers, who do good work for the family. Friends of his parents. Friends of his friends. To all those people, he must be loyal. He would not refuse his help if they ever asked.

In the fifth circle there is society. Society includes the third and fourth circles, but it is also an entity of its own—an abstract crowd of people and judgments and obligations. Society's opinion should be respected, of course.

Then, there is the rest of the world. It is endless. When he was young, he was curious. Scotland was so fascinating. Now, curiosity has died.

The rest is already so heavy to bear.

But back to her.

Elizabeth was fire. (She is white fire still.) But she was blazing, burning, when he met her— he was already walking in the shadows, three ghosts as his daily companions. And she, fiery with life and light and laughter. He did not have the right to take her, of course. He could not buy her and bring her home, because of the third, fourth, and fifth circles.

Elizabeth would have been good for the second circle, though, Darcy was thinking, at the time, at Netherfield and at Rosings, when he was watching her and listening to her with quiet desperation. She would have been perfect. A good friend to his close friends. A good mistress of Pemberley—she would have helped him carry the load—and of course, in the first circle, in his arms, she would have... She... The sun would have risen.

But no. It would have been selfish. Marrying just to please himself—what an idea! For love? How self-centred. Egotistical. No.

Then he got her, despite everything. When he realised what he had done to her, after their wedding night, the third, fourth, and fifth circles disappeared from his view. Society is still there somewhere, of course, moving like a big, ever-hissing snake. But he cannot see it any longer—the night is absolute on that part of the plain.

That night, after he berated her. When she sat

down on the bed, raised her eyes to him, and said, "Very true," to all his insults. Brutally, he could not remember. Why the judgments and the opinions of those circles had even mattered. Why he had even listened, even for a second, to the hiss of the snake. All his fears of misalliance and gossip crumbled, reduced to nothingness and rubbish—

—when he realised he had destroyed all his hopes of ever seeing the dawn.

How God must laugh.

So, yes, he is very unhappy.
It is well. He deserves to be

(Georgiana's ghost is sitting by him, with a shy smile.)

And then Elizabeth puts her hand on his chest. And it is real.

And it is true.

And it is burning like hell.

Elizabeth's hand lingers for a few moments. Then she smiles and walks away. She says something about tea. The door opens, tea is served, they drink, they talk, politely, then she goes away, to sleep.

It is morning. The breakfast parlour. She arrives, she sees him, and smiles.

He smiles back.

They go walking. (Crocuses everywhere.)

He is very happy.

No, it is not happiness. It is a sort of fever.

He is burning.

Waiting for her next smile. Her next touch.

He does his tasks for the day. They are not flies. He does not swat them. Everything is connected and makes sense. It is just that there are a lot of them, and they are heavy.

In the evening, when he goes home, Elizabeth smiles at him again.

In the morning, they walk.

They mostly stay silent. But sometimes he points and explains. The history of that chapel. Of the village. Of that farm. Of that man. There is a tree, and a bench. They sit there. Across the lane is a beautiful old stone cross, half buried, with a broken Virgin Mary. A remnant of more Catholic times. Faraway, the old abbey—in ruins. He tells the story.

Before their walks, they (the bench, the cross, the farm, the man, the abbey) were hazy. Now, when Elizabeth sees them without her husband, they vibrate with the sound of his voice, with the feel of his presence, with the knowledge imparted.

They glow. They are secret and special.

One day her husband touches her.

He has forgotten his gloves, and when he

realises it, they are already far under the white and silver sky. It is not that cold. They go on. She has her arm in his, so his hand, his bare hand, reposes on her wrist. It does not have to, really, but somehow, it is.

There is a naked part between her coat and her gloves. His fingers trail on her skin.

It is barely a touch at first.

She does not say anything. She does not pull away.

They keep walking. In perfect silence.

His fingers touch her skin again.

They keep walking.

He does not say a word.

Next morning, she enters the breakfast parlour, and smiles. He smiles back—then he is serious—his eyes follow her, when she sits, when she fills her plate, when she pours coffee. His gaze is intense. In that way he has, in that way he always had, Elizabeth suddenly realises. Even when they were not married. When they were just acquaintances.

"Would you like some more coffee, Mr Darcy?" she asks. (Nobody could say that Elizabeth Bennet—Darcy—is not always perfectly polite.)

"I was thinking," he answers. "You said you like colours."

"I do."

"This winter is endless," he says. "And very grey."

"It is getting better," she says, raising her eyes to him.

She thinks he stops breathing there for a while. But maybe it is her imagination. Maybe it is all in her imagination. The wrist, the glows. The shirt. 'Dearest'. Maybe she is grasping at straws. Worse. Maybe there are no straws.

It is a while before he speaks again. "Well, I was thinking," he finally continues. "About colours. It is still the Season."

He hesitates. Then, "How about going to London for a few weeks?"

Chapter 7
London

London is brittle and beautiful and dangerous. Cutting like a crystal shard.

Julia Fitzwilliam. Darcy's cousin. Twenty-eight, fashionable, funny, married to the Fitzwilliam heir. Taking Elizabeth shopping.

Noise, busy streets, yelling, strange smells, carriages, expensive teas in expensive establishments. Gorgeous fabrics. Deep, shimmering hues. A new maid, sent by Julia. New dresses, new gloves, new shoes, new shawls, new words. London words. Silks. Satins.

No time to think. Elegant ladies with pearls being introduced to you on the pavement.

Julia is perfect because she is new. She does not know about Elizabeth. About the melancholy, about the grey, about the doctor and the screaming in the closet. Julia does not know about the Elizabeth of before (in Hertfordshire), she does not know about the Elizabeth of after (at Pemberley), she just knows about the Elizabeth of now.

So, Elizabeth of now can try a new skin. (Julia will not know it is new.) The new skin is joyful, witty, sophisticated. Almost like the Elizabeth from Hertfordshire, but that Elizabeth (from before) was not a skin. That Elizabeth was real.

∞ ∞ ∞

Elizabeth does not see Darcy much during the day. He has a lot of business in the city. And she has Julia.

But at night…

They are always out, together. She and her husband. Theatre, dinner, dinner, ball, theatre, concert, dinner, repeat.

Elizabeth is drinking life. Sucking it, like a vampire sucks blood.

See, Elizabeth does not feed on loneliness. She feeds on people. Like…like her mother, really. (Dreadful thought.) Elizabeth feeds on conversation and laughs, friendships and crowds, connections and humans. On parties and ideas and irony. Her husband, she suspects, feeds on loneliness. Well, maybe on solitude. Nobody really feeds on loneliness.

He is right about London colours—she drinks them too. She is sucking them hungrily. Colours in actors' costumes, garish wallpapers glowing in the candlelight, the infinite gay nuances of the masquerade's crowd. Colours are intellectual too; Elizabeth finds them in phrases of music, in poetry readings, in political debates, in literary discussions—in colourful insults overheard through a window.

(Hearing them, treasuring them, storing them for grey days to come.)

It is raining a lot. Elizabeth likes it. London is hazy, like a modern painting.

So yes, together, she and Darcy, every night. For hours, from seven till midnight, often later.

He never touches her—except when she is taking his arm, of course. Other husbands, they touch their wives on the elbow, the arm, the shoulder, the waist. Her husband almost does it, once—when they enter their theatre box—his hand moves towards the small of her back. He hesitates—the hand moves away.

Elizabeth has a red dress. Crimson. He bought the fabric for her. ("I thought you might like this," he says. She does.)

He does not touch her the evening she is wearing the dress. But she feels like she is wearing him. Like he is touching her all over. (Unnerving thought.)

She sees Julia a lot. They laugh a lot. Elizabeth tells her about the doctor.

It is still raining. The grey in the streets

glimmers. They have tea. She and Julia. Again.

Elizabeth's new skin (joyful, witty, sophisticated) is far from perfect. There are dinners where Elizabeth feels fragile, lost. She falters. She says something—that does not fit exactly. That is just a little to the left, or to the right, like a missed throw at cricket.

"I apologise," she says to Darcy, in the carriage, afterwards. "I lack practice. I fear I played a few fake notes in the conversation."

"I do not think anybody notices."

"You do."

"That is because I knew you before—I can see the difference. But even with…" He pauses. (Even with what? Elizabeth wonders.) "Even now," he continues, "you are more charming and clever than any woman present."

She is speechless.

The Matlock dinner.

Darcy's family. Who elegantly, sharply disapprove of her. Not of her, exactly—her they could not care less about. No, they disapprove of the 'circumstances'. The incident, the damage, the marriage. All of them do, except Colonel Fitzwilliam; but Colonel Fitzwilliam is getting slaughtered at Waterloo. So, they feel free to slaughter her.

(Julia is present, but she does not intervene.)

It is done with needles.

Long, thin, metallic needles (sentences) piercing Elizabeth just where it hurts.

Elizabeth of old would have laughed. Elizabeth of old would have parried the needles with ease. This Elizabeth feels naked.

She parries, though. She smiles. She makes neutral, amiable answers. (Nobody could say that Elizabeth Bennet—Darcy—is not absolutely...you know.)

But she gets paler and paler.

Suddenly, her husband's hand is on her shoulder.

She does not see him coming. But yes, suddenly, he is at her side, in the drawing room, touching her.

Dinner. Darcy puts his hand on her arm often. On her elbow. Or even, once, on her shoulder, around the chair. (A bold move.) He talks. He is very calm. He catches most of the needles in the air and lays them serenely on the table, near Elizabeth's plate.

As a gift.

But he cannot catch them all. At the end of the meal, Elizabeth is getting tired of catching. She is beginning to miss some. Darcy's hand is warm though.

"Sadly, Mrs Darcy, a life in the country—with such a family—may not have prepared you for all the pressures of London," Lady Matlock says.

"You are very right, Lady Matlock, it did not," Elizabeth answers. "But my father always said that navigating the daily absurdities of a small town would teach me to survive in any society."

Julia smiles. "Of course, you needed a doctor to survive Pemberley's society, Elizabeth. So I wonder whether your father was right, and whether you will really be able to navigate this one."

People laugh. Elizabeth sits petrified. No words come.

"See?" Julia adds. "And here we all thought you had an answer for everything."

Two weeks of shopping and tea and 'intimate' conversations. And now, wielding the blade, waiting for Elizabeth to be weary, and…strike.

Then, at the end. Near the drawing room door. "Shall I come tomorrow to fetch you, Elizabeth?" Julia asks. "We still have to go to that fitting —the green silk. It will go perfectly with your complexion."

Elizabeth cannot insult Darcy's cousin. To be honest, she does not feel strong enough. "I am so sorry, your ladyship," she whispers. "I am not sure I shall have time tomorrow."

"Come on," Julia protests. "Is it 'your ladyship' now? I am sure—"

"What my wife is too polite to tell you, your ladyship," Darcy interrupts, "is that you are not welcome in our house any longer."

Everybody hears.

The carriage. The night.

It is still raining.

The carriage gets stuck in the street.

The water has risen somewhere, near the river. Some streets are impassable. They are stuck. They are sitting side by side, shoulders touching, under the blanket.

Elizabeth should say thank you. She cannot say thank you.

Wait. Why can she not?

"Thank you," she breathes.

He looks at her. She cannot really see him in the dark. She imagines the look. So many possibilities.

Silence. Then she says, "You never told me how your sister died, Mr Darcy. It seems… Is there… something…I do not know about?"

It is a hunch. Things she overheard in the

Matlock drawing room. The ladies' faces when they pronounced the name "Georgiana," or rather, when they did not.

(It is a hunch, but Elizabeth knows she is right.)

New silence.

"There was a man…" Darcy starts.

"Oh my God." Elizabeth shivers.

(Georgiana was fifteen.)

"He was the son of my father's steward," Darcy explains. "He was raised with us—Georgiana trusted him. He seduced her." Elizabeth is silent. "They spent a few nights in different inns together, then the carriage had an accident on the road to Scotland. They both died."

Elizabeth cannot speak.

She should take his hand, she thinks. She cannot.

Wait. Why can she not?

She cannot.

Men are talking near the carriage. Coarse voices. Street conversations. Darcy listens. He asks the footman to open the door, he gets out. He speaks with the men. Elizabeth cannot hear.

It is still raining.

When Darcy comes back, he says, "There have been storms in the North. I am worried."

"For Pemberley?"

"Yes. I think we should go back."

The rain is falling harder.

Chapter 8
Water

They find an express at the house. Pemberley has been flooded; the situation is dire. Darcy leaves on horseback the next morning; Elizabeth will join him with the carriage.

"I apologise. I thought your London stay would be more pleasant," he says, when he is at the door.

"My stay in town was very pleasant," Elizabeth answers. "I enjoyed it immensely."

He stares at her, trying to divine her thoughts, her emotions. Trying to interpret her smile.

Trying to guess whether there is...more.

"I am talking, of course, about yesterday's dinner," he adds, with a smile of his own. (Apologetic. A little shy.) "My family's behaviour, and Julia's, was unpardonable."

Elizabeth shakes her head. "It is of no importance. None whatsoever." Then she hesitates, and it is her turn to look shy. "I mean—I understand their judgment is of great importance to you, and..."

WHO IS ELIZABETH BENNET'S SOULMATE?

"No," he interrupts. "No. It is not."

It is in direct contradiction with what he told her on their wedding night. They look at each other; there is so much more to say, but Pemberley is waiting.

(It is a lie. The truth is, he is terrified.)

"I hope we shall come back to town sometimes," Elizabeth says softly.

"We shall."

They are still looking at each other.

Darcy does not know how to say good-bye. (He does not want to.)

So many things to tell her.

They say good-bye. He leaves.

Four days later, in the morning, Elizabeth's carriage arrives at Pemberley. Near Pemberley. Because she has to travel the last mile on foot.

Three villages flooded, and the main house. The water has receded now, and Elizabeth can enter the...her... She can come home. She is aghast at the damage.

It gets worse. After the first flood, a dam broke uphill, she learns, creating a second disaster. Now Lambton is underwater, and another village, and…

No time for grey. No time for self-reflection or melancholy. Darcy is in Lambton. She does not see him. Elizabeth's duties are food and shelter, for more than two hundred people. Women and children.

People everywhere in Pemberley House. On Pemberley's ground floor, the part that has not been flooded. Half of Pemberley's first floor.

Fires and warm soup and running around with Mrs Reynolds and the servants. It is like they are allies in a war, she and Mrs Reynolds, giving orders, making hard decisions. Thinking in essentials. One woman has seen her three children drown before her eyes. News come from Lambton, and it is bad, and it is night. Darcy does not come back. Then it is morning and people are coughing. Elizabeth thinks of pneumonia, of children dying. "They ingested unhealthy water," the reverend explains. "Miasma." Fires, blankets, hot tea, hot remedies. One baby has a high fever. He is near death. He vomits. The Elizabeth that once looked for colours in the snow seems to be a thousand years away.

If she ever existed.

It is raining again.

The men are still in Lambton and the other village, trying to save what they are able. They need food. Elizabeth and three kitchen maids (and mules and a cart) go there, taking everything they can.

Elizabeth has not seen Darcy since he left the house, in London.

In Lambton it is water and mud and dead bodies. (Lying in the mud.) 'Only' a dozen. (It could have been so much worse, everyone says.) The activity is dwindling down. It is over, mostly. People who could be saved are safe, the others are dead. The water will recede.

(If it ever stops raining.)

Darcy is nowhere in sight.

She looks for him.

He is that way, someone says. No—he left to inspect Brooks's house, someone else explains. Someone talks about the church cellar. Then apparently, he is helping to empty the Andersons' barn.

Except he is nowhere.

The sun is going down. Elizabeth panics.

She walks north, following the water. Someone said Darcy left that way, an hour ago.

She walks.

The noise and voices of the village fade. She keeps walking, calling him.

Nothing. No one.

∞ ∞ ∞

Only water and flooded houses and darkening skies. The world is brown and silver. A universe in dual tones. The sky is an endless mirror.

Emptiness and death. She keeps walking. She goes farther and farther, the only spark of life in a perfectly still world. In fact, she has never felt so alive. In the worst way possible: pain, exhaustion, fear. Searing fear.

She keeps calling him.

The rain falls harder.

"Here!" Darcy's voice.

"Where?"

"Here!" he repeats. "Hurry! The boy is trapped!"

The house. The flooded house, in the middle of the river—there was a whole hamlet there, now Atlantis. She enters the freezing river—feet, calves, knees. It is getting dark. There is a wall, and the door is open, but it is flooded to the lintel. It is the only way in. Grey, mud, cold. She cannot swim.

"Hurry!" he says. "I am not going to be able to hold him when…"

She dives under.

Chapter 9
Earth

She is in.

Cold. Dark. A very small room. Very low ceiling. Dwindling light, through the broken window. Water gets to Elizabeth's chest.

The head of the little boy is hardly visible; Darcy is deep in the water, holding him.

"His foot is stuck in…" Darcy starts. Elizabeth tries to look. "No," Darcy whispers, "hold his head, let me."

She holds the child. She is so cold. She talks to him, trying to reassure him. Darcy dives into the grey, muddy water, once, twice. "I cannot see anything," he grumbles, and suddenly—something must have happened, somewhere, maybe uphill—maybe another dam has broken, because of the rain—there is a wave, water bubbling by the entrance. Darcy has dived again. The child gasps; he is free. Darcy reappears.

"The water is rising!" Elizabeth cries, in case Darcy is too dazed to notice.

"Damn," Darcy mumbles, then, "Go!" he orders.

The boy dives down in the direction of the door and disappears. They hear him yelling something outside; he sounds safe. Darcy turns to Elizabeth—but it is already too late.

The current is too strong. They see it by the window. The river has grown huge. The water is rising fast. Soon it will touch the ceiling.

"Damn," Darcy repeats. Elizabeth's feet hardly reach the bottom. She is shaking from the cold. He takes her in his arms. They stand immobile for a moment, heads very close. Even her thoughts are frozen.

"Elizabeth," he begins. Then, "Wait."

He disappears underwater.

She stays alone.

He reappears.

"Do you know how to swim?"

She shakes her head. "No."

"There is a passage down there, leading to the wine cellar. You have to dive down and then up. I shall help you."

"No. I cannot do it. You should go. You will come back later," she lies. "With help."

"Down, and up. I shall hold your hand," he repeats. "Now."

Underwater they go. It is not difficult. Now they are in another room, looking exactly like the one they just left. Stone walls, low ceiling, the water is even higher.

"We shall have to do it again," Darcy explains. "The wine cellar is connected to another, and then I think we can reach the Jones's farm. It is on higher ground."

She cannot protest any longer. She follows him. Then they must do it a third time, going through a completely flooded room, no air at all.

Underwater. For an eternity. Oblivion. She is moving through living darkness.

The underworld. Liquid.

They come out in what was a courtyard and is now a lake. She can breathe again. The world is real again. They move forwards, holding on to the walls. They get into the (flooded) farm.

The water is still rising. It is almost night.

Darcy disappears for the second time.

"To the east," he says when he comes back. They make progress, along the walls, going east. He is right, the ground is rising. When they arrive in the other part of the farm, Elizabeth's feet touch the ground.

It lasts for another eternity—following him, going from house to house. Soon they can walk, waist high in the cold water, and suddenly they are on dry land (not dry, very muddy) on an island (not an island, a hill, now surrounded by water). There is a house. They run. Well, she tries. In truth, she can hardly walk. Her dress is so soaked, she is carrying lead.

Then Darcy breaks something—a wood shutter maybe. They get inside.

A drawing room, lost in shadows. Maybe a rich farm, or some nice cottage, deserted. The air is humid. Darcy fumbles in the shadows, looking for the tinderbox.

"Get out of your clothes," he orders.

She does not demur. It is life or death. Except, she needs him, because she cannot remove her dress alone. He helps her, then he starts the fire. Soon, she is down to her (soaked) shift; she looks around, climbs on a table, she reaches the curtain, and pulls it with all her might. It comes crashing down.

The flames are getting higher.

"I shall help you," she says in return. Men's clothes are so tight. She helps him out of his boots, out of his breeches.

He is totally naked. He hangs his clothes and hers to dry.

The fire is burning brighter, but she is still shaking. She grabs the curtain. "We should try to keep warm," she says.

He nods. He gestures at her shift. "You should

take that off."

She does. He hangs it to dry also. He takes her in his arms. They wrap the curtain around them.

They sit down near the hearth.

At first, she does not think.

Exhaustion does not even begin to describe it. Cold does not even begin to describe it. She is not even really conscious.

Slowly, it gets better.

∞∞∞

Her thoughts were frozen too. They begin to wake up.

She is naked, in the arms of a naked man. She should be horrified. She is not.

It is not important.

What is important is they are both alive.

Getting warmer.

Time passes. One hour, maybe two.

Her eyes are closed, but she can see them from afar, like she is a bird. The two of them, near the fire, both naked. She imagines the light of the flames dancing on their skin (in truth, they are huddled under the curtain, but that is how she sees them). She pictures the yellow and orange lights, the infinite nuances of their flesh, the shimmering of the velvet curtain.

Then (in her mind) they are not in a drawing room any longer, but in a cave, deep down in the earth. They are near the fire—another fire. Strange paintings on the wall—bronze and ochre and coral.

Time passes.

∞∞∞

He is in the first circle, and she is in his arms.

He feels the grass under their feet, the crude grey stones around. The night and the Scottish stars. It is raining, softly, but they are somehow protected. Or maybe it is raining for real, out of doors.

The other circles do not even exist. They are alone, on the top of the hill, under the white moon.

Now she begins to feel conscious of him.

His legs against hers. Her back against his chest. His head touching hers. His stubble, caressing her cheek.

His heart beating.

He feels her skin under his fingers. Her breast, above his wrist. The softness of her belly. He imagines the whiteness of her thigh.

He feels her breathing.

Their right hands are so close to each other.

Elizabeth takes his.

Their fingers intertwine, and his whole body tenses. Then he kisses her neck, her right shoulder; he is feverish, desperate. Her cheek, her temple. She leans into him. He moves a little. She turns to her left; she nuzzles her head into his shoulder. (He is kissing her head, her brow, her face.)

She falls asleep.

Chapter 10
Moments

The sun is rising.

Warmth, light. Elizabeth wakes up.

She rises slowly—she is alone. Her clothes are dry. She dresses.

Everything is slow and beautiful.

The rays of light, through the broken shutters. The water outside. So peaceful.

She hears her husband in another room (the kitchen, she guesses). She does not want to go and see him yet. She does not know what will happen, and she wants to hold on to beauty for a while. She wants to hold on to the previous night, to the fire, to the curtain, her dreams, and the cave. To his touch and his embrace. To what happened before she drifted off to sleep.

The moments—the memories—are floating in a bubble. It is fragile (and silver).

Elizabeth sits on the sofa. She closes her eyes. She imagines the room, the subdued colours around her. The shimmer of the bubble floating in the air. Fairies are stuck in it.

She wants the present to last forever.

She goes to the kitchen. Darcy is trying to toast some stale bread. It smells like coffee and bacon.

"Oh, God bless you," she says, laughing.

"Yes," he answers. There is light in his eyes when he looks at her. "I do not remember being so hungry in my entire life."

(She is ravenous.)

She helps him prepare breakfast; she finds preserves in a cupboard. They go back. There is a dining room; she opens the shutters, he puts the food on the table. They eat. They talk. Not about the flood. About…coffee and bacon and butter and honey and other breakfasts, at Longbourn, at Pemberley, or in London. They talk about the family that lives in the cottage. He smiles. She laughs—food tastes so good.

They talk about eating from expensive plates with silver spoons, on their own private desert island, in the middle of the muddy water. How strange it is, to be guests and ghosts in someone else's house.

He cannot take his eyes off her—does not even try.

"You saved my life," he says.

Elizabeth is very surprised. "Not at all, Mr Darcy. I believe it is quite the opposite."

"No. I could not have left the boy to his fate. He would have drowned, and then it would have been too late for me to escape—the water would have been too high."

"You still could have swum to the next farm. Without being burdened by a terrified, helpless woman. I am, of course, always loath to contradict my husband, but I do believe you are the hero of this story, sir."

"Well," he answers, smiling. "Maybe this is a disagreement we do not really need to settle."

She smiles in return. "Indeed."

"Are we going to be trapped here for a while?" she asks, when they are at the window, looking at the water.

"We could be. We have enough food to survive for a week. But someone will come along."

Someone does. Five men, on the opposite bank, calling, looking for them. Darcy hails them. An hour later, a rowing boat comes.

Pemberley.

It is a day of a million tasks, a million moments. As soon as they set foot in the house, they are engulfed. Half of the families of the estate are still sleeping on the ground floor. Darcy organises the men; he sends letters and expresses—asking for help, buying food. Buying new seeds for spring—most of them are lost.

Water begins to recede around noon. Fast.

Houses reappear from Atlantis. People are sent to save what there is to save, begin the clean-up process. Elizabeth has only one task: taking care of everything, for two hundred and fifty-three people (Mrs Reynolds counted them).

Elizabeth and Darcy—they are together, but never together. She is running around. He is talking to people and giving instructions.

She is too busy to think of the silvery, shimmering bubble. She wonders whether it has split.

And then…

Darcy is talking to his steward and two other men. She is walking through the room.

Their eyes meet.

It is like he has been waiting for this—yes, for their eyes to meet. Like she has been waiting also.

Now she is burning.

She cannot look at him any longer; she cannot even breathe. She flees down to the kitchen. "You should have some tea, Mrs Darcy," says Mrs Abbott, the cook. "Sit down here with us for a while. It is a jungle up there."

It is a jungle up there. Elizabeth laughs and sits down. She drinks the tea; she talks and jokes. She tells the story of the boy and the cottage and the water. The boy is alive, by the way. Safe and sound, at Pemberley, with the others.

She longs to go back upstairs. To see whether she can meet Darcy's eyes again.

She goes upstairs. Their eyes meet again.

Forget about the bubble. Spikes of burning metal, hope, and fear. She smiles and nods and walks away. Darcy follows her into the hall, moments after. He calls to her, walks to her, takes her hand in his. He begins to say something. Someone comes along; he has to let her go.

Then that is what they do all day. Their jobs.

Their eyes meet. They steal moments. In halls. Between two doors. They touch. A quick squeeze of the hand. A brush on the shoulder. A hand on her waist, in passing. He always initiates it.

She burns.

She almost cannot believe it.
And then she begins to doubt it.

It is a wave of grey. Of panic.

"Elizabeth, I have to speak to you," Darcy says, in a hall, between two doors, her hand in his. "Please. I want to… Tonight?" he asks, and she just nods.

Panic rises higher.

She does not know why, really. She is a rational being, and if she thinks rationally about what happened over the last few days (weeks? months?) the verdict seems clear. She is twenty-two, not an innocent in the ways of the world.

The Elizabeth of before has flirted at dozens of balls and is (or was) perfectly capable of sparking interest and recognising attraction.

But the Elizabeth of before had not drowned in grey.

This Elizabeth is afraid—of hoping and losing hope, of giving herself and being trampled upon, of loving and being spited. This Elizabeth sees it, though. She sees how beautiful it could be; she sees the possibilities and the grace. She wants to cry at the idea that it could not happen. It would save them; it would save both of them. She knows now how near he is from drowning too, how maybe he has already drowned, and she is the one that can drag him back. Yes, she is so desperate she wants to beg.

So she does.

Night.

When she retires to her chambers, her hands are trembling. She sits on a sofa in her parlour; she watches the door. The one that leads to his chamber, to the blue shirt, to books and mahogany.

He enters. He is pale and nervous. She politely asks him to sit down. He does.

Then she kneels before him.

"I do not know what you want to tell me, sir, but please—listen to me first."

She sees him freeze. But she has to go on. "I know that you despise me—not me, exactly, maybe," she adds quickly, "but my family and my connections—but... Please listen." He is livid, petrified. "Please—I beg you—let me be a wife to you. I can be a good wife to you. I can help you. I can be your companion, your confidante. I can love you. We can both..." She shakes her head; it is difficult to find the words. "We can both..."

She loses her voice. Then she finds herself standing up—she does not know how. He has his hands on her arms; his grip is so tight.

"There is nothing I want more," he whispers, and she does not move—she is frozen too now, hardly breathing, their foreheads so close, everything so close. "Elizabeth, there is nothing in the world that I want more," he repeats, his voice breaking. "I..."

He is caressing her arms. He stops.

"But you are in the throes of a misunderstanding," he says, his voice still broken. "That is why...why I have to speak to you."

"I am not sure I follow, Mr Darcy." (She has no voice either.)

"Please, sit down."

She does. She is scared again. He paces the room.

"When I came back into Hertfordshire," he begins. She simply listens. "When I came back into Hertfordshire, the second time. I..."

Chapter 11
A Little Lace

"When I came back into Hertfordshire, the second time," Darcy says, "it was to see you."

Elizabeth frowns. "I…am not sure I follow."

He does not meet her gaze. "I fell in love with you very early on. Even before you and your sister came to stay at Netherfield, I believe. But I was convinced that the disparities in our families' situations made an alliance between us impossible. Then I saw you again at Rosings Park, and…"

Darcy raises his eyes to her—she is petrified. He is very pale; his voice is low, tentative.

"I remember each of our dinners, each of our walks. Every detail—every word, every gesture of yours. I was struggling. I walked to the Parsonage a dozen times, wanting to propose, but then—I…" His voice breaks. "I was a fool."

There is a pause. The fire crackles. Somewhere below, two hundred and fifty-three people are trying to sleep. Somewhere east, houses are still submerged under freezing water. Elizabeth feels stretched between two times, two realities. Her mind is going to tear, like a sheet of paper.

"I left—again, for London. I could not forget you," Darcy explains—it is almost a whisper. "I came back home—to Pemberley—but I could not forget you here, either. I saw you in every lane, in every room."

Elizabeth closes her eyes. She can see it too, her ghost, near the lake, under the lime trees. In the hall, near the eastern window. Down the stairs, looking up at him. She feels like crying.

"I heard about the death of your father. Bingley was already betrothed to Amelia… But I…" Darcy stands up, begins to pace the room. "I knew the house was entailed. I had heard that money was—that you were in reduced circumstances. You had to move away, to give room to your cousin. Miss Bingley informed me with a sort of—glee."

Elizabeth could see it. Could hear it—Caroline Bingley's voice. Coming through a fog. It was all very far away.

"I mention the glee," Darcy adds, "because that moved me. I imagined the worst. I saw your situation as even more dire than it really was, I suppose. I imagined the Miss Bingleys of the world, sneering at your family. So I had to see you."

Elizabeth is very still. "To propose?"

"Maybe—yes—I do not think I had reached a decision, one way or the other." He shakes his head. "I suppose I deliberately placed myself where I would not be able to resist my feelings for you."

"But..." Elizabeth protests. She cannot make sense of his words. Everything is upside down. The geography of the past, falling apart, like pieces of a jigsaw puzzle. "I... You did not even visit—did you?"

"I did."

Elizabeth stands up too. "I apologise, Mr Darcy," she says. "After my father's death, after Jane's marriage, I... Everything I remember is hazy."

She takes a few slow steps. It is raining in her mind. Pieces of time, of reality, falling around her, crashing to the floor. In that tiny cottage, near her aunt Phillips—a cottage they were not sure they could really afford, that they were not sure they could really keep. Her mother, screeching. In the narrow halls, under the low ceilings. Saying—screaming—that it was Elizabeth's fault Jane had to marry so low (a reverend—rather poor). Screaming that if Elizabeth had accepted Mr Collins, they could have waited. Jane would not have been forced to throw herself away.

Loud accusations. Incessant. Ghastly. True.

"I visited the day after my arrival," Darcy says, "to offer my condolences to your family. Then a second time—I do not recall the pretext I used. Your mother rang for tea. You were there—in the drawing room—but you did not speak. You were wearing a black bombazine dress—with a little lace, just here…"

He moves his hand in the direction of Elizabeth's collarbone—the gesture is so tender. So gentle. Sadness is choking her again.

"I am sorry," she repeats. "My memory is all a haze."

Her turn to pace the room. Trying not to walk on the pieces (her past, lying on the floor).

"So that is why you agreed to marry me," she says.

"Yes."

"After the scandal…" Elizabeth hesitates. "After you found me in that barn… It was clearly an accident—and, even so, after Lydia's elopement had dishonoured us all, you could not have been expected… You were not honour bound in any way to…a daughter of such a family. All the blame would have fallen on me. And yet…you acceded to my mother's every demand."

"I loved you. I still do."

He cannot keep his eyes away. He is staring at her, studying her with such an intensity as if he wants to see through her skin—straight to the inside of her soul. To see every movement, every thought.

Silence falls.

"But…" Elizabeth massages her temples.

The wedding night.

Darcy's anger, his insults.

"But then…"

She does not have to say it aloud. He sits down. He seems very tired. "Dearest, I cannot explain myself," he whispers. She hears despair. Fear. "I… My conduct does not make sense to me, either."

Two hundred and fifty-three people, trying to sleep downstairs. And both of them, now.

"You have to understand how…miraculous it all was," he explains. "The barn, your mother's pleas—they were the perfect pretext. I had been struggling between love and duty, and suddenly, both were aligned. You were ruined, I had to marry you. But I still…"

Family. Society. Expectations. Circles. The snake, hissing in his ears, telling him how selfish he was.

"There is no excuse for the way I acted that night. I was not thinking straight. I suppose— if I have to find an explanation…" His voice is low, again. "I suppose I believed that if I voiced my misgivings aloud, we would fight. You would be offended, furious. You would tell me how ridiculous I was."

"You wished to lay it all to rest," Elizabeth says, slowly. "You wanted to give me your black pebbles of doubt, so I could laugh at them and crush them and reduce them to dust."

"I… That is a strange way to define it, but, yes. I suppose you are right."

"And instead, I…"

She stops.

"And instead," he says, "I crushed you."

The conversation ends there. He stays on the sofa, watching her. She is pacing the room, kicking pieces of time as she goes. Memories changing their skins. Worlds shifting and restructuring. It is an unpleasant process. She sees herself through Darcy's eyes: a silent, sad maid sitting in a parlour, in a black bombazine dress—whom he wants to save. Whom he wants to hold in his arms and cherish.

He sees her ghost in every lane, and then he saves her, and he gets the ghost.

She returns to that moment in the parlour —that piece of her past that she does not even remember. She sees it like a scene in a play. Her mother is serving tea. Kitty must be out, visiting. Mary must be in the other room, reading—there is no pianoforte for her to play. Mary hates Elizabeth now. Elizabeth not marrying Mr Collins is the reason there is no pianoforte for her to play. After the barn, Elizabeth begs Mary to stay silent—to not go to her mother—but of course Mary does her duty. So much resentment in her sister's eyes.

But back to that moment (the one Elizabeth does not even remember). The parlour. Darcy's second visit. She is sitting on the beige sofa, far away from her mother. Far away from him. Maybe it is a sunny day, light filtering through the glass, dust dancing in the air. Her black dress, with a little lace around the collar— Elizabeth is not talking. Darcy is looking at her.

A false image, from a false memory. It changes the past, though. A little. It cannot change her father's death, her mother's hatred, her sister's bitterness. Jane's loss. But—Elizabeth was so lonely. And now she knows, there was somebody who—who loved her.

Those grey days begin to take on a fragile, silver hue.

"Elizabeth," Darcy whispers, now, at Pemberley. (He cannot take his eyes off her. Like in that memory. The false one.) "Elizabeth, I can bear anything—your anger, your reproaches— but not your silence. Please, I beg you—tell me what you are thinking."

There is no anger. Instead, she feels her heart is bursting. She wants to stand up back in that drawing room, in the tiny cottage, in her black dress, with her mother watching. She wants to walk to him and tell him that she is so sorry— for everything that has not yet come to pass— that she did not understand him before but that she understands him now. That they can avoid months of pain; that she wants to love him now.

She looks at him in the present. What he sees in her eyes is enough. He stands up and walks right to her—then stops (love and shyness and fear). She puts her hand on his heart—on the light blue shirt (except, it is not really the light blue shirt, of course).

He covers her hand with his.

Their first night is very awkward and very tender. Everything in the dark. The candle on the side table has burned out. Elizabeth keeps her shift; he keeps his shirt. His gestures are tentative, and she does not know what to do. It does not hurt, but it is so odd. Out of her realm of experience. She has no words, no context for what is happening.

The room is different, she realises, while their bodies are intertwined. He is kissing her. She

feels his skin and his weight. Her bedchamber—
it was grey—it had been grey for months. Now…
well, it is still dark, with the curtains drawn, but
—it is different.

He stammers words of love in her ear and she—
she holds him so tight.

The sun has risen.

She opens her eyes. He is sleeping besides her.

She hears him breathing. Everything is so still.
She stays still, too. Moving is a risk. The moment
could shatter.

Memories move in the air, a slow silver dance.
The sad ones, the new ones. Melancholy. Joy. His
words. His embrace.

Images of the night. The closeness and the
flesh—again, she has no words—a gentleman's
daughter does not learn those. She wonders
whether she will ever get used to this strange,
gorgeous, barbaric ritual. She wonders if women
who—fallen women—when they—if they ever
become blasé about such intimacy.

She feels like she never will.

Elizabeth starts. The sun is warmer—it must be late. Two hundred and fifty-three people and the servants, waiting—her maid and Darcy's valet are helping downstairs. She rises up from the bed as silently as she can. She dresses as silently as she can. She braids and twists and pins her hair as silently as she can.

The result is...commendable. Twenty-one years at Longbourn, five sisters, one maid.

"You look beautiful." His voice.

"You must be in love, Mr Darcy." She laughs. No jewels; she is wearing an old dark-purple dress. The fabric can survive sick children, stew, and crying widows.

She sits on the bed. To smile at him. He grabs her by the waist. "You are not thinking of leaving, I hope."

"It seems I cannot." She lies down on the cover, alongside him. Rising on one elbow, studying his face. She kisses him, once, on the lips.

"You must understand, I would like to leave," she states. "I very much desire to speak to Mrs Reynolds about mildew, sickness, and soup. But would a dutiful wife disobey her husband?"

She thinks he is going to answer in kind, that he will joke along, but he does not. He keeps watching her.

"I am so happy," he says, slowly.

She is very conscious of the stillness of the

room. Of the rays of the sun, on the bed.

"I should not be," he continues. "People have lost everything—lost loved ones. It will be years till they recover. The estate will suffer substantial losses. It will be years till we recover."

"I shall be by your side," Elizabeth says.

She feels sadness again—tenderness too strong in her heart, the desire to shield him against the future and the past, against exhaustion and heartbreak. She caresses his cheek; she touches her lips once more. Afterwards, his eyes are a little too bright. He puts his hand on her nape, draws her closer.

Kisses are silver and endless.

"Still, I do not feel guilty," he says. "My thoughts are too full of you."

Elizabeth reflects for a while. "The flood is not your fault," she muses, after a moment. He looks at her ponderingly. "You feel everything is your responsibility," she explains. "But this disaster is the will of providence. It is not mismanagement."

"It is mismanagement," he grumbles. "But not mine." Elizabeth heard it downstairs—the dams, it seems, were not well maintained.

"That is why you can allow yourself to be happy in this moment."

"Your mind works in bizarre ways," he

whispers. Before drawing her close again.

She goes downstairs. She enters the summer drawing room. The large glass doors are open; they connect the east parlour and the music room beyond. Elizabeth freezes.

The image is so striking, she can hardly breathe.

Colours, inching closer.

This part of the house was flooded during the first rising. The waters have receded, leaving everything covered in mud—a lost, monochrome world.

This morning, clean-up began.

On the right, greyish beige, everywhere. To the left, servants moping and wiping and washing and polishing—exposing golden oak floors, blue sofas, red tapestries, lavender walls.

Colours, eating the grey away.

Metaphor, embodied.

Her husband comes down. He stands behind her; he puts his arms around her waist again.

Together, they watch. Mrs Reynolds walks through the room, giving instructions to an army of helpers. She seems exhausted, and it is only ten.

She hardly notices them.

"You know," Elizabeth whispers to her husband, when the housekeeper has gone, "you are right. My mind works in bizarre ways indeed." She hesitates. "I… Sometimes, I see the world differently."

He hesitates too. Then, "So do I."

He tells her about the circles. She tells him about the colours.

Excerpts

The "What If?" Darcy and Elizabeth Series

Four Proposals Of Marriage

Elizabeth sat down. She laughed again; it was nervous.

"I feel like I just made a decision I may regret all my life, Mr Darcy. In ten years, you will be married to the most elegant lady there is, and I shall be an old maid, entertaining your children with the mythological tales Father told me."

Darcy forced a smile. A gentleman took rejection well. A gentleman did not show weakness when a lady refused his hand. "You will be as charming at thirty-two as you are now."

"How gallant. This is all Jane and Charles's fault, you know. If not for them, for the beauty of their union, I would have gladly accepted your offer. But... When I see them together..."

There were tears in Elizabeth's eyes again. "I am a silly, stupid girl, and I want a marriage of affection, not a union of reason. Do you remember their wedding day? I want my husband to look at me with the same passion in his eyes as when Charles saw Jane that morning. I want to look at my husband and think, this is the man I love, with all my heart. You are finding me ridiculous."

"No." Something hurt in Darcy's chest. "No."

The Governess

"Your situation has a very obvious solution," Colonel Fitzwilliam stated, while they were playing billiards in Darcy's house in London. "That is why the concept of 'mistress' was invented. You buy Elizabeth Bennet a little house, you give her a generous allowance... Of course, you hide her existence from your wife, when you will get one."

"I have thought about it."

"And...?"

Darcy was silent for a while.

"Elizabeth might refuse."

"Ha." It was Colonel Fitzwilliam's turn to play.

"Well, you know what John would say. Arrange for her to lose her place. Once on the streets, she will be desperate enough to beg you—to do anything—for a morsel of bread."

"John is the true portrait of a gentleman," Darcy answered. He hit the ball with cold, restrained anger.

His cousin raised his hand. "Understand, I am not suggesting that at all—I quite like Miss Bennet. It's not the governess position that bothers me, nor her sister's fall. Just give her thirty thousand pounds, and, you know—I would see you at the altar."

"Of course, if she had thirty thousand pounds, she would not be in that situation."

"No," said Colonel Fitzwilliam, rather indifferently.

Do You Love Me?

Darcy caught Elizabeth's hand, he held it for a few seconds, till Elizabeth regained her footing —or maybe it lasted more than a few seconds— then he had to let her go.

The situation was unbearable.

That accidental touch haunted Darcy all night. It had been weeks, months now, that he was living only to see her, to be near her, to listen to her—his life was a series of grey parenthesis with only her presence as touches of color.

His heart would soar when she looked at him —he would despair when she was silent, or if he imagined he had offended her in some way—and all of this, without any possible future. "The last man on earth I would ever be prevailed upon to marry," she had said, all these years ago.

Yes, they were friendly now; her opinion of him had changed, she had even said as much, and it had filled his heart with such despair and happiness—with frustrated passion—yes, it was unbearable. No woman could pass from such bitter hatred to the point where she could return his love—he had to regain control over his life— love was a curse, he would go mad if he didn't fight it, or flee—but letting go was so difficult.

He had no hope. None.

All These Years I Dreamed Of You

"My address to you will certainly seem quite strange, madam. I know you have already refused me once, and I swear, if you do so again tonight, I shall never bother you again—but I have to try. I still admire you as much as ever

—and—I would be honoured if you would agree to be my wife. I am conscious that if this were the case, I would receive only your hand, and not your heart, but it would be with the hope that the years we would spend together would give me many opportunities to soften it."

In any other circumstances, Elizabeth's shock would have been comical to behold. She stood petrified for a moment, before taking a step towards the fireplace.

"I— That— Well, Mr Darcy, you are quite… reckless." She shook her head. "We… You know, of course, it has been three years since we last met."

"I am, indeed, keenly aware of that fact."

"Well," she repeated. "Who would have thought, seeing you in society, that you would be prone to such impulsive, rash behaviour?"

"You might, perhaps."

Elizabeth coloured. "Yes. I suppose I had reasons to be aware of this aspect of your character."

Modern Pride and Prejudice Variations

Games Of Love And Cruelty

Same hotel room.

When Darcy tries to take Elizabeth in his arms she steps away. She puts her hand on his chest and pushes him toward the wall. She gets very, very close. Her lips almost brushing his, but not quite. He wants to kiss her. Elizabeth takes a step back.

"No, no," she says, smiling. (Not her usual smile. This one is tense, unhappy.) "No, no... Let's not pretend we..."

A pause. (That is when Darcy notices the screaming.)

"Do not kiss me," she orders. "I have the right to kiss you. You don't."

Then she plays with him, stripping him. Soon Darcy is nude and Elizabeth is grazing his chest with her fingertips. Her hands go downward but her face stays so near, her lips caressing his cheeks, his jaw, his neck, his lips again. Never quite kissing him and—it's crazily erotic, awful —he's desperate, his brain firing.

So, the next day, Darcy brings a date to Netherfield Game Night.

Revenge.

Obviously, Darcy does not think of it under

those terms. He just wants to hurt her.

(Screaming, in his brain.)

Pemberley

"I am in love with you," he said. Elizabeth appeared stunned. "I, hum, I tried everything to stop it—I mean, it is ridiculous—so irrational in my position, but I cannot shake it—I really tried —so I was thinking, seventy a week, or even eighty, if you want—"

"Sir—" Elizabeth started, but he didn't even notice.

"You will have to be discreet, of course. If people knew, it could harm my standing at Pemberley. And Ms Debourgh, she would think I've lost my mind—"

"Sir," Elizabeth repeated, this time, with more force*. "Because I still think you saved my life that night, I will not dwell on how offensive this proposition is," she said, icy cold. "But I am afraid I must decline. I have no intention of taking a protector, ever."

"What?" he breathed, at last. "What do you mean, you won't ever take a protector?"

"Did I ever give the impression that I would prostitute myself?"

"What the hell are you waiting for? Marriage?"

"Well...yes," Elizabeth said, a little flustered.

"Why wouldn't I meet someone who—"

"Oh, don't be ridiculous."

Printed by Amazon Italia Logistica S.r.l.
Torrazza Piemonte (TO), Italy